UNDERGROUND

LINDA NELSON

Published in 2025 by Provoco Publishing who own the publishing rights.

ISBN: 978-1-7395012-3-5

Cover Design and Artwork - © Provoco Publishing
Logo Design - © MJC at Martyn Carson Creative
Photographs reproduced under license
Edited by Jane Murray

DEDICATION

This book is for my dear husband, Carl, there are
no words that fill the emptiness you left, just the
ones in this book, with all my love x

Chapter One

The letter arrived first thing. I'd been expecting it, but my stomach still flipped when I saw my name printed on the envelope. Bold black on cream. Daniel Bennett.

It had been Miss McGowan's idea. Every Art lesson, "You can do it Danny," "You don't know until you try," "It's a chance in a lifetime." It did my head in, but I kind of liked it too. Finally, I'd given in and filled in the form. It needed Mum's signature, but that didn't matter. I could do it better than she could; I'd had enough practice. When I told Miss McGowan I'd sent it off, her whole face sparkled. At that moment I truly loved her. Not in a weird way, but because she actually gave a shit. That didn't happen much.

The paper felt thick between my fingers. I turned it over in my hands as if the power of touch might tell me what it said. Envelope still unopened, I walked through to the kitchen. Last night's take-away lay on the table, congealed patterns of left-over food swirled across silver cartons, an abstract work of art. Along with the dirty dishes, I pushed them to one side. I laid the letter flat on the table and stared down at it. Torn between wanting to know what it said and not, I savoured the moment of possibility, those seconds when you can believe something good might happen.

From the living room, the hum of the TV rippled across the quietness. Mum must've fallen asleep downstairs - again. I'd leave her for now. My fingers trembled as I slowly peeled open the envelope.

St Cuthbert's College of Arts
St Cuthbert's Square

London
W1 2CN

Dear Daniel,

Following consideration of your application I am delighted to invite you to attend an interview at St. Cuthbert's College of Art with a view to offering you a scholarship on our Sixth Form Course for promising young artists. I would be grateful if you could return the attached form indicating your acceptance. On receipt of this I shall contact . . .

I didn't read any further. I was floating. Me, Danny Bennett, Sixth Form at St Cuthberts College of Art!

'Mum!' I shouted through to the living room. The only reply was the buzz of the TV. 'Mum!' I shouted louder. Still no answer. Excitement propelled me towards the living room. In my head I was already at St Cuths, sat at an easel, paint brush in hand, the lecturer stood behind me, nodding her head in full appreciation, "A true masterpiece Danny!"

Leaning against the door frame, my fingers trembled, waving the letter in my hand, 'Look what I've got!'

A sudden surge of heat rushed through me at the scene before me. Curtains drawn, the light of the TV flickering against them and Mum, flat out on the sofa; wasted. The memory of screaming and shouting that had kept me awake last night flashed back to me. Mum and Meggsie, her waste of space, on-off boyfriend, arguing till the early hours. Paper crumpled in my clenched fist. What was the point? It didn't matter what the letter said, I wasn't going anywhere. I had to look after Mum; we only had each other. I walked back to the kitchen and threw the screwed-up envelope hard against the wall. It rebounded on to the worktop, landing in a spilled puddle of tea. I watched the edges slowly turning brown.

My stomach gave a low rumble at the leftover take-away. Too grim to heat up, I opened the cupboards to see what else there was. Nothing hopeful. Bread or cereal. I went for cereal. Cereal without milk. On a good day, we had both. There weren't many good days. A laugh caught my throat. If I ever did become a famous artist, I'd buy a cow, then we'd always have milk.

I ran the taps to wash up a bowl and waited for the sink to fill. Rising steam hit my face. I squirted in the last of the washing-up liquid and plunged my hands into the hot water, thinking about Mum and how I wished things could be different. Different for her, different for me. Maybe, if we'd been born into a different life?

My mind wandered to make-believe better places, as I watched the bubbles trickle down the plates resting on the draining board. I caught sight of the crumpled-up letter on the worktop. It would have been good, but that was Miss McGowan's dream, not mine; besides, things like that didn't happen to boys like me, boys off the Kingsmead.

I carried on with the washing up, one ear listening out for any signs of movement from the living room. In the newspapers or those crappy magazines Mum used to read, people always said they knew something was wrong, could sense it. At first, I couldn't quite catch what was out of place, then it clicked. It was the voice. The News. I hadn't taken much notice of the TV when I'd seen Mum flaked out on the sofa, but her world was reality TV and soaps, not the news.

Hands dripping, I ran to the living room. She lay on the sofa, exactly like she was before, only this time I saw the blue tinge of her lips, all the more blue against her paper white skin. My legs became weak. I felt like I'd been punched in the stomach. One word banged in my head. *Why, why, why?* Why hadn't I looked properly? Why hadn't I taken those couple more steps to check she was okay? Why had I been pratting about with a stupid letter that was never going to be real? This was all my fault. I wanted to puke, but there was nothing there.

I knelt down beside her. Wisps of blonde hair lay across her face. I knew what she'd feel like before I touched her. Warm but clammy. In situations like this, every second counted, there was no time for panic. Above the guilt, automatic pilot kicked in. The stillness of the room settled on me, and hands shaking, I punched the numbers into my phone. A sharp voice on the other end answered.

'Emergency, which service?'

'Ambulance,' I said in a voice that wasn't my own.

At the hospital everything was slow motion and full speed at the same time. People appeared from nowhere, barking out orders I didn't understand. At some point I was ushered to a seat in the waiting area by a pair of firm hands. The sick feeling moved from my stomach, lodging itself in my throat. I scanned the seats. A sea of faces unable to hide they'd rather be somewhere else.

My eyes focused on the clock hanging on the wall opposite, trying to slow my heart with each tick. One, two, three, four, five – waiting for someone to come and get me, tell me what was happening. Uneasily, I shifted on the orange plastic seat. I tensed my leg to stop it jigging up and down, then dug my hand into my jeans pocket, pulling out the small pad and pencil I always carried with me. My fingers wrapped round the wood, but the usual calm didn't come. Eyes falling on the woman behind the reception desk, I carried on anyway. Mind still elsewhere, I began to doodle. Her name badge said Rosemary. It suited her pinkness, I thought, adding shade to her apple cheeks.

Another glance at the clock, and another five minutes gone. Still nobody had come to see me. I needed to see Mum. The snap of paper cut across the waiting room as I slapped my sketch pad shut. I licked my lips, trying to rid my mouth of its dryness, ready to talk to Rosemary.

'Excuse me,' the words scratched my throat.

'Yes, my love,' Rosemary looked up. When she clocked it was me, she couldn't hide the pity in her eyes.

'Can I see my mum yet?' I asked.

'You'll be able to see her shortly, dear. The nurses are making her comfortable. If you want to go back to the waiting area, they're sending someone to make arrangements for you.'

Blood pounded in my ears. I turned to go back to my seat. I needed to see my mum. Why did nobody get that? I slumped back into my seat. Making her comfortable? They'd had plenty of time to make her comfortable. And what did Rosemary mean, *making arrangements for me?* A blanket of coldness wrapped around me. A steely tingle crept up my back. I'd been so worried about Mum, I'd not thought about me. What would happen to me? *Making arrangements;* I knew exactly what it meant. I could see Rosemary looking over. Her pink cheeks reddened when her eyes caught mine, her mouth twisted into a strained smile. Pin pricks of panic jabbed my skin. I had to do something, but I didn't know what, so I sat, still and cold as a statue, and waited. Waited for the inevitable.

Chapter Two

The inevitable arrived exactly eighteen minutes later dressed in a suit.

'Hi, I'm Annie.'

She stuck out her hand. I didn't take it. Her eyes flicked towards her watch. 'I'm the hospital social worker,' she explained without needing to. 'Your Mum's a bit out of sorts.' An understatement, but I let it go. 'It might be sometime before she's back on her feet and I understand there isn't anybody else at home.' I didn't know if she was asking me or telling me. I looked at her blankly. She looked at her watch again.

'Strictly speaking this isn't my remit. I usually work directly with patients so I'm contacting a colleague to get someone from the Children's Team to come and see you.'

My face remained blank while inside, a helpless rage churned. We didn't need her or her colleagues. We didn't need anybody's help. We were doing all right on our own. It was like Mum said, they'd never helped us before, they'd only made things worse.

Annie's voice carried on nipping at my head.

'Let's take some details.'

She pulled a purple pen and a swirly patterned notebook out of her bag. Flatly, I answered her questions. Name. Address. Date of birth. Next of kin.

'Any other family members who might be able to help?' she asked, a hopeful look on her face.

There was nobody unless you counted Mum's brother, Uncle Tony. We hadn't seen him for ages. I didn't have a clue where he was.

'My Uncle Tony's around.' The lie was jagged in my

mouth.

'Well …' Annie stopped short and looked up, her face brightening with relief. Perhaps I wouldn't be such a problem after all. 'I'll pass that on to the allocated social worker. I'm sure they'll be able to arrange something' She snapped her notebook shut. 'All done!'

'Can I go see Mum?' I asked.

She carried on, ignoring my question.

'I'm not sure how long it will take for the social worker to get here, and I've got a meeting to get to, but you'll be okay waiting here.' She didn't wait for an answer but then, it wasn't a question. A fake smile split her face as she shoved her notebook in her bag and headed off to her meeting.

The sick feeling inside swelled. Memories sparked in my head. Spiked and cracked. A man with a grey beard, a woman with red hair. Smiling faces, soft voices, Mum crying.

'This is the last time. It will never happen again. I promise!'

The judge promised too. If it did, they'd consider putting me in to care. She'd tried so hard, no drink, no drugs, just me and her. She'd kept her promise, for a while anyway, until things started to go wrong again. It wasn't her fault. She lost her job, but we still managed. Then Meggsie turned up, wormed his way in, ruining everything. The big man promising her a whole load of lies. By then, I'd worked out how to play the game, worked out how to look out for me and Mum. Keep my head down, get on with things, don't get into any trouble. It was enough to keep them away. Now they'd come poking their noses in. No way could I let them take me away, Mum needed me. I couldn't let her down. I stood up. I had to see her, let her know I was okay. We were okay.

I took a deep breath and walked over to Rosemary who was back behind the reception desk.

'Can I see my mum yet, before the social worker gets here?' I asked.

'They're still getting her sorted, if you can wait a tad longer.' She was apologetic, understanding - but she didn't understand. There wasn't time to wait. I didn't have to blink too hard to force the tears to spill from my eyes. When they did, her lips twisted with sympathy and indecision.

'I'll make a quick call,' she said lifting the phone to her ear, turning her back so I couldn't hear what was being said. It didn't take long for her to get an answer. When she turned round, I could tell by her face that at last, something was going right for me.

'The doctor says you can see her for five minutes, no more.'

Rosemary re-arranged the papers on her desk. Wiping away the tears, my foot tapped against the linoleum floor. We needed to go. A sharp breath escaped my lips when she finally came round the other side of the desk.

'Follow me,' she said.

My eyes fixed on her sensible shoes as they squeaked the short walk down the corridor.

'Here,.' Rosemary indicated to a side door. I swallowed hard. Mum wasn't in a ward; it must be bad.

Fingers pressed against the dispenser; hand gel slipped across my sweaty palms. Rosemary flashed her key fob across the black box beside the door. Its red light flashed and turned green. The sharp smell of disinfectant itched my nostrils as I pushed open the door.

I'll be off then,' Rosemary said. 'And don't worry, I'll keep an eye out for your social worker.'

Don't bother, I wanted to say, but all I could do was stare at the curtain ahead of me, pulled around the hospital bed, knowing that behind it was Mum, not knowing what I was about to face. Ears buzzing, I counted, one, two, three … by the time I got to ten a dull, empty calmness had spread over me. I prepared myself for the worst and walked towards the curtain.

As I neared, I heard voices coming from behind it. A man and a woman. I leaned forward, straining to hear what was being said.

'An accidental overdose is problematic in itself, but with these additional complications …' the man's voice was low. A gasp of air hit the back of my throat as I strained to hear more.

'Pulmonary embolism... pneumonia.... could be critical.' His words floated in and out of my ears like someone was messing with the volume. I tried to stay focused, but everything was a jumble in my head.

The woman spoke next, 'We'll need to keep her in until she's stabilized, but on a positive note, she's reacting well to the medication.'

I took another step forward, clinging onto the small bud of hope which had taken hold inside me, when the curtain swished back.

My feet faltered, a hot flush travelled up my neck, embarrassed at being caught eavesdropping.

'Can I help you?'

The woman who was wearing a white coat looked at me in a way that said I shouldn't be here. The quick flash of her eyes took in the room, giving it a once over, like she thought I might have nicked something. The flush on my neck started to prick with anger. Where did she get off? It was my mum in there, I had every right to be here, but the voice that came out of my mouth was nothing like the one in my head. It was barely a whisper.

'It's my mum,' I hesitated. 'I'm Danny, her son.' I gathered my voice, pushing the words out. 'When can I take her home? I need to know what to do, how to look after her.'

For a brief moment the doctors eyes met mine, then she looked above me, to the side of me, anywhere but directly at me. Awkwardness dripped from her, a silent gulf between us. It was the other doctor who broke it.

'You're a good boy Danny, but your mum needs specialist support and she'll need a lot of support when she does leave hospital. It's not going to be easy.'

I let his words hang in the air. What did he know? It was me and Mum, like it always had been. We didn't need anybody.

'Can I see her?' I asked. I didn't wait for the answer, I pulled back the curtain and went through, but I didn't miss the same look of pity I'd seen on Rosemary's face pass between them.

My insides froze. Tubes and wires snaked across Mum's body. My legs were lead as I moved towards her. If only I'd gone into the living room sooner. My eyebrows pulled tight. This was all my fault.

'Mum,' my voice was brittle and cracked. 'Mum' I repeated. 'I'm here.'

Her eyes flickered beneath their lids. Slowly she opened them, a watery gaze focusing on my face. I slipped my hand into hers and gave it a gentle squeeze. Her fingers twitched against my palm. As her mouth parted, her chest rose with a jagged intake of air. Shallow breaths rasped against her dry lips.

'D... D...' Her chest fell back down with the effort.

I bent down, my face next to hers. 'What is it, Mum?'

'I'm sorry, Danny, so sorry.' Her words were light and breathy.

'It's not your fault, I'm sorry,' I tightened my hold on her hand and took a deep breath. 'Mum, they're sending a social worker to see me.'

Her glazed eyes widened. Her voice was thin, but her nails pressed hard into my skin.

'No, they can't take you away.' The tremor starting in her hand spread over her body, her breathing quickened.

'Shush, shush,' I stroked her arm, trying to calm her. 'It's going to be ok.' The words were forced out with a confidence I didn't have.

'No, they'll take you away for good this time.'

'They won't, I've got it all worked out. I'm going to stay with Uncle Tony,' the lie tripped easily off my lips now, 'until you're out of hospital.'

She looked at me through a fog of confusion.

'Tony, our Tony, yes, stay with him, but...'

'Don't worry, they won't be able to find me and when you're out of hospital it'll be fine, they'll see we're okay. Stop worrying about me, concentrate on getting better.'

I was convincing myself as much as I was convincing her. I had no idea what I'd do, but I'd think of something, I had to. What mattered was Mum was okay.

A weak smile hovered over her lips.

'You're a good boy.' Her eyes drifted around the room, taking it all in.

Tears trickled down her cheeks. 'I'm sorry. I know I've got to change. This time I'm going to do it, really do it. I can't keep letting you down.' The pain in her eyes wasn't only from the effort of speaking, it was from the words themselves.

I squeezed her hand tighter. I wanted to believe her. I

had to believe her. Her eyes held mine, and despite the weakness in her body, I felt her strength when she squeezed my hand back.

'You don't have to worry. When you get out of here, we'll be fine, everything will be back to normal,' I said.

I could barely hear her the next time she spoke.

'I promise, this time. I promise. I love you.'

Her eyes fluttered as she drifted off to sleep, but I'd seen the fire in them. This time it would be different. This time she meant it.

I sat holding her hand, looking at her, willing her to get better. I didn't notice the nurse come into the room.

'I think it's time to go,' she said, smiling kindly.

'One minute,' I replied, pulling my pad and paper out of my pocket.

Quickly I sketched an outline of me and Mum, faces smiling. Underneath I wrote *I love you too*. I folded it and placed it in the palm of her hands, gently bending her fingers around it. Without looking back, I left the room. Teeth gritted; I walked back down the corridor. Rosemary was back behind her desk.

'The social worker's here,' she called out, nodding in the direction of the waiting area.

'I need the loo,' I replied, not looking at her or the social worker.

'You're going the wrong way!' Rosemary's voice followed me down the corridor.

Eyes fixed on the door, heart thumping against my chest, I carried on walking out of the hospital - then ran.

Chapter Three

By the time I got back to the Kingsmead, I'd decided finding Uncle Tony was my only option.

Back home, I let myself in. The take-out cartons were still there, a thick skin forming over one of them. I took the stairs two at a time, mentally ticking off what I needed. Top of the list; art stuff; crayons, charcoal, pencils. I took it all. Clothes: I figured two of each. Sleeping bag, I doubted Tony would have anything spare. I stuffed everything in my rucksack, one thing after another. I didn't stop, I didn't want to think about what I was doing. I didn't want to change my mind.

Next was money.

Back straining, I pulled the wardrobe forward. The rip of the plastic bag, taped to the back, was satisfying as I pulled it off. Almost three hundred pounds. It had taken nearly a year to save. Working weekends, stacking shelves at the supermarket on the estate. It wasn't hard. The hard work was keeping the money from Mum. Somehow Meggsie always managed to persuade her to hand it over, so they could be snorted away. He said she needed it; it made her better and she believed him. There was always a promise to pay me back. I was still waiting. The hiding place behind the wardrobe had been a good one - it was too heavy for her to move.

I split the notes in two. Rolled them up and shoved a wad down each sock in case I got mugged or something. I'd seen it in films. No doubt they'd seen the same ones too, so it probably didn't matter. I checked my pocket for my phone then stopped. I heard a bang, and it was coming from downstairs.

Shit! The social worker! But they'd knock, not walk

right in? I strained my ears. Drawers and cupboards were being open and shut. Whoever was down there was looking for something. That was no social worker. My heart knocked against my chest. I knew who it was. It was worse. Meggsie - and that could only be bad news.

Slowly I crept to the top of the stairs. Stepping left then right, avoiding the creaks, I made my way down. At the bottom, I looked into the living room. I was right. Meggsie with his buzz cut, fake Armani t-shirt, and knock off trainers. My fingers curled into fists the sight of him, bringing with it a reminder of Mum laying in her hospital bed. In my head I'd give him a kicking because of what he'd done. In reality I wouldn't stand a chance. My fingers uncurled as I watched him, bent over peering behind the TV.

If I was quiet, I could slip through the kitchen and out the back, but as my hand connected with the door handle Meggsie's connected heavily with my shoulder.

'All right, Danny?'

His hand gripped tighter, icy coldness washed over me. I was going nowhere. I turned around.

'Meggsie,' I said it like he was a mad dog, trying not to show my fear. 'If you're looking for Mum, she's not around.'

'Yeah, heard she had a funny turn,' he said.

Fists clenched; a flash of anger burned as I pictured Mum in the hospital. If it wasn't for him, she wouldn't be there. I wanted to grab him and shake him. Inside I raged. This was his fault, him, and his stupid drugs. I wanted to shout it out, but the words didn't make it to my mouth. I wanted to keep my teeth, and it wouldn't help Mum.

'Thing is, son,' Meggsie began.

I grimaced inwardly, wishing he'd stop calling me son. He carried on.

'Yeah, thing is son, she owes money and not just me.' He was smiling but his voice was savage, 'Don't suppose you know where she keeps it?' I shook my head. Mum didn't have any money, he knew that. He looked at me through slanted eyes, his fingers dug deeper into my skin. He'd finished being nice.

'Thing is Danny, if your Mum's not here to sort it out, it's down to you. She's well over-due her payments and it's starting to cause me problems. I can't have that.'

I shook my head. 'I don't have any, honest!' The rolls of cash stuffed down my socks pressed into my ankles. The smell of alcohol hit me as Meggsie brought his face close to mine, pushing me hard against the wall.

'Well, you better find some then,' he hissed. I retched, not sure if it was from fear or the glob of spit landing on my chin. You know it's not in my nature to be violent.' His face twisted as he shoved me harder into the wall. 'But these other people, well, I can't say what they might do. Nasty people, wouldn't think twice about hurting your Mum, or you for that matter.'

The hate I felt for Meggsie was overtaken with sheer dread of what might happen to Mum if we didn't pay him. I'd seen the results of getting on the wrong side of him and his so-called mates and it wasn't pretty. This was serious stuff. Pulling my body tight to stop the shaking, I wiped my face with the back of my sleeve and spoke in a voice I hoped didn't show my fear.

'I'll go look upstairs, see if I can find anything.' I wanted to be as far away from him as possible. Give me time to think.

'Good idea, son.' Meggsie's menacing smile returned. 'I'll carry on down here.'

In Mum's bedroom I sat on the unmade bed, took a deep breath, and tried to calm myself. Downstairs the rummaging turned to desperate banging and crashing. I quickly rolled up my trouser leg and pulled out the wads of cash. So much for my savings. I peeled off enough notes to get me to Uncle Tony's and to get some food. Thought about it, then peeled off another two for emergencies. That should be enough. I stuffed it back down my sock as far as it would go, took another deep breath, and shouted, 'Meggsie! I've found some.'

The crash was replaced with feet bounding up the stairs. Meggsie burst through the bedroom door.

'How much?' he asked, face expectant.

'Dunno,' I said, handing the money to him. 'Haven't counted.'

Meggsie's smile faded as his grimy fingers leafed through the notes. When he'd finished counting, he shook his head and pulled a small black book out of his pocket. He turned over the pages until he found what he was looking for. I wasn't expecting him to share his sketches with me, but neither was I expecting this.

'See here.' He stabbed his finger at whatever was written there. 'Three thousand, that's what it says.'

My head lightened. How could Mum owe that much? There's no way we could pay that back. Meggsie sat down on the chair opposite the bed and started shaking his head.

'It's not looking good Danny, your two-fifty's not nearly enough.' He waved the bundle of notes at me like it was nothing. 'That'll cover this month's interest.' With each word the finger that had jabbed the book jabbed my chest.

My mouth opened - nothing came out. There was nothing to say.

'You've got a month to get the rest.' He got up to leave, then turned back, his face pure evil, 'and like I said if you don't pay up, I can't say what's going to happen to your Mum.'

Chapter Four

With the slam of the front door, relief seeped through me – for a second. Meggsie might have gone, but he'd be back soon, and when he was, I needed to have three thousand pounds. I wanted to cry, but instead I laughed as the whole shitty situation hit me. I kept on laughing. I couldn't stop. Three thousand pounds! Where the hell was I going to get that? Eventually, the laughter turned to tears I'd been holding back. I let them roll. I didn't care. My whole body shook, thinking about Mum and what they might do to her when I didn't get the money.

With that thought I jumped up; I wiped my face with the back of my sleeve. I had to do something, but I didn't know what. First, I'd find Uncle Tony's address. Head twisting frantically, I looked round the room, like it was going to jump out at me. It didn't, but my eyes fell on something black, snuggled between the cushion and the arm of the chair where Meggsie had been sitting. His black book.

I snatched it up, flicking through it desperately as if somewhere in the lists of names and scribbled amounts of money was the answer to my problem. No luck there, either. The only thing that leapt out was Mum's name with a fat £3000 written next to it. I stuffed the book deep in my jacket pocket. I didn't know how, but it might come in useful. I might be able to use it to protect Mum. Insurance or something. If nothing else, it made me feel I'd got one over on Meggsie. Hopefully he wouldn't realise where he'd lost it. I heaved the rucksack on my back and went downstairs.

In the living room I kept my eyes off the sofa. I didn't need reminding of what happened earlier. I sifted through papers and envelopes piled on the windowsill. No address, only take-away flyers, and unpaid bills, then I went through to the kitchen and pulled open the drawer next to the sink. I rifled through string, dead batteries, a whole load of other crap we never used and eventually found it. A photo of Uncle Tony, face beaming out beneath his blonde fringe. He looked like Mum, like me. The 'Signature Bennett look,' Mum called it, blonde hair with brown eyes. Mum was tiny, but I'd got my dad's build, not that I'd know. I'd never met him. He was long gone by the time I was born. It was the only good thing he'd given me, so Mum said. Tall, but not too tall, slim, but not skinny.

The photo was a few years old, but when I turned it over, I knew it was the right one. Scrawled on the back was an address. If everything else hadn't been so crap, it would have been worth a fist pump.

I laid it down on the worktop, flattening out the creases so I could read it properly. "242 Gladwell Way," it had a hopeful sound to it. Yeah, some hope, I thought, my eye catching the letter I'd screwed up and thrown there earlier this morning. That was a lifetime ago. I picked it up, now decorated with a swirl of brown tea stains. Slowly, I unfolded it. It was never going to happen but for a minute I wanted to read it and be one of those kids who did have stuff like this happen, one of those...

My jaw dropped as my eyes travelled down the paper. I blinked to check I was reading it right. I hadn't read the whole thing this morning. I did now.

... I would be grateful if you could return the attached form indicating your acceptance. On receipt of this, I shall contact you to confirm an interview date. I would also like to draw your

attention to the Matthew Vaughn Scholarship Fund. A bursary of £3500 will be given to three promising students. If you would like to be considered, please send a portfolio of work to the above address by July 31st ...

My heart missed a beat. This was it. This was how I'd pay Meggsie back and get him out of our lives. Without him around, Mum would stand a chance. I looked at the letter again. I'd get everything sorted by the time Mum was out of hospital. There was just the small matter of winning the scholarship. It was a long shot, but it was the only one I had, and I had three weeks to do it in.

It was early afternoon, but the tube was still rammed. I pushed myself against the wall at the back of the carriage, head down, making myself as unnoticeable as possible. Shutting out the noise, I started to think about ideas for my portfolio. Excitement pushed through the urgency of the situation. It had to be something different, something special, to make me stand out. I was going to do this.

The tube doors hissed shut. As it pulled out of the station, I lurched forward. Wedged between two men in suits, on one side the smell of freshly showered skin, on the other stale cigarettes, I steadied myself, gaze firmly on the floor, concentrating. Some work with charcoal might be a good idea. Ms. McGowan said I 'excelled' at that.

While ideas whizzed around my head, heat gathered round my neck, a mixture of stuffiness and nerves. The further I got away from Meggsie and poxy social workers, the better I'd feel. The last thing I needed was to puke my guts up on the tube. I squeezed my arm round my front and pulled down the neck of my hoody, letting in some air. Stale cigarette man's eyes fixed on me when I accidentally jabbed him with my elbow. He might wear a suit, but his eyes looked mean. My hands felt clammy. I smiled, trying to look apologetic; I didn't want any trouble. I wanted to be off this train and at Uncle Tony's. My fingers were itching to make a start on my portfolio.

Carefully, I squeezed my arm back through and checked my jeans pocket. The photo with the address was still there. I knew it off by heart anyway, but Tony's scrawly writing made it real. 242 Gladwell Way, it definitely had a good ring to it. I sketched a picture of it my head. Flowers and window boxes, nothing like the Kingsmead.

I looked up to check how many more stops. Only two. Turning my eyes back to the carriage, it was the paleness of her face against jet-black hair that caught my eye, a good face to paint. She stood about three people in front of me, piercing blue eyes sparkled straight ahead. She wasn't looking at anything, more concentrating really hard. Like me, squashed in a sea of people, she didn't notice me looking. I dipped my head and carried on watching; she carried on staring into the air. I almost missed the slight flick of her wrist I was so fixed on the brightness of her eyes.

Face still blank she stared into nothingness, then snake-like moved her hand along the jacket of the man flattened against her. Her fingers fluttered across the top of his pocket. In a blink, birdlike, she plucked out his wallet. Then, like magic, it disappeared into the folds of her own jacket. I waited for the man to turn around, to shout, to grab her. He didn't. I blew out a gasp of air. Her face stayed motionless, but triumph glinted in her eyes. It was wrong, but I couldn't help feeling relieved for her.

Then bad timing, bad luck or what? At that moment, the man put his hand in his pocket. Confusion spread across his face. His hand pushed through the tightness of bodies around him checking his other pocket. Understanding replaced confusion.

'Who the hell's taken my wallet?' he shouted. His head spun round, eyes falling on the girl with the black hair.

Silent unease rippled across the carriage. All eyes down, feet shuffling. The man's eyes remained locked on the girl. Defiance shone from her as she stared back, trying to front it out. It was the slight dip of her eyes to the breast of her coat that gave her away. The train lurched to a stop and the man grabbed her by the arm. As bodies jostled against each other, he lost his grip. She took her chance and pushed forward.

'No, you don't,' the man shouted, trying to grab her. Her eye caught mine as she carried on pushing, launching herself towards the opening doors. The man's arm reached out and grabbed the hood of her jacket. Anger pulsed through his clenched fist. The look she gave me wasn't fear or pleading, she looked like she could handle herself. It was more expectant.

I didn't feel sorry for her, but I don't like seeing people in trouble and I honestly don't know if I meant to do it. It might have been the swell of people pulling me forward, but the next thing I knew the man had tripped over my foot.

'Sorry,' I muttered. He lunged forward, stumbling into the crowd in front, losing his grip on the girl. She turned, flashed me a smile, then headed off into the throng of people.

The man looked at me, then in the direction the girl had disappeared, undecided whether he should go for her or me. I wasn't hanging around while he made up his mind. I slipped into the moving crowd, hoping she was ok, knowing she would be.

Heading up the escalator I caught a glimpse of the girl again. A sharp, penetrating whistle cut through the noise of the station. Her head turned, trying to locate it, then she was gone.

Chapter Five

The breeze on my face felt good after the stuffiness of the tube. Standing outside the station, I gulped in the fresh air then punched Uncle Tony's address in my phone. This was it. Ready to go.

Gladwell Way was a ten-minute walk. Keeping my eye on the phone, I followed the blue line on the map. Even with the weight of the rucksack, my step lightened. Everything was going to plan. I'd stay at Uncle Tony's, get my portfolio ready, get the scholarship money and pay off Meggsie. By the time Mum was out of hospital, everything would be back to normal and somebody else would be Meggsie's and Social Care's problem.

As the blue line brought me nearer, I got the feeling Gladwell Way wasn't the place I'd drawn in my head. For starters, there were no window boxes. Open streets with small, terraced houses, the odd cafe and food shop sandwiched between them, disappeared as taller buildings overtook, their shadows darkening the road. By the time I reached the blue dot on the map, the tower blocks were a solid concrete mass.

The little blue man hovered, not quite able to pinpoint the exact location, or perhaps he didn't like the look of the place either. It was worse than the Kingsmead, but it didn't matter, Uncle Tony was here, and that's what mattered. Trying to keep the lightness in my step, I walked through an alleyway running between two blocks of flats. It was more like a tunnel. The air was heavy, layered with a sour smell of vinegar rising up from a half-eaten, discarded tray of fish and chips. I breathed as I came out to the other side, where it opened on to a grassy square. On each of its sides were rows and rows of balconies, stairways randomly placed. A vertical maze.

'Hey, Danny!' someone shouted over to me from the play area on the other side of the grass.

I knew that voice. Shit! My leg muscles tightened, ready to run. It was Meggsie. He must have followed me. The red hoody he wore screamed danger. He wasn't on his own, he was with his sidekick, Gizmo. Meggsie brought Gizmo along for one thing - his muscle.

'Think you've got something that belongs to me!' his voice echoed off the buildings.

Shit again! His book, I'd forgotten I had it, now it burnt in my pocket. My mind raced. Give it back or keep it? Even from a distance I could sense their malice. I'd get a kicking either way, besides if he wanted it that badly maybe I'd been right; I could use it as insurance to protect Mum. My eyes shifted, darting from side to side. The tension thickened. Their movement was slow but taut, ready to strike. Decision made – run.

My feet moved but didn't know which way to go. They weren't my own, dancing from side to side. I heard the thud of their feet bouncing off the concrete. Laughter ricocheted from wall to wall. A laughing Meggsie was more dangerous than an angry one. They were out to get me. Without looking back, I ran for one of the stairways. For what seemed like the billionth time today, my heart raced. At the top of the stairs, I crouched behind a balcony wall. Every part of my body prickled, alive.

Hunched below the wall, I looked down the walkway at the stairs to the next balcony. Venom filled with laughter was getting closer. I needed to run, but I couldn't let them see me. Still crouching, I did a sort of squat run past the flat doors to the next stairway, then on hands and knees clambered my way up. At the top I made a sharp left, still stooping as I ran to the next set of stairs.

"Come out, come out, wherever you are!" It was Gizmo jeering.

I didn't stop. At the top I turned a sharp right along to the next set of steps, but this time I went back down the next set, trying to throw them off. The tops of my thighs burned. I kept going. Back down on my knees, concrete grazed against my skin, but I didn't have time to worry about the hole that had worn in my knees. Along and down, along, and up. My muscles were on fire. I could still hear the pounding of feet, but the laughter wasn't as close now. At the next set of stairs, I risked stopping. My breath came back in gasps.

Pressed flat against the wall, I chanced a glimpse over the top. A flash of red and I pulled back. I didn't know what to do. I could end up being chased all day. Like hounds with a fox, they'd tire me out then move in for the kill. Desperately, I looked around for a way out, but was met with a wall of doors, stairs and balconies. Then I saw it, right in front of me. A sign. "235 - 245 Gladwell Way." Underneath an arrow pointing straight on and to the left. I was here.

Back pushed as close to the wall as I could get, my rucksack scuffed against it as I shuffled along. Some doors had missing numbers. I counted on in my head. 236, 238, 240. Yes, 242! It was around the corner. If I could get past the bend without being seen, I'd be home safe. I dragged myself along the floor. A metre to go. I didn't believe in God, he'd never done anything for me or Mum, but I muttered a silent prayer. Uncle Tony had better be home.

The door to flat 242 looked like someone had tried to

kick it in. It was dirty red, but the numbers shone out like gold. I almost cried. I'd made it. Daring to get up to a half standing position, I catapulted myself from the wall to the door. There was no sign of Meggsie or Gizmo, but I knocked gently, just in case. My knuckles brushed against the wood. No answer. I knocked again, then again, louder.

A voice answered. It wasn't Uncle Tony.

'Wait on! I'm coming!' It was a woman's voice. Maybe his girlfriend, whoever, they sounded slow and heavy, like they weren't coming anytime soon.

Impatient now, I knocked again, throwing a look over my shoulder, checking I'd not been spotted. The door flung open. Glazed eyes peered through straggly red hair. Her skin was grey. She reminded me of Mum on a bad day. Uneasiness crossed me. She looked at me vacantly, then nodded her head at me to come in.

'Ritchie, it's for you,' she called down the hall. What? It was like they were expecting me, but Uncle Tony didn't know I was coming, and I didn't know any Ritchie.

Without looking at me, she sauntered back down the corridor. She sloped in to one of the rooms as a man came out of another. It must be Ritchie. He looked like he'd just got out of bed. His hair was a mess, a stale smell lingered behind him.

"Yeah, what'll it be?" he asked.

Was he confusing me with somebody else? The uneasy feeling grew. I pushed it down. This was Tony's flat. It was going to be ok. It had to be.

'I'm here to see Tony,' I said, sure this would explain everything.

I was wrong. Ritchie's face clouded.

'What are you looking for that shit for? Don't tell me

31

he owes you money too?'

'No, I'm…' but before I could finish, he carried on.

'Do you know where he is?' He took a step forward. 'Cos if you do ...' He grabbed hold of my jacket and pulled me close. Rancid breath hit my face. I shook my head struggling to get my words out.

'No, I don't. I've not seen him in months I'm just...' my words trailed off. What was I doing, I didn't know?

'Well, if you do, tell him from me he better not come back here, 'cos if he does, he's dead.'

I stood there not sure if I was better off staying with Ritchie and his death threats or going back out to face Meggsie and Gizmo. The choice was made for me when Richie pushed me towards the door.

'Go on, get out and don't forget to tell him.'

He drew his finger slowly across his throat.

Chapter Six

Back out on the balcony, the weight of reality crushed me. Tony's flat wasn't an option. Tony wasn't an option. I had no idea where he was. Panic rose in my throat. My brain fizzed unable to fix on one thought. The sour stench of the flat clung to me and a wave of exhaustion settled on my shoulders. I threw it off when a familiar flash of bright red caught my eye. For now, my priority was Meggsie. I'd think about what I was going to do next once I'd got away from him.

Peering over the railings, I watched him, and Gizmo make their way back to the play area. They'd not seen me, perhaps they'd given up. I doubted it, but if I went for it now, I could get down the stairs and get away without them seeing me. The burn in my thighs returned as I crouched down. I'd be ok until I got to the bottom then I'd have to pelt it.

My knee clicked at the last step, not a good sign for the sprint ahead. From where I squatted the distance to the alleyway out of the estate wasn't far, but it might as well have been miles. I was fast, but I had my rucksack, and I couldn't leave it behind. It was everything I had.

I counted - one, two, three. I was off. Panting heavily, I didn't bother to check if they'd seen me, if they were following. I ran, eyes fixed on my way out. Legs and arms pumped; my rucksack slammed against my back. My thighs ached, but I carried on. I had that feeling when you know you're about to win a race, butterflies in your stomach. I was going to make it.

Too soon! The slapping of feet on concrete and the manic laughter sounded behind. They were on me. I pushed myself harder, chancing a glance over my shoulder. Gizmo had given up, head bent down to his knees, body heaving, but Meggsie was flying, only a couple of arm's lengths away. So close, I could hear his breathing, each gasp forcing itself out. My insides tightened. He'd be on me in seconds.

A forceful pull on my rucksack jerked my head and shoulders back. Blind panic took over. Twisting and turning, I tried to loosen myself from its straps. I caught a glimpse of Meggsie's face. Pure fury. Fear spurred me on. I had no choice. I wrenched my arms backwards then forwards. My body lightened as the rucksack fell from my back. I don't know what hurt most, the pain where the straps had jarred my shoulders or the leaving behind everything I owned, my art stuff. Whatever. I was free.

Momentum kept me moving. One step, two steps, I didn't have time to stop.

Smash!

'Whoa, whoa!' The man I'd slammed into held up his hands, then gently maneuvered me back, his hands still on my shoulders.

'Slow down, my friend. You'll cause someone an injury.'

I looked him straight in the face, sure he'd see the panic in my eyes, then turned to look behind. Meggsie was kneeling on the ground pulling everything out of my rucksack. Clothes, art stuff, my worldly possessions strewn over the floor. Meggsie's hands all over them. I wanted to run back and rescue them, but my feet wouldn't let me. I had to rescue myself first.

Turning back to the man, I expected to see that look on his face, the one that said, "*Oh shit, what have I walked into?*" But he was smiling. I looked him up and down. He was about the same age as Mum, slightly bigger than average but he wouldn't stand a chance when Meggsie and Gizmo gave him a kicking, along with me. I was about to tell him to run for it when he spoke.

'Have you got a problem with my friend here?' he was talking to Meggsie - he was talking about me! His voice was soft, calm, no hint of fear in it. He was either a black belt in karate or a total mad head. I was going with mad head.

Meggsie didn't even bother looking up. 'This thieving little shit's got something that belongs to me. If I were you, I'd keep your nose out and do one.'

Relief for the man rubbed against rising panic. This was his get out.

He didn't move. I stared at him, willing him to turn around and leave.

'I have to admit I'm slightly uncomfortable leaving this young man alone with you,' he said to Meggsie, then turned to me, the smile still on his face.

God! Was he a complete buffoon? Chest so tight I thought I'd suffocate, my voice was a high-pitch squeak when I squeezed out the words, 'Here, have it.' I reached into my pocket and pulled out Meggsie's book. If I gave it to him maybe he'd go, or at least leave this bloke alone. I didn't want some randomer's blood on my hands. Using the book against Meggsie, it was a stupid idea. What had I been thinking? Meggsie would get it whatever. I held it out towards him. The squeak from my mouth moved up a pitch when the man's hand shot forward placing it on my arm.

'I don't think he deserves it with an attitude like that,' he said, gently taking the book out of my hand.

Oh, my God again! What was this bloke on? Meggsie slowly lifted his head, a moment of disbelief overtaken by a flash of anger. Eyes shining, Meggsie moved to get up. I looked at the man, hoping he'd give him the book or just do one. My legs screamed run, but my feet stayed rooted to the ground. This wasn't going to end well. Even so, I couldn't leave him, he'd been trying to help me. This was my fault. Eyes closed, I stepped forward and steeled myself for whatever was coming.

I waited, but instead of the sound of breaking bones, a whistle pierced the air. It sounded familiar. Slowly I opened my eyes. From out of nowhere a lad had appeared, standing beside the man. He was older than me, about eighteen, and he was ripped, pure muscle. He ran his fingers through his thick black hair, pushing it out of his eyes.

'Problem, Mike?' he asked, his face looked like grit.

The man, Mike, gave Meggsie a hard stare. 'I don't think so?' he said it like a question, but it wasn't.

The vein in Meggsie's neck was pulsing. He looked at muscle boy then gave a glance over his shoulder. He was looking for Gizmo, sizing up the situation. Gizmo and Meggsie together against Muscle boy might be a fair fight, but Meggsie on his own? My money was definitely on the boy. Gizmo was still crouched over, shoulders heaving up and down, sucking on an inhaler, no use to anyone.

Meggsie turned back, the vein pulsing in his neck ramped up a notch. He was desperate for blood, but he wasn't stupid. He was evil, not a fighter, he let other people do that for him.

'I'll be back.' One by one he gave each of us that killer look of his I knew so well, then turned and walked away.

'I'll very much look forward to it,' Mike replied. For a minute I thought Meggsie was going to turn round and go for it anyway, but he didn't. I watched him walk back to Gizmo still desperately sucking on the inhaler.

Meggsie snatched it out of his hand, threw it on the floor then gave him a crack over the head. I winced for him, but at least for now it was Gizmo getting it, not me.

Chapter Seven

Air worked its way back in to my body. I filled my lungs. I could breathe again. I looked at the man who'd saved me. He didn't look much like a saviour, with his mousy hair. I couldn't work him out. He looked like he'd walked out of classroom at Kingsmead High but was hanging around with a kid who looked like he'd never been in one. I tried not to think about it. It didn't matter. Meggsie was gone.

'Well, that's that sorted,' Mike said it like he'd finished the washing up. He smiled across at the boy. 'Thanks for your help, Grits, you can get back to what you were doing.'

'Right, Mike.' The boy jerked his head and, without looking at me, left like he'd arrived, quickly and quietly. I could have dreamt the whole thing except Mike was still in front of me, flicking through Meggsie's black book. He frowned, eyes moving up and down the pages, probably trying to work out what it all meant. I don't know if he knew what was in it and he had no idea Mum was in there, but my face reddened with shame, then guilt. It wasn't Mum's fault.

'Yours, I think.'

He snapped the book shut and handed it back to me. Maybe he didn't get it. He bent down and started gathering up my things. I bent down to help, picking up the pencils scattered across the floor.

'Mike Fielding, pleased to meet you,.' From a crouching position he held out his hand.

Not knowing what else to do, I held out mine.

'Danny,' I offered back, 'and thanks for the help.'

'It's nothing. Glad to be of service.' e took my hand

and squeezed it tight. 'So, what brings you here?'

The light I was basking in after Meggsie's disappearance clouded over. My plan had gone up shit creek. I had no idea what I was doing or where I was going. Uncle Tony wasn't here, and it wasn't likely he'd be back anytime soon, if ever. Mike might have got rid of Meggsie for now, but he'd be back. He wanted his book, and he wanted his money.

My insides trembled as reality took hold, but I re-arranged my face to look like I didn't care and shrugged my shoulders. I wasn't giving anything away. I had no idea who this bloke was. Mike didn't seem bothered I hadn't answered. He chatted on.

'Going on a trip?' he said, handing me one of my spare hoodies., 'Take it it's not a holiday.' He gave a knowing look.

I pushed the hoody back into my rucksack. I was grateful, but he didn't need to shove his nose in like one of those social workers. A stone dropped in the pit of my stomach. Shit, maybe he was!

'It's not that I want to interfere, but I could be of help.'

It was like he'd read my mind. He passed me a pair of socks, then pulled a card from the inside pocket of his coat and handed it to me. Printed on it was *Mike Fielding Community Youth Worker*. I was drained, but my body stiffened, ready to run again. I was right, he was a social worker - more or less.

For the second time he read my mind.

'Don't worry, I'm not going to report you or call the police or anything like that.' He gave a short laugh, 'Like I said, I might be able to help. I only wanted to show you my credentials, so you know I'm an okay guy. You can't be too sure these days.'

My body eased, but only slightly, as I listened to what he had to say.

'You look like you might need somewhere to stay. I could organise a bed for a night or two. I run a hostel for kids not too far from here.' He paused, then added, 'It's all fairly unofficial, so no questions asked, if that's what you're worried about.'

It wasn't like I had much choice, but I took a firm hold of the desperation rising in me, pushing me to jump at the chance, and tried to weigh up what he was saying. On one hand, this guy had saved me from Meggsie, but on the other, he could be anyone. I didn't know if I could trust him, then again, a couple of nights somewhere would be good while I tried to figure out what I was doing, and it would give me some space to start work on my portfolio.

The debate in my head was interrupted by a low whistle from Mike.

'Wow, these are good!' He was flicking through one of my sketchbooks, slightly bent from the force Meggsie had thrown it to the ground.

'It's a hobby,' I muttered, embarrassed but chuffed he liked them. I'd never really shown anyone my art, well only Mum, and Miss McGowan. They said it was good, but they would.

'This is more than a hobby. You've got real talent.' Mike paused while he looked through the rest of my sketch pad. 'You really should think about doing something with these,' he paused again. 'Probably best to get your current problems sorted first. The kids I help out are like you, they need a hand while they get back on their feet. I can help you with a bed for the night, and if you've any other problems,' he dipped his eyes, 'I might be able to help with those too.'

I doubted it unless he had a spare three grand knocking around which he fancied handing over.

Mike carried on. 'It's all off the record of course. You don't need to decide now. I've got a few errands to do, so what if we meet back at the cafe on the corner at about sixish? You'll have seen it on your way in. That'll give you time to have a proper think.'

I knew the cafe he meant. I gave a slight nod. I wasn't making any decisions yet.

'Come on, then.' He put his hand on my shoulder and guided me towards the passage out. We walked in silence while I tried to work things out in my head. His hand felt reassuring, but it didn't sit easy with me, Mike, and Muscle boy. Fair enough, he might have saved me from Meggsie, and he might not be about to do me in, but that didn't mean he was okay.

'Well, this is where we part company,' he said, when we arrived back at the main road. 'Don't forget, six o'clock.'

'Yeah, six,' I repeated.

Then, as an afterthought he turned, pulling something out of his pocket.

'Here, take this.' He handed me a crisp five-pound note. 'Get yourself something to eat.'

I thought of the money shoved down my sock, but I took it anyway, I might need all the cash I could get. Fiver in hand, I watched him disappear. Maybe he was one of the good guys?

Then again, maybe not. I looked at my phone. It flashed 4.13pm. Thirteen, unlucky for some. A sign, an omen. I should get out of here and never come back.

Chapter Eight

I ended up on the tube. If Meggsie was on my back, there'd be too many people around for him to do anything and I could easily lose myself in the crowds. I went up and down the Piccadilly line. The thoughts in my head going backwards and forwards, like the tube. I wanted to believe Mike was okay, that he'd help me, that I'd have somewhere to stay, get my portfolio done. Job sorted. But really, I had no idea who he was. Right now, he could be phoning social care, or he could be some cult leader reeling me in. Or maybe he was just a good guy. I had nearly two hours to decide what I was going to do.

As people left the tube, I grabbed myself a seat. Leaning back, I felt the ache in my muscles from all the crouching and running. Legs stretched out, I studied myself in the window opposite. Blonde hair, brown eyes, the tilt of my chin. I looked the same, but everything was different. When I left home this morning, I'd got it all worked out, but things hadn't exactly gone to plan. The argument about Mike carried on in my head. I could always hole myself up somewhere for a few weeks. If I was careful, I could pay for a room for a few nights. I reached for my sock to touch the reassuring bulge of money.

My hand didn't make it, it didn't need to. I could already see it had gone. Still, I patted my ankle, checked my trousers, hoody pocket, checked my socks again. Socks, trousers, hoody, Frantically I repeated it again - then again. I don't know why. I knew it wasn't there. It must have dropped out while I was running.

I shot up from my seat, ready to run back and find it,

then sat straight back down. What was the point? It would be long gone. I was well and truly stuffed. I sank into my seat. At least I had the fiver Mike had given me. Body and mind exhausted I closed my eyes, partly to stop myself from crying, partly to block everything out. I wanted to fall asleep and forget this was happening.

There was no chance of that. A warm breeze brushed my face when the tube stopped, and the doors swished open. Laughter bounced down the carriage. I opened my eyes. Two boys tumbled in, pushing, and shoving each other. One was about my age, the other younger. Dressed in shirts and blazers, they smelled of cleanliness and money. I watched their reflection in the window.

One was trying to hook a hockey stick round the other one's ankle. No boy at Kingsmead would be seen dead with a hockey stick and the girls mainly used them for hitting each other. The other boy carried a black violin case. I tuned in to their conversation.

'Mum's going to absolutely murder us if we're late,' the younger one said.

'Murder you more like. We wouldn't have been late if you hadn't been kept behind by Harrington. She'll hit the roof when she finds out you've bombed your French test,' the older one replied, giving him an extra hard dig in his ribs.

Still laughing, the younger one pushed him back.

'Not as much as Dad will murder you when I tell him you've been dropped from the cricket team.'

The older boy gasped.

'I have not! You're the one dropped because you're horrendously useless.'

Their banter carried on. It was a different language.

At the next stop the boys tumbled out. I don't know

why, but I left my seat and followed them. Maybe I wanted to see what their life was like. For a few seconds pretending it was mine, that I was with them rushing to meet my Mum. Outside the station they turned a corner. I sped up, keeping them in sight. Ahead a large, white four by four pulled up at the side of the road, engine running. Through its window I saw a woman, waving at them frantically, mouthing at them to get a move on. I stopped and watched them run to the car. When they got in, she leant across the seats giving them a quick hug before pulling away from the kerb. They drove off, a car full of happiness.

My stomach hardened. I wished I had a mum who knew I had homework, never mind cared I'd actually done it, that I had a life where the worst thing that happened was getting kicked off the cricket team. Instead, I had a mother who was so spaced out, half the time she didn't know I was there. Was it luck or had I done something really bad in a previous life? It must have been pretty bad considering how shit my life was right now. I brushed my hand across my face, trying to wipe away the frustration and anger. Maybe this was my chance - maybe Mike was my chance? Why should boys like them get it all? Why not me? I looked at my watch - five thirty. I better get a move on.

I was going to meet Mike.

Chapter Nine

By the time I got to the café, guilt had pushed through my anger. I shouldn't be so hard on Mum. It wasn't all her fault; life had thrown so much shit at her. Things hadn't always been so crap, before the drink and the drugs. Her laugh, the one I hadn't heard for so long, sounded in my ear. Memories surfaced. Bonfire night at my old primary school; her arms pulling me into her, saying I was keeping her warm when we both knew it was because I was scared. Flinching, with every bang and crack, her arms got tighter. Her spending all morning turning the house upside down, searching for my precious He-Man figure, then I found it in my pocket. She'd laughed about that for the rest of the day, eyes brightening every time she remembered.

When had it all got too much? There wasn't a single thing, a single point when it had all changed, but what I knew was once Meggsie got his claws into her, there was no turning back. The anger rushed back this time mixed with fear. This was his fault, not hers. I had to find a way to get him away from her. Me getting the bursary was a start, and to do that I needed somewhere to stay. I needed Mike.

With Mum on my mind, I took my phone out of my pocket to see if she'd messaged me. There was nothing. I tried not to worry. Those tubes and bleeping machines, she wasn't in any state to be sending messages. Still, I didn't want her to worry. My fingers bounced off the phone. EVERYTHING GOOD. HOPE YOU'RE OK. LOVE YOU. D xx. I pressed send. It was going to be okay. I was going to make it okay.

Phone still in hand, I checked the time. Two minutes to six. I leaned into the shadow of the cafe wall and did a quick scan. A woman walked by pushing a pram, a toddler dragging behind; a couple walked out of the café, arm in arm. As far as I could see there were no social workers, no police waiting to pounce - but there was no Mike, either. Damn! I'd been so busy arguing with myself whether or not I should come back, I hadn't thought Mike might change his mind. I pushed back the panic, there was still a couple of minutes. I was about to check the time again when a voice called my name. This time I didn't recognise it. It belonged to a girl; she was walking towards me.

Unlike her voice, her face was vaguely familiar, but I didn't know anyone round here. She must be calling another Danny. I looked around. There was no one else about. I dropped my head and studied my trainers, at the material wearing at my toes. I expected her to walk straight past. She didn't. She stopped right in front of me.

'Danny?'

I lifted my head. Close up, recognition kicked in. Pale face and black hair. Stood right in front of me, she looked even prettier. My face reddened at the thought, imagining she knew exactly what I was thinking. It was the girl from the tube. Confusion overtook embarrassment. I knew who she was, but that didn't explain how she knew my name.

'Mike sent me,' she said. Question answered, but it opened a whole load more. How did she know Mike for starters? If he was a youth worker, maybe he worked with her and Grits. It sort of made sense. If he was, he might not be too happy with her nicking off people in the Underground. Well, I wasn't going to tell him. Even though she didn't know it, her secret was safe with me. Somehow that made me feel good.

'Something came up Mike had to deal with, so he sent me to get you. I'm Skye.'

She must have taken my blank stare as disinterest when she asked, 'That's if you want to come?'

'Yes,' I said, finding my voice. 'Till I get things sorted.' This was temporary. I needed to make that clear.

'Yeah, like you were sorting things earlier with the bloke in the red hoody?' A smile hovered over her lips.

My eyebrows lifted. This was getting weird now. How did she know about that?

'You didn't think Mike turned up by accident?' she asked, the same sparkle in her eyes I'd seen on the tube.

Actually, I did, but didn't say. I already felt enough of an idiot.

'Lucky for you I was meeting Mike over this way and spotted you were in trouble. I persuaded Mike you could do with a hand. Think of it as my way of saying thanks for helping me out with that goon on the tube.'

'Yeah, suppose we can call it quits,' I said, not feeling quite as stupid, even though helping her out had been more of an accident than the knight in shining armour thing, but she didn't need to know that.

'Ready to go, then?' Skye asked, walking away from the cafe.

This was it. My insides danced across my stomach. My feet moved forward, but my head still wasn't too sure.

'So, Mike. He's okay?' I asked. Falling in beside her, I stepped up my pace. She was smaller than me, but her legs moved fast.

She turned and looked at me like I'd asked her if the sky was blue.

'He's more than okay.'

'There must be a catch?' I pushed. Nothing came for free, or it never had in my life.

'The only catch is we all look out for each other,' For a second her eyes lost their shine. 'If it wasn't for him, I don't know where I'd be.' Quickly, the shine returned. 'It might not seem it, but today could be the luckiest day of your life.'

I wasn't sure I'd go that far but things were getting better. If Mike was all he was cracked up to be, maybe things would carry on getting better, but for now if it meant somewhere to stay tonight that was good enough for me.

'This is us,' Skye said, half an hour later when we reached a piece of scrubland hidden behind tatty billboards. Odd bits of rusty machinery, old tyres and the usual nicked shopping trolley were scattered around. My eyes fell on an abandoned mattress. Covered in green moss, it lay on a slant across a pile of rubbish and a load of discarded planks. Was this where I was staying? I know he'd said it wasn't official, but I wasn't expecting this. Then again, at the end of the day, it's not like I was spoilt for choice. I swung my rucksack off my back. It wasn't going to be forever. I'd be home soon. The thud of the bag as it landed echoed the thump of homesickness in my chest. I thought of my bedroom at home. Nothing fancy, but it was mine.

When I was about six, I'd watched one of those TV programmes where some celebrity DIYer had gone to a kid's house and done up their bedroom. When they'd finished, it was like a spaceship, controls and panels fixed to the drawers, planets hanging from the ceiling. They even had an alien bursting out of the wardrobe door. I wanted that bedroom.

I nagged at Mum even though there was no way she

could afford it, but she did something better. She was like that then. I remember her shouting me up to my room. Everything was covered in old sheets and newspaper, pots of paint, all different colours, piled on the floor. I found out later she'd been round the estate blagging everyone for any old paint they'd got.

'Right, Danny,' she'd said. 'The world's your oyster, or your universe!'

Then we painted and painted. One wall was a swirl of colours, the inside of a shooting star, she'd said. Another we did purply- black, then made foil stars and stuck them all over. We painted aliens, spacemen, spaceships. When we finished, it was amazing. Mum was good at art, "It's the only good thing I've given you," she'd sometimes say when she was on one of her downers. She didn't even say that these days.

I grew up and grew out of space stuff, covering the walls with different drawings, sketches, some of my paintings. It was still there, underneath, but the thing that stuck in my mind wasn't what was on the walls, it was the laughing and the hugging while we'd done it. Like the space bedroom, that had disappeared, hidden away somewhere, but like the walls, if I peeled back the layers, I'd find it. I knew I would.

The memory of how Mum used to be sparked my determination. If helping her meant sleeping on a grotty mattress, that's what I'd do. At least here I'd be safe. There'd be other people around.

'So where does everybody else sleep?' I asked, trying to sound like sleeping out in the open on a mattress of mold was something to look forward to.

'What?' Skye took in the rucksack on the mattress. A smile spread across her face, 'You didn't think you were sleeping there?'

'Well, no, I, er…' It was obvious I did. Not that I was trying to impress her or anything, but great start, I looked like a total idiot.

'There's no way Mike would let any of us sleep on that. I'll show you where you will be sleeping,' she said, then put her fingers to her mouth and whistled, the same piercing whistle I'd heard before, on the tube, then again when Grits had appeared. Before I had time to think what it meant, there was a rustle from the bushes by the billboards. Somebody pushed their way through. It was Muscle Boy.

'Hi Grits,' I said. I didn't know him, but it was good seeing another familiar face.

He obviously didn't feel the same.

'You've found Picasso then?' Ignoring me, he looked at Skye. The stone face I'd seen earlier wasn't one he'd put on for Meggsie's benefit - it was his face.

'Mike's been raving about your drawings,' Skye said, explaining the Picasso dig.

'Oh, they're nothing,' I said, but underneath the embarrassed laugh, I glowed. I know Mike had said they were good, but he must really mean it. It made me want to get to wherever we were going and start on the work on my portfolio.

'Not from what Mike said, he's…'

Grits cut her off before she could finish.

'Come on, we haven't got all day. We don't want anyone seeing us hanging around.'

I wanted to ask him why, but I kept quiet. I got the distinct impression Grits didn't like me.

'Here, put this on.' Roughly, he thrust a scarf into my hands. I was right, he really didn't like me.

Chapter Ten

I looked at the scarf in my hands, then at Skye, not sure what to do.

'Over your eyes,' Grits snapped before she had time to say anything. I looked at Skye again, like it was a joke, but I knew it wasn't. This was turning out to be some weird hostel, official or not. My mouth felt dry. I was thinking maybe this wasn't such a good idea.

Skye moved towards me, 'Don't worry, it's a precaution. Security.' The touch of her hand on my shoulder added a flutter to my already churning stomach.

'We don't want every shit for brains homeless kid knowing where we are, and you might not want to stay.' A satisfied smile twitched the corner of Grits' mouth. Despite the poison in his voice, I almost smiled back. *I might not want to stay.* At least I knew that leaving was an option.

'Really, it's fine,' Skye said, trying to reassure me.

I ignored Grits' digs. Skye's reassurance didn't exactly work but what did I have to lose? I eased my rucksack on my back then wrapped the scarf round my head and over my eyes, pulling it in a tight knot at the back.

'Just checking.' I heard Grit's say, then a sharp yank and rough hands pulled the scarf tighter along with my hair.

Grits pushed me forwards, gentler hands hooked through my other arm. That must be Skye. They guided me along, one side carefully steering, the other jostling. Under my feet the ground changed from concrete to grass then to rubble. I wobbled on the uneven surface, steadying myself when the ground changed again, gravelly now but even.

'Keep going.' Grits shoved me forward; Skye squeezed my arm. Small stones crunched beneath my feet as we carried on. Then suddenly we stopped. Grits let go of my arm. I heard what sounded like wood being dragged across the floor, followed by a metal clank. The next thing Grits' hands pushed down hard on my head. I reached out my hands to stop myself toppling over, the roughness of broken brick work scraped against my skin. Grits pushed me down even further.

'Move to the left,' Skye said helpfully.

I eased myself through what felt like a small hole, my rucksack catching against its sides. Once through I stood straight again. Cold air shrouded my body. A dank, dusty smell hit the back of my throat.

'Go on,' Grits pushed me out of the way as he followed behind. I stumbled to the floor. Rough stones dug into my knees.

'Concentrate, Picasso,' he said, hauling me back up.

Skye's voice came from behind.

'Give him a break. It's not like he can see where he's going.' Skye's concern made the push almost worth it. Grits' grip on me eased, replaced by the tension pulsing in the silence that followed. It was broken by a repeat of the noises I'd heard before, the pulling of wood and clanking of metal, only this time the other way around. A door being open and shut.

We started moving again. Under forced blindness, my other senses were on high alert. I felt the closeness of walls around me. The back of my hand brushed against dampness; feeling my way forward, I breathed in the mustiness. Now wasn't the time to get claustrophobic. Grits' feet shuffled on the gravel; behind me I heard Skye's gentle breathing.

As far as I could make out, we were in a passageway or a tunnel. Under the clamminess I smelt a trace of something familiar, metallic-like. Dust and grease covered the coldness. Then, out of nowhere, came a loud rumble. The floor shook beneath my feet. Skye's hands grabbed at me as I stumbled forward. I straightened myself up, hoping Skye didn't feel the tremor in my knees. This was like some horror movie blind man's buff. I did not know where I was or what it was. It could be anything. I could be anywhere.

We stayed motionless until the noise travelled past and the floor became firm again. When the stillness returned, we carried on moving forward without speaking. The thunderous juddering happened twice more before we finally stopped. Grits pulled roughly on the knotted blindfold. I winced inwardly when my hair caught between his fingers. I didn't want to give him the satisfaction of knowing it hurt.

With the scarf off, I blinked, accustoming my eyes from total blackout to the dingy light cast by the torches Skye and Grits were holding. Although the blindfold was off, I was no nearer to knowing where I was. I was right; we were in a tunnel, but Grits had no worries, I had no idea how we'd got here. Through the gloom, I took in my surroundings. We'd come to a dead end. Panic rose again. The walls were pressing in on me; it was almost better when I had the blindfold on. I felt like I was suffocating. I took a deep breath, pulling in the stale air. It didn't make me feel much better. Grits kicked aside some old sacking spread across the floor. In the dimness I made out a manhole cover.

'Give me a hand,' Grits grunted, bending down.

I knelt beside him to help prize it open. His scathing look told me he didn't think I was helping much.

Shoulders straining, it didn't feel that way to me. Slowly, we edged it back revealing a set of rusty ladders leading down to God knows where.

'You go first Skye, get them to open up,' Grits said.

'See you down there,' she said, disappearing into the hole.

As soon as she was gone Grits took a step towards me, his face twisted. I moved my feet, ready to dodge whatever was coming, a slap, a fist in the face. The dank wall pressed against my back and my fists curled automatically, not that I stood a chance against him anyway. But he didn't hit me. His eyes gleamed as he brought his face close to mine.

'We've built something good here, we've worked hard for it, and we don't want some new kid messing it up. We don't need you. We're fine as we are. I don't even know why Mike asked you.' His eyes bore into me. 'Take this as a warning. Mess things up and you'll have me to answer to.'

I wasn't a fighter but if I had've been, I'd have pushed him away and told him, tough shit, Mike had asked me, and I was doing this for my mum, so he better not mess it up for me. But I wasn't a fighter, and anyway he had no worries, I wasn't going to be here long. Once I'd got a plan together, I was out of here. So, I stayed quiet. Why cause any aggro? I needed somewhere to stay. I'd put up with Meggsie long enough. Putting up with Grits for a couple of days was nothing.

He motioned towards the ladder, 'Go on, get down.'

The ladders wobbled as I moved from rung to rung. I looked down into the darkness. I could just about make out the floor. The last couple of rungs were missing, so I jumped. A cloud billowed in front of me when my feet landed on a bed of ash. I coughed through the swirling fog. After my run in with Grits, Skye's smile was as bright as the beam from her torch.

'Over here,' she shouted.

I followed the light to the heavy metal door she stood beside. Above, Grits grunted and groaned pulling the cover back over the manhole. Skye picked up a small metal bar lying on the floor and tapped out a rhythm on the door, waited, then repeated it. A code.

From the other side heavy bolts were drawn. The door opened slowly. A head appeared from behind it. I couldn't see its owner; the peak of a baseball cap hid his face.

'It's us, Chip. You letting us in?' Skye asked.

'Only if you 'av ze secret password, Mademoiselle.' The boy laughed and lifted his head. Now I could see him properly, he was probably about my age but smaller. Blonde hair, almost silver, stuck out from beneath a cap. Now I could see it properly - red and white with a gold cannon on the front. An Arsenal fan.

'The only thing you'll be getting is a smack in the face if you don't get a move on,' Grits said, appearing behind me.

'Sorry, just having a laugh,' Chip answered.

Grits pushed past without looking at him, 'Hurry up and get this door shut.' It wasn't just me he didn't like then. I don't know if that made me feel better or worse.

'Hurry up and get this door shut,' Chip mimicked under his breath once Grits was out of earshot. He sounded exactly like him.

I shuffled through the door, too late to worry whether I'd done the right thing. It clanged shut with a bang of finality.

Chapter Eleven

'Welcome to The Warren!' Skye said, sounding genuinely pleased I was there.

In the glare of the strip light, I blinked away the darkness of the tunnel and tried to make sense of where I was. The shuddering noise I'd heard earlier made sense now. We were in an Underground station, but not one I recognised. An ancient clock, missing a hand, dangled from the ceiling. Stuck in time, everything was cloaked in mustiness. I wanted to capture its broken history on paper. The cracked tiles, the curve of the ceiling. Maybe there'd be time for that later. I'd heard about these tunnels, some built but never used, others closed and forgotten. It was spooky, but when I thought about Meggsie and where I could have been, spooky was good.

The boy who'd opened the door looked up at me from under the brim of his cap. 'Chip. How do?' His eyes twinkled. He was as friendly as Grits was unfriendly.

'Danny,' I offered, returning his smile.

'Never mind that crap. Mike's waiting for you in the dining hall. Get your backsides down there,' Grits interrupted.

'Sure thing!' Chip mock saluted, pulling a face at Grits back as he walked away. 'Better go before all the scrans gone,' he said, setting off in the same direction as Grits.

Skye tutted, 'Yeah, never mind keeping Mike waiting, it's all about your belly.'

My rucksack was weighing on my back as I followed them across what once would have been a busy platform. We passed through an archway sign posted

XIT; the E dropped off long ago.

A sharp smell cut through the grease, twitching my nose. I sniffed at its familiarity.

'My favourite,' Chip breathed deeply.

I sniffed again. That was it - chicken korma. I could almost taste it. My stomach whined, remembering I hadn't eaten all day. Voices mingled with the spicy smell wafting down the tunnel. We rounded a corner into an old entrance foyer, now blocked off and looking more like a school canteen. Groups of kids sitting round tables. About fifteen to twenty in total, chatting, shoveling food in their mouths.

'What'll it be, guys?' asked a girl, her hair scooped up in a ponytail, standing behind a longer table which was set up like a makeshift kitchen. Steam rising from pans bubbling away on camping stoves.

'Everything for me,' Chip said. 'Twice!'

'I'm Mim,' the girl smiled, handing me a bowl piled high with curry.

'Danny,' I said, taking the bowl.

The curry looked as good as it smelt. Balancing it in my hand, I followed Skye and Chip, squeezing between the tables. Friendly faces nodded their 'hiya's' as we made our way over to a table where Mike sat.

'Good to see you!' Mike stood up to say hello. I wasn't sure if it was the distant shudder of another train going overhead or nerves at seeing Mike again which made the bowl wobble in my hand. 'Sorry I couldn't meet you earlier. Something came up. Sit down and tuck in before it gets cold.' He pulled out the chair next to him. 'What do you think?' he asked.

I didn't know if he meant the food or The Warren, but either way the answer was the same.

'Great!'

Not that I'd ever stayed in a hostel, but this wasn't what I was expecting. More dormitories and school dinners. This was surreal. It was hard to believe a few hours ago I'd nowhere to stay, no money and was about to get battered by Meggsie. Now I was in a weird version of Alice in Wonderland, fallen down a hole into a completely new world. Sat here safe and dry, eating top quality korma, with a bunch of kids who were clean, happy, and well-fed. I pushed back the voice telling me if it's too good to be true, it probably is. Instead, I sucked up the warmth of curry and friendliness spreading through me.

'When you've finished, Skye and Chip can show you where you'll be sleeping,' Mike said. 'It's not the Ritz, but it's warm and dry and above all it's safe, and you'll have space to sort out what you need to do.'

'Is Danny coming out with us tomorrow?' Chip asked through a mouthful of food.

Mike looked at me, eyebrows raised. 'Might be good to have a break, give Chip and Skye a hand, see how things rock and roll down here?'

'I'm only here till I get things sorted' I answered, more to Chip than Mike. They needed to know.

'Ah, come out with us. It'll be a blast.' Chip sounded like he really meant it. I hardly ever went out with mates anymore. I'd stopped saying yes when Mum got really bad. I'd got pretty inventive with excuses for people not to come round the house. Everybody had sort of drifted off, but it didn't matter, Mum came first, like she did now.

'I'm not sure, there's things I've got to get on with,' I needed to get my head down and start this portfolio.

Skye looked up from her plate, 'That's a shame.'

Unlike Chip, I wasn't sure if she meant it, or it was

just one of those things you said. Either way, a tug of regret pulled at me. She was nice. She'd been kind to me. Spending a day with her would have been good. I liked her, but then again, that's not why I was here. I was here to sort things out for Mum, and the quicker I did that, the quicker things could get back to normal.

'Maybe Danny can help us another time if he's got things to do,' Mike gave me a knowing look. 'Talking of which…' He put his hand under the table and pulled out a carrier bag.

'Here.' He offered it to me.

I took the bag from him. It was flat and folded over, it squashed between my fingers. I had no idea what was in it. I pulled it open and peered inside. It only took one look, and I knew exactly what it was. A carrying case for my artwork, but not just any, it was top quality. The leather was soft to touch as I took it out.

'What is it?' Chip asked, looking as unexcited as I was excited.

'It's for his art stuff, philistine,' Skye answered. 'You put your work in it, then roll it up, stops it getting damaged.'

'Exactly, Skye,' said Mike. 'It's a shame to think Danny's pictures could have got damaged earlier today.' He turned to me. 'It will fit in your rucksack without getting squashed. Talent like yours needs protecting.'

Not quite believing it was for me, I turned it over in my hands.

'Look inside,' Mike said.

I laid it on the table and rolled it open. If I was lost for words before I was even more lost now. Wrapped inside was a set of Blackwings. Even school couldn't afford quality pencils like that.

All I could get out was, 'Thanks!' I hoped Mike could

hear in that one word how much I meant it.

'Any time. Anyway, I better get going, no rest for the wicked!' Mike laughed, getting up to leave.

'I'll help out tomorrow,' I got it out quickly, before I changed my mind. It was the least I could do. Mike was giving me a roof over my head, feeding me and now this. One day wouldn't matter.

'That's great,' Mike said. 'If you're sure, an extra pair of hands is always a help.'

I was sure, and the smile on Skye's face made me even surer.

I watched Mike walk away, everybody hanging on to his words as he chatted, passing their tables. I looked down at the holder again. I still hadn't worked him out, but maybe he was one of the good guys, maybe they did exist.

'Anyone for seconds?' Chip held up his empty plate.

'Not for me.' I was so full I could barely move.

'Never mind seconds, we need to show Danny where he's staying,' Skye said, snatching Chips plate from under him. For someone so small he certainly packed it away.

'Ok, but if I faint with hunger, it's your fault.' Chip grasped his stomach.

'So, what's the crack tomorrow?' I asked, following them out of the dining area and down another tunnel.

'It's like a collect and delivery service.' Skye answered.

'Easy as chips,' Chip laughed. 'You'll get the hang of it in no time.'

It didn't sound too difficult, and, as I kept telling myself, it was only for one day. After that I'd get on with putting my portfolio together. I looked down at the art case I was carrying, still stunned by such a generous gift. My stomach felt warm and full. It wasn't just the curry. I had a plan.

'We're here,' Skye said as we approached a new tunnel. This one had no tiles or posters just grey walls and pipes, more like a service tunnel. Along one wall ran a line of old hospital screens. Chip pulled back the orange patterned curtain. A pain stabbed, sharp in my chest, the swish triggering a picture of Mum, tubes protruding from her, machines bleeping. The curry in my stomach churned. I steadied myself on the metal frame of the curtain.

'Are you okay?' Skye took hold of my arm. 'Why don't you sit down?' She motioned to the roll-up mattress on the floor, laid out with sleeping bag and a blanket.

I lowered myself down.

'It's not that bad, is it?' Chip quipped.

Skye gave him a disapproving look.

'No, it's great. It's the hospital stuff, it reminded me of someone.'

Skye and Chip waited for me to go on.

'My Mum, she's not well.' I wasn't going to tell them the whole story. I'd got too used to the sideways looks, people making up their minds about her when they didn't even know her. 'That's why I'm here. It's only temporary. She'll be out of hospital soon, then things will get back to normal.' I was reminding myself as much as telling them.

Chip nodded his head. 'Same. I had to get away from my mum and poxy stepdad. My real dad is in the army, a bit of a hero,' his chest swelled with pride. 'But once he's back, I'm outta here - not that it's not great, of course.'

It felt better knowing there was someone else who wasn't here long term.

'What about you?' I looked at Skye.

In the awkward silence that followed I didn't miss the glance that passed between her and Chip.

'I'm off to the loo,' she said, bending her head, but not fast enough to hide the tears in her eyes.

I gave myself a mental slap. I'd only been there five minutes and somehow, I'd managed to upset her.

'Was it something I said?' I asked Chip, as she headed off back down the tunnel.

'Yep!' he said, not pulling any punches. I looked at him, waiting for more. 'Not everyone's lucky like you and me, not everyone has a family they can go back to.'

I kicked myself, I should have realised. Every person here had their own story. As good as this place was looking, it was no holiday camp, no-one was here out of choice.

'Shall I go find her, say I'm sorry?' I asked.

'Nah, don't worry, she'll be back in a minute.' He brushed it off easily while the guilt stuck to me.

But he was right, by the time I'd opened my rucksack and emptied it out on the roll out mattress, Skye was back.

'You okay?' I mumbled, not knowing what else to say.

'Yeah,' she replied, her mouth smiled but the redness around her eyes said different.

'I'm sorry, I didn't…' She didn't let me finish.

'Honestly, don't worry it's fine,' her voice was as gentle as the hand she placed on my shoulder. The same flutter I'd felt earlier passed through me. I automatically pulled my stomach in tight, afraid Skye might notice. Someone like Skye would never be interested in me that way, I wasn't exactly great girlfriend material. Not that I was thinking that way, I wasn't here to get a girlfriend, but it would be good to have Skye as a friend.

'I'm glad you've got your Mum to go back to.

Anyway,' her voice brightened, moving on from the subject. 'We'll get off and let you sort your stuff out.'

'Yeah, get some beauty sleep. You'll need it, busy day tomorrow.' Chip winked as they left.

I started folding the clothes I'd taken out of my rucksack, still feeling the warmth from Skye's touch. It turned cold when I picked up my spare jeans - under them was Meggsie's black book. It was small, but it filled the mattress, a reminder of Mum's debt and what Meggsie might do. I took a breath and pushed it deep into the bottom of my rucksack, out of sight. I rummaged through the rest of my things, pulling out the letter from St Cuths. Even in its tea-stained glory, it took away the bitter taste Meggsie's book left in my mouth. I read through it again. I could do this. I folded it back up and slipped it carefully into the inside pocket of the art case Mike had given me. The Blackwings shone out. I might as well make a start now.

Sat cross-legged, I made myself comfortable on the mattress and lay out my pencils. The sounds of overhead tube trains faded into the distance as hope flowed from my hand to the paper. The pencils glided across it, capturing her eyes and the neat trim of her hair. She was right. Maybe this was the luckiest day of my life.

Chapter Twelve

'Wit woo!'

Chip's shrillness broke through my morning fog head. I felt like I'd slept for years.

'You got it bad, man,' he laughed.

I rubbed my eyes, focusing my half asleep-half awake vision. Chip waved a piece of paper at me. 'Pretty good, though!'

I wanted my sleeping bag to eat me up. In his hand was the drawing of Skye I'd done last night.

'I like drawing people,' I muttered, face reddening. 'I'll do one of you,' I added, trying to make it less of a thing. It didn't work.

'Don't worry mate, your secret's safe with me.' He gave a knowing nod.

I was about to argue when he grabbed the bottom of my sleeping bag and shook it.

'Get your love-struck backside out of here, we've got work to do. Oh, and a word of advice. Don't let Grits know you've got the hots for Skye. His eye's well and truly on her.'

Maybe that explained why he had such a downer on me.

The smell of sausage and bacon from the dining area was as good as yesterday's curry. Plate piled high; my eyes roamed looking for somewhere to sit. Chip gave me a dig, 'How about over there?'

I followed his gaze to where we'd sat last night, where Skye sat now.

'If you want.' I tried to look unbothered. It didn't work - again. His puckered lips squeaked as he kissed the air.

I shook my head at him, turning away. Great timing, so much for the warning about Grits. He stood behind me, face like thunder.

'Move it, Picasso, we haven't got all morning. I need to sort out what everyone's doing.'

I moved out of his way and followed Chip to the table taking the seat opposite Skye.

'Ready for today?' she asked.

My firm nod didn't give away the worry circling in my stomach. I still wasn't quite sure what we were doing. My appetite sank even further when Grits sat down in the seat next to Skye. The smile on his face made him look almost human. It was obviously for Skye, not me.

'Your list for today. Dexter's Electrics off the High Street. Thought it would be a good place to start if you've got Picasso in tow.'

'Yep, he's gonna learn from the maestro!' Chip said, plonking himself down next to me.

'Don't go teaching him your bad habits,' Grits snapped back, the smile disappeared from his face. 'Skye's in charge. We don't want any of your cockups. Try not to draw any attention to yourself - if that's possible.'

Chip laughed, trying to cover his embarrassment, but he couldn't hide the pink flush of his cheeks as Grits carried on, 'When you make mistakes you don't just put yourself at risk, you put everybody and everything we're doing here at risk.'

He was talking to Chip, but his hardened eyes connected with mine. 'And you, Picasso, remember - watch it. You've been warned.' The worry in my stomach gave another swirl. What did he mean about Chip cocking things up? How hard could collection and delivery be?

'Where does he get off?' Chip grumbled as we watched him leave. 'If my ad heard him speaking to me like that…' His words hung in the air. I glanced at Skye, worried the mention of parents would upset her, but if it did, she didn't show it.

'Don't worry about Grits. He's always nervous when someone new joins us. He doesn't want anything to go wrong,' she explained, ignoring Chip.

'Yeah, like it did before he met up with Mike. He ran his own group, but they all got busted. He reckons someone snitched on them to the police and that's why they got caught. Funny how he was the only one who got away.'

Irritation deepened on Skye's face. 'That's not fair, Chip. You know Grits is gutted about that. It's why he's so tough on us. It's because he cares.'

He had a funny way of showing it, but that wasn't what was taking up my headspace. I was trying to make sense of what I was going to be doing today. The unease creeping up my back didn't have time to settle. Skye looked at her phone.

'Eat up, time to go.'

Blindfold back on, I was in the tunnel again. The smells and juddering were more familiar this time, my feet moved more confidently. In what seemed like no time we were back out on the scrubland.

Blindfold off, I sucked in the morning's freshness, coughing out the dust of The Warren. Skye took out the list Grits had given her and passed it to Chip.

'The usual stuff, nothing fancy. We go in, collect, then out. Remember what Grits said.'

'Grits schmitts, what does he know?' Chip replied, barely glancing at the list she'd handed him. I was beginning to understand what Grits meant.

Skye rolled her eyes at Chip, then looked at me. 'Danny, you watch for now. Look and learn, don't draw attention to yourself. Anything goes wrong, we'll meet round the corner from the shop. Don't panic.'

Don't panic. I could already feel it rising.

Then we were on the move again, speed walking up the High Street. Skye's words played over in my head, 'If anything goes wrong…' The unease wasn't creeping now. It was stamping. Still, I followed. Her words unnerved me, but what unnerved me more was being out here, outside the safety of The Warren. Every flash of red I saw was Meggsie. I had to keep on moving.

By the time we arrived at Dexter's, my heart was racing, and it wasn't the fast walking. A combination of fear of Meggsie and what I was about to walk into. I kept telling myself it was simple; we were picking stuff up. Still, it didn't stop me thinking something wasn't right. I hovered at the doorway, debating whether to face the unknown or stay out here and risk Meggsie appearing.

'Danny, you go first. Find somewhere to stand where you can watch us.' Skye gave me a gentle shove. I was through the door.

Aisles stretched out before me. Washing machines, cookers, small electrical goods, computers. A swift look and I positioned myself by the iPads. I had a clear view across the shop, nothing to do with it being next to the door, ready for a quick escape.

When Skye and Chip came in they didn't look like they were together. Skye marched in, a girl on a mission. Chip sauntered behind, head down, glued to his phone. I made out I was playing on the screens in front of me, but my eyes flitted from side to side, trying to keep up with their movements around the shop. My heart beat in my ears. No way was this picking up a collection. Skye strode up and down the aisles searching for something without much joy. Chip ambled along. He picked up a camera, turning it over in his hands, not really looking at it. He went to put it back on the shelf, but at the last minute slipped it into his bag.

I turned stone cold. They weren't collecting, they were shoplifting, but truthfully, I already knew that. I just hadn't wanted to believe it. Skye nicking that bloke's wallet, she didn't need me to keep it a secret from Mike, she was doing it for him.

My head screamed at me to get out. I was Danny Bennett; I kept my head down, kept out of trouble. That's how me and Mum got by, and now more than ever I needed to keep a low profile. The last thing I wanted was to get caught nicking.

I shouldn't be here. I looked towards the door, readying myself to make a run for it. A flash of red whizzed by. My heart lurched. Meggsie. I told myself to stop being paranoid. He wasn't the only person to wear a red hoody. I breathed deeply, trying to think straight. If they got caught, nobody knew I was with them. I'd sit it out then decide what to do.

I risked a glance over at Chip. Totally blasé, he did it again, picked up another camera, put it straight in his bag - three times it happened. I was no expert, but he wasn't even trying to hide what he was doing. Then I noticed the security man, his eyes fixed on Chip. I wanted to puke. He'd been sussed, but the look on Chip's face told me he'd clocked him, too. Blood pumped round my body, watching, waiting for Chip to run. A low groan rumbled in my throat. Chip, at the same slow pace, carried on walking down the aisle.

Frantically, I scanned the shop floor, looking for Skye.

She'd know what to do. Like before, she was walking along the aisle, fully focused on whatever she was pretending to look for. I willed her to look at me so I could warn her, but my telepathic powers weren't working. Or maybe they were - she didn't look at me, but she turned and started walking towards Chip. For a split second I lost sight of them behind a display of hair dryers. She'd warn him. I sucked the breath of relief straight back in when they reappeared from behind the tower and Skye walked towards the door. Chip didn't follow, instead he walked right back towards the security guard.

This was it. He was as good as caught. Panic rose. Why hadn't Skye done anything? I didn't know what to do, but it was too late anyway. When I looked back, the security guard had hold of Chip's arm.

Stay or run? The question exploded in my head. Before I could decide Chip's voice, well, one of them, rang across the shop floor.

'How dare you! I think you will find you're mistaken.'

He could have been one of those posh boys with the hockey sticks I'd seen on the tube. Head down, I risked another glance.

My jaw dropped. What was he thinking? Chip opened the bag to show the security guard. No way could he blag his way out of this. The guard put his hand inside and started pulling things out. My jaw dropped further. A book, a pencil case, a half-eaten sandwich. Not one camera!

For a second the security guard looked as confused as me, then when he saw Chip's smug expression, I thought he was going to punch him. Chip gave one of his best smiles, 'Don't worry, I won't be filing a complaint.' And he walked out of the shop swinging his bag.

I stood wide eyed, everything clicking into place. They'd swapped bags behind the stack of hair dryers.

'What you staring at?' The gruff voice of the security guard brought me back. Time to leave. I smiled weakly, hoping my shaking legs would get me to the door.

Chapter Thirteen

Out in the open, I still felt trapped. The world closed in on me. Head twisting and turning, inside and out, I wanted to run, but where to? Whichever way I went it was headlong into shit. Mentally. I kicked myself again and again. I'd known The Warren was too good to be true. I could run now, forget I'd met Mike, but there was Meggsie, and my stuff. It was all back at The Warren. I took a breath, a minute to think what I should do, clenching my hands to stop them from shaking. I'd go back, get my things, then decide. Every bit of me was on high alert, I made my way to the meeting place.

'You've seen the maestro at work then,' Chip greeted me. 'Think you can do it as expertly?'

'Yeah, clever,' I answered, avoiding the question, hoping it didn't show this was the last place I wanted to be. On the outside I'd stopped shaking, inside was tremor city.

Skye was busy fumbling in the bags, taking things out of boxes and putting them back in different bags. The bag with all the nicked stuff in was lined with something that looked like metal foil. She pulled it out.

'That's what stops the alarms going off. It needs taking out, then we split the stuff between us, so it doesn't look as dodgy if one of us gets stopped.'

She picked up one of the bags. It burnt like hot coals when she thrust it into my hands. I wanted to launch it as far away from me as possible. It was heavy as lead in my hands on the walk back to the tube station. Chip chatted away, making up for my silence,

'Mike will be well pleased with this lot. We'll get it back, move it on and bang - party!'

'You make it sound like we're living the high life,' Skye shook her head, then looked at me. 'Anything we make is used to keep The Warren going, to keep us safe, to give us a better start in life. He's going to help me get to college, train as a nurse.' For a split second, the sadness I'd seen on her face the night before returned.

'There's no way he's getting me to college, however hard he tries. I'm working with my dad when he gets back' Chip butted in.

'Mike's rule is, we only take from those who can afford it, who won't miss it. A redistribution of wealth.' Skye explained.

'Yeah, like Mike says, they've got more than enough. It won't hurt to share a bit with us,' Chip added.

The bag lightened slightly in my hand. I got what they meant, but it was still stealing, it was still wrong, and I still couldn't risk it. Disappointment filled me. I wished it were different. It felt so right walking down the street with Skye and Chip, and even if Mike was doing something wrong, it was for the right reasons. He was a good bloke; I could see that.

My mind was pulling in different directions when the voice sliced through me before I saw him.

'Danny, son, fancy seeing you here.' The red of his hoody filled my eyes as the colour drained from my face.

Chip looked confused, not sure what was going on, recognition flashed across Skye's face. My knees weakened; resignation set in. There was no use running, no offence to Skye or Chip but there was none of Grits' muscle to save the day. I looked at them both, my eyes telling them to run for it. They might as well save themselves. I was getting a beating whatever. Skye and Chip were too busy exchanging glances to notice my look. Something unspoken passed between them. Suddenly Chip ran at Meggsie, pummeling at him with his fists. No surprise, Meggsie batted him out of the way like an irritating fly, but it gave me the opportunity to run.

I didn't need to look back to know he was behind me. I had a built in Meggsie radar and he wasn't going to let me get away that easy. There was no way I could outrun him. Ahead of me, the shopping centre loomed, a beacon of safety. If I made it inside, I might be okay, more chance of me losing him, and if he did get hold of me, less chance him laying into me with all those witnesses about. Head forward, energy surging through me, I torpedoed through the doors. Warm air and relief rushed at me. I didn't stop to see if he'd followed. Weaving in and out of the crowds, backtracking on myself, up the escalator then straight back down, in one shop door, out of the other, I tried to shake him off.

After what seemed hours, but was actually minutes, I slipped behind a screen advertising toothpaste. A smiling mouth, filled with gleaming white teeth looked down on me. I wished it would swallow me up. Daring to look, I poked my head out. No sign of red. I took a deep breath. I couldn't stay here all day, I had to get back to Skye and Chip, back to The Warren, back to safety. I pulled my hood tight over my head. Sweat cold against my skin, I stepped out. Nerves shot; I focused on the door beyond the top of the escalator. My way out.

Moving up the stairs, my head rotated like a searchlight. Still no Meggsie, I was nearly there. Then as my eyes levelled with the floor, a wall of red stood blocking my exit. In blind panic I turned, trying to make my way back down, but the escalator moved up quicker than I could get past the column of people blocking my way. There was no escape. Before my feet had chance to connect with the floor, he'd hauled me off the escalator.

'Danny son, where've you been?' For the benefit of everyone around his voice was deep with concern while his nails dug through my clothes into my skin. This was it. I was a goner. I didn't even try to pull away, there was no point fighting.

Then through the noise of the crowds I heard it. The whistle. Skye and Chip were here, I wasn't sure where or what they could do, but the fact they were near made me feel I could cope with what was coming. A movement caught the corner of my eye. Sidling up to me out of nowhere, was Skye.

'Pervert!' Her voice rang out above the crowd. 'He touched my bum!'

She turned and whacked Meggsie on the arm. I couldn't believe it. Skye taking on Meggsie for me. If I liked her before, I liked her even more now.

Meggsie looked stunned, but still had a firm hold of me.

'Stop touching me!' Skye shouted out even louder.

Heads turned, the beginnings of a small crowd gathering around us.

'You should be ashamed of yourself,' a woman weighed down with shopping tutted as she pushed past.

Meggsie's stunned face was furious, 'Bitch, I haven't laid a finger on you,' he hissed at Skye.

Over the top of Skye's head, I saw a security guard walking towards us. Meggsie had seen him too. His grip slackened; another hand pulled at me. It was Chip.

'Go!' he said, pushing me from behind. Automatically I pushed back, glancing at Skye, then turning to Chip.

We couldn't leave her with Meggsie. 'She'll be fine,' he hissed, teeth gritted. His hand forced me along, relief at my escape overshadowed leaving Skye behind arguing with Meggsie and the security guard.

'I'm not staying here to be abused by a low life like you,' Skye's voice travelled across the shopping centre.

The relief came when a few seconds later, I felt her breath on my neck

'Keep moving, don't stop.'

And we didn't, not until we were well out of the shopping centre, and we were sure Meggsie wasn't following.

'That's one you owe us,' Chip puffed out between short breaths, when we finally stopped running.

'Totally.' I heaved. 'Big style.'

Skye looked at me, 'You owe us nothing, Warren kids look out for each other.'

Her words sliced through me, a double-edged sword. It was true, they'd totally looked out for me. That hadn't happened to me in a long time. I'd been saved again. I so wanted to stay, but I couldn't - I couldn't risk being caught. The smile I gave back came from the bottom of my heart, but it still felt false. In a couple of hours, I'd be gone. For me they'd be a memory, one of those you drag up when you're not feeling too great. No doubt they'd forget I ever existed.

Chapter Fourteen

The thump in my chest slowed with the clang of The Warren door. Safety wrapped around me. Even Grits' bark was a welcome compared to what could have happened. The last thing I wanted to think about was how soon I'd have to go back out there. I shivered. The blanket of safety began to slip.

'Where've you been?' Grits accusing eyes fell on me.

'We ran into the idiot that's after Danny, the one from the estate,' Skye answered for me.

The mention of Meggsie set my heart thumping again.

Like a death ray, Grits' eyes bore into me. 'He better not have followed you back.'

'No, we lost him,' I muttered, trying not to think about what might have happened if he had.

'We gave him a real run around, no way did he follow us,' Skye echoed.

The look of obliteration left Grits' eyes when he answered Skye.

'Good job you were there. Go get a break, you deserve it after putting up with these amateurs.' The steeliness returned when he looked back at me. 'Help Chip unload this stuff, then Mike wants to see you in his office. Chip can show you where it is.'

'Thanks for all your hard work, you've done a great job,' Chip muttered under his breath as Skye and Grits walked off down the tunnel.

Chip's impressions of Grits didn't lighten my mood. We stacked the boxes from our 'collection', one on top of another, next to a mountain of iPads, phones, DVD players and car Satnavs. The pile got higher and so did my stress. I wanted to be as far away from here as possible, but at the same time I wanted to stay. I had no idea what I was going to say to Mike - or more to the point, what he was going to say to me. I still had no idea when Chip led me to Mike's office. I wanted the journey to take forever so I didn't have to disappoint Mike, so I didn't have to think about leaving, but we were there in the blink of an eye. Chips' knock on the door echoed like a death knell.

'Come in,' Mike answered. I pushed the door open leaving Chip behind.

The buzz from the light hanging on the ceiling filled the windowless room, which at one time must have been a ticket office. Along one wall sat a blue torn sofa, along the other shelves packed with cardboard boxes, stuffed with papers. Mike sat behind a desk. He motioned for me to sit on the sofa.

'Good to see you,' he said.

I squirmed in my seat, about to throw everything he'd done for me back in his face.

'Good day?' he asked.

'Yeah,' I replied. The falseness I felt earlier magnified.

'Grits told me about your run in with Meggsie.'

My mouth dried at the mention of his name,

'I hope you decide to join us, for a while at least. It would be a weight off my mind knowing you were here safe.' Mike waited for an answer.

'Well, er…' I stumbled. Mike's kindness made it even harder to find the words I wanted to say.

Mike's face dropped. He knew what was coming.

'I know what we do here doesn't always sit easy, and I sincerely wish there was a different way, but sometimes we don't have a choice. We have to break the rules. I'm sure Skye and Chip have explained we only take from those who can afford it, to give to those who can't. You kids.' He looked at me, stressing the words that came next. 'All for the greater good, Danny. That's our motto.'

When he spoke again, he had a faraway look in his eye.

'Before you make a decision, I want to tell you a story. I hope it might help you understand.'

It wasn't what I was expecting, but I eased back into the sofa, ready to listen, glad to put off the point I had to leave.

'It explains why I do what I do.' Mike leaned back in his chair, chin resting on crisscrossed fingers.

'John Somers, a troubled boy I knew, ended up on the streets. Not a strong lad, but he survived.' A flash of pain crossed Mike's face. 'One freezing night he went to a homeless shelter, but there were no beds, so the support worker turned him away. He knew John was struggling, but rules were rules. He told him to come back early the next morning and he'd book him a bed for that night.' Mike lowered his head. 'John never came back. The next day they found him dead on the street.' Mike's voice cracked. 'It was a long time ago, but that support worker was me. I let that boy down and I vowed I'd never let it happen again.'

The name John Somers pricked my mind. I'd heard it before but couldn't think where. I shrugged it off, probably on the news or something.

Mike cleared his throat. 'I talked to the powers that be, reasoned, argued for more resources, but nothing changed. Kids like you, like Skye and Chip, out on the street. Sometimes you have to make things happen. I owed it to John to do something - rules or no rules. So, I did this. A safe place, so I'd never have another John Somers on my conscience. I made it happen, Danny.'

My reflection glinted in the glassy film settling on

Mike's eyes. I didn't know what to say. Pink spots surfaced on his cheeks. I felt for him, not in a "what a saddo" way, but in a "what a great guy" way. He leaned forward, staring directly at me. 'That's my story. That's why I want to help. You can share yours if you wish, but no pressure.'

I started to talk, and when I did it was like I'd taken a lid off and couldn't put it back on. I told him about Mum, about Meggsie, the overdose, the money we owed, Meggsie's black book, the fears about what might happen to Mum, art college, my plan for paying back Meggsie. I told him it all.

Chapter Fifteen

I sank further into the sofa. Speaking it out loud left me exhausted. Mike looked straight at me, not with pity, but with strength.

'That's some story. I'm impressed at how you're working things out and totally understand why you don't want to stay. You're right, your Mum comes first. Stay tonight, that's fine. In the morning I'll get some food packed up for you, enough for a couple of days. I'll feel better knowing you're not going hungry, for a while at least.'

The relief I felt that he understood that he wasn't disappointed, swamped me, but slap bang behind it was a solid red lump of fear - Meggsie. I was going back out there. He'd found me once, what's to say he wouldn't again? The effort it took to push me up from the sofa was as big as the pull to stay. It tugged harder as I walked to the door. Hand stretched towards the handle, it felt like I was about to walk off a cliff.

'Danny.'

I turned. The pain in Mike's face was the same as when he'd spoken about John Somers.

'It's hard for me to say this, but I'm going to because I care,' he pursed his lips, head tilted to one side. 'Your art is amazing. In a fair world you'd win that bursary hands down, but this system's not set up for people like you. You won't get it, Danny. It's as simple as that.'

His words shot through me A dead weight smashed down on my already heavy chest. I wanted to shout he was wrong, he had to be. This was how I was making things right. This was the plan, the only plan, it had to work, but his words echoed inside, pulling me down. I tried to drown them out, but I couldn't because deep down I knew he was right. Who had I been kidding? I wasn't one of those hockey boys I'd seen on the tube. I was me. Danny Bennett. Boys like me didn't go to art school. I was desperate. I was sinking.

'I am sorry for saying it as it is,' he paused, 'but there may be another way we can sort this out.'

'How?' I grabbed at his words like a lifeline.

Mike looked me straight in the eye.

'I'm sure Skye and Chip will have explained what we do with the money we make from selling on the goods that we "collect".'

I nodded. I knew it was all for the right reasons, but I still couldn't risk it. I had to think of Mum.

'The bulk of the money helps us to live the lifestyle we do here, feeds us, clothes us, keeps us warm. Any surplus, and there usually is some, is put towards good causes. If you join us, did your bit, we could use some of it to pay off your Mum's debt. I'll be honest, there's a risk, but it's small; everyone at The Warren will be looking out for you. You'll be kept safe until it's time to go home.'

Deep inside a whisper took root, gradually growing louder. Maybe Mike was right. This was a surer way of getting the money, and they'd saved me from Meggsie - twice now.

Mike carried on, 'I can help you in other ways. I've got contacts in the council through my youth work connections. You and your Mum need a fresh start. I could put a word in for a new house, a new area, get you away from that lowlife Meggsie.'

'You'd do that for us?' Disbelief and hope surged through me. Me and Mum, in a new house, a new life. Away from Meggsie. Put like that, Mum could definitely do this. I knew she could.

'Of course, anything I can do to help. And if you're worried about your Mum, it will be easy enough to keep a check on how she's doing, and we can let her know you're safe.'

I was finding it difficult to keep up with what Mike was offering alongside the argument going on in my head. It was risky, but there were so many reasons to stay. Mike had everything covered.

'You don't need to decide now, sleep on it and let me know tomorrow,' Mike said.

My mind mush, I turned to leave.

'Oh, I almost forgot, your drawings,'

I turned back.

'I don't want you to feel disappointed about art college, it truly isn't that your works are not good enough. Like I said, life isn't fair, but an acquaintance of mine owns a café near London Fields, Café De Lucia. Some of the local artists display their pictures there to sell. I spoke to him and he's more than happy to showcase yours. He thinks they'll really appeal to his clientele.'

My mouth opened to speak, but all that came out was a choking gasp. Had I heard him right. My artwork for sale.

'It's not the Tate, but it's a start,' Mike said.

I didn't care. My work was going to be hung on a wall for sale, for people to see. Who needed St Cuths? I tried to push the thought of it out of my head.

'I don't know what to say!'

'Say nothing. You might not go to the right school, talk with the right accent, live in the right house, but you've got talent and if there's anything I can do to further that, I will. You deserve a chance.'

82

Indignation fueled me. He was right. I deserved a chance. I thought again about the boys I'd seen on the tube, with their musical instruments and posh voices. It wasn't fair that they got it all! I was going to do this. I'd make it right for Mum. Maybe not in the way I'd thought, but I'd make it right. I know what Mike did wasn't strictly legal, but he was doing it to help. He was making things equal. It's a good job there were people like Mike about. Nobody else was helping me. He might have to break the rules, but he wasn't hurting anyone. It wasn't like they were out mugging old ladies. If I sold some of my sketches and helped at The Warren, I might be able to pay Meggsie back before Mum left hospital. I took a deep breath. The words came out firm and strong.

'I'll stay.'

'You will?'

I nodded.

The skin around Mike's eyes creased as the smile spread across his face.

'That's brilliant! Let's make this happen. You won't regret it.'

After all he'd done for me already, he still managed to make it sound like I was doing him a favour.

'Welcome to The Warren,' Mike leaned across his desk, grasped my hand and shook it firmly, 'All for the greater good.'

Chapter Sixteen

I was bouncing, walking back towards the dining room with Mike. I'd done the right thing.

'I can't tell you how glad I am you're staying. We'll get this issue with your mum's debt worked out in no time,' Mike sounded as happy as I felt. 'I understand now why that low life was so keen to get back that black book. Living off other people's misery.' Mike stopped mid-step, 'Just a thought, it might be an idea to let me look after it. I can lock it in my office, keep it safe. It also means I can keep tabs on how much of your Mum's debt's being paid as well.'

'No problem,' I replied. I didn't care. The mention of Meggsie's book and what was in it didn't make me feel quite as sick anymore, now I knew it was going to be sorted.

'Might as well get it now. No time like the present, hey?' Mike said.

Back in the sleeping quarters, I rooted around in my rucksack, trying to find the black book. My hand rubbed against the soft leather of the writing case Mike had given me, now packed with my drawings, the Blackwings, the letter from St Cuths. For a second, I wavered. St Cuths. It would have been so good. Was I good enough? Miss McGowan had thought so. My hand fell on Meggsie's book. Mike was right. It was a dream. This was my reality. This was how I was going to change things.

Back in the dining area, tables were pushed back, the smell of bacon grease hung in the air. Everybody sat around chilling. It was hard to believe less than three hours ago I was here having breakfast, no plan, no idea what I was going to do, and now it was all falling into place.

'Can I have your attention!' Mike didn't really have to ask; all eyes were on him. The room buzzed in anticipation of what he was about to say.

'I'm pleased to tell you we have a new recruit. Danny has agreed to join us.'

Any doubts I had were blasted out when the room erupted into applause with the odd whistle thrown in.

'Welcome bud!' Chip bounded over, slapping me on the back.

Skye was behind him.

'Nice one.' The spark in her eyes lit a spark in me.

'If Danny's staying, you can take him to get kitted out.' I didn't miss Mike's glance at my threadbare clothes. I hadn't really thought about it before, but for a bunch of homeless kids, everybody looked pretty smart.

'We're on it, boss,' Chip said.

'Before you go, have you got the book?' Mike asked.

I pulled it out of my pocket and handed it to him. Goodbye black book - goodbye problems.

Mike's fingers lingered over the book, 'I'll lock it in my office, keep it safe,' he said.

From the dining area, I followed Skye and Chip through to another tunnel. At the end was a door, blasted across it was a yellow sign - HAZARD STRICTLY NO ENTRY.

'In there?' I asked.

'No, that one,' Chip pointed to a smaller door tucked away in the corner opposite. 'That one's out of bounds,'

'It's dangerous, full of electrical stuff, keeps The Warren going,' Skye explained.

'Ta dah!' Chip threw open the other door. A stock cupboard, half filled with broken crap, the other half piles of clothes, all new. Shoes, trainers, hoodies, joggers - good stuff. A mini-JD sports.

'Help yourself,' Skye said.

'What, for real?' I'd never had clothes like this before. I remember once Mum got me a pair of Nikes, not the real thing, but I wore them till they were done in, until there was no more room for my toes to grow.

As I rifled through the clothes, my eyes fell on some tins of paint stacked on the shelf above. Automatically, my hands went to them.

'What are these for?' I asked.

Chip looked closely, 'Paint! All these clothes and you think about paint. You're nuts!'

'Hey, leave him alone. He's an artist,' Skye joked. 'It's all rubbish. It'll be thrown out when someone gets round to clearing it.'

There wasn't much I could do with emulsion anyway, so I carried on looking through the clothes. It didn't take me long to choose, ending up with trainers, trackies, a hoody and a massive smile.

I was still smiling that evening at dinner. I'd never looked so good.

'Nice' Skye said, which made me smile even more.

'Very suave,' Mike nodded in approval when he sat down to join us. 'You just need this now.' He pulled something black and chunky out of his jacket pocket and handed it to me. It wasn't until I had it in my hand that I realised it was a phone. A prehistoric one.

'It's ok, I've got one.' I handed it back, hoping I didn't sound ungrateful.

'It's for you to use while you're in The Warren.' Mike pushed it back towards me, 'I'll take yours for safe keeping.'

I didn't get it. I looked from Mike to Skye.

'Safety,' she explained, 'Can't risk anything being plastered over social media.'

Mike nodded. 'Not that I think anybody would do it on purpose, but accidents happen.'

My phone was my most treasured possession, the only decent thing I had. Giving it up would be like giving up a limb. And what if Mum wanted to contact me? I glanced at Skye again.

'It's no biggie, you'll get it back when you leave. Safety comes first. We've all got them.' She pulled her phone out of her pocket. I hadn't taken any notice of how old it was before. 'No camera, just text and talk. All it's got is a direct line to Mike. And a torch of course, that's probably what we use most.'

My own phone wavered in my hand.

'If you're worried about contacting your Mum, don't be. I've got some news,' said Mike.

My grip on my phone slackened. I steadied myself for the news - good or bad.

'She's okay, still in intensive care, but almost ready to be moved to the main ward.'

I didn't realise I'd been holding my breath, when I let it out the lightness made me feel faint.

'My friend went to see her, let her know you were okay. She said to tell you she loves you and she's glad you're safe.'

My skin stretched with a smile that cracked my face.

'She might be out soon then?'

Mike nodded, 'It's early days but knowing you're safe is one less thing for her to worry about.'

I looked at the phone in my hand. What was I thinking? Mike had given me clothes, food, a roof over my head. If I was in, I had to be all in. My phone didn't matter. I was here for Mum, and I'd do whatever it took to get things back to normal.

'There you go,' I handed it to Mike.

That night I lay in bed thinking about Mum, about how soon we might be home. I imagined handing the money over to Meggsie and telling him to get stuffed. I tried not to think of the right or wrong of it, only that Mike was making it possible. I wished there was something I could do for him. Then I remembered - the paint! It was going to be thrown away, nobody would miss it, and Mike said he liked my work. I'd do a mural on the tiles, my present to him, and when I left it would still be here to remind him how grateful I was. There was no time like the present. I eased myself out of my sleeping bag.

The spookiness of that first night in The Warren returned as I crept down the tunnel. While everyone slept, history took back over. White tiles shone in the dimness, lighting the way. At the dining area I got my bearings and headed off to the store cupboard. I passed the yellow glare of the hazard sign and went to the cupboard I'd visited earlier. The metal lids of the paint glinted in the light shining through the door. I pulled them out; two tins of white, a blue, a green and a black. Already I was mixing colours in my head. I glanced at the shelves opposite. I needed brushes. I was about to rummage to see if I could find any when footsteps echoed faintly off the tiled floor.

Hands frozen in mid-air, I tilted my head, trying to work out where they were going. I wasn't doing anything wrong, but I still felt guilty, and it didn't look good sneaking around in the middle of the night. I switched off the torch on my phone and waited. I needn't have bothered, there was only one place they were heading – here.

My mind whirred trying to come up with an excuse for what I was doing here. I told myself to stop being stupid, I didn't need an excuse. I was here getting the paint. There was no need to panic, say it as it is. I was ready to face whoever it was when the footsteps stopped. I waited for them to start again. They didn't. Instead, I heard a key turning in a lock. There was only one room that could be, the hazard room - which was out of bounds. When I heard a door opening, I pressed my face against the gap between the door and the frame. Through it I could see Mike, a briefcase in his hand. In the room, he stood at a table and opened the briefcase. My eyes widened. I'd never seen so much money!

I carried on watching. Mike flicked through the bundles of cash, counting it out. He then put it into envelopes, replacing them in the briefcase. With a smile on his face, he snapped the briefcase shut. I moved back from the gap; afraid he might see me.

I waited a few minutes, and breath squeezed tight, I looked back through. Mike had gone. Air escaped slowly from my mouth, thinking about what I'd seen. From the look of it, there was enough to pay Meggsie back and more. I know Mike said the money they made was for running The Warren and any left-over went to good causes, but if that was the sort of money they were bringing in, I had no worries.

Back in my bed I tried not to think about why Mike would need to sneak about in the middle of the night, or that Skye had told me the room was too dangerous to enter. All I needed to know was I'd made the right decision. I shut my eyes and shut out those thoughts. I was going to pay Mum's debt.

Chapter Seventeen

Paintbrush resting in my hand, I stood back and checked out my handiwork. It was okay, but I could do better. The angle of Mike's chin wasn't quite right. I tipped turpentine on to the rag and rubbed at the paint.

'Phewee!' Chip's voice sounded behind me. I turned to see his nose scrunched up at the smell of spirit filling the tunnel, 'Someone's gonna get high down here!'

'All in the name of art,' I said, screwing the cap back on the bottle.

'Looks good enough to me,' Chip nodded in appreciation.

'Not quite, but it will be in a second.' I slid my brush across the tile. 'That's it done.'

I'd been working on the mural for the past three days in between going out and taking 'lessons' from Skye and Chip. I'd not actually 'collected' anything yet. I still had half an eye out for Meggsie, but now Mike and The Warren had my back, that worry took more of a back seat. I'd let Skye and Chip in on my idea for the mural, the surprise for Mike. They'd helped keep it under wraps, but now I'd added my finishing touches, it was time for the big unveiling. Skye was on her way with Mike.

My foot tapped against the floor as I waited. Maybe it needed a bit more shading at the top, more definition. I snapped my head away. It was too late for changes, but I wanted Mike to like it, to appreciate what I was trying to say.

'You can open your eyes now,' she said as she guided him in front of the mural.

Hands gripped together I leaned forward. Eyes wide, Mike stood there in silence. Oh God, he didn't like it. I swallowed my disappointment.

'What can I say? I'm blown away!' Mike took my hand and shook it hard. 'What a wonderful surprise!'

Relief seeped out of me. He liked it. I swear I saw a tear in his eye.

Across the tiles I'd painted a tube symbol with The Warren Crew emblazoned across the top. Underneath was written, *All for the Greater Good,* and holding all this in cupped hands was Mike.

'Now it's my turn to surprise you,' Mike said. 'Today's the day. No more observing, it's time to put what you've learnt into practice.'

Now it was my turn to be lost for words. I'd known it was coming. Even so, my legs felt like they were about to buckle.

'You okay with that?' He must have sensed my nervousness. 'We'll start you off with something easy. It's all about confidence, Danny. Walk straight and tall, look like you belong, and people think you do. You're just another kid shopping.'

My insides spun like I'd been on the waltzers ten times in a row. Before I had time to pull myself together, Mike spoke again.

'And now for surprise number two,' he said.

The waltzers gave an extra spin. I didn't know if this was going to make it better or worse.

'It's your mum, she's been moved to the main ward. Give it a week or so and hopefully she'll be heading home. She sends her love.'

The spinning stopped, the fear of the day ahead evaporated, pushed aside by a swell of confidence. I could do this. I was doing it for Mum.

'Can I go see her?' The words tumbled out in excitement.

Mike paused before he spoke. 'That would be lovely, but my friend said there's a social worker sniffing around. We should definitely arrange it for later, though.'

He was right. I didn't want to blow it. She was doing okay, and she knew I was okay. That's what mattered. That and me getting the money, and that started right now.

'Come on then,' I said to Skye and Chip. 'Let's go do this.'

By the time we were in the tunnel, the swell of confidence had deflated. Now that I was part of The Warren, I didn't need the blindfold. Without it, the tunnel was even more claustrophobic. Damp clammy walls pressed in on me. The only reassuring thing - it looked solid. I counted every step, each one bringing me closer to daylight, shuffling along, my hands feeling their way along the walls, trying to keep up with Skye and Chip, scurrying along like moles.

Part of me wanted to get this over with, part of me wanted time to drag. Either way, we were through the tunnel and outside quicker than ever. I'd learned a lot from Skye and Chip. I wasn't stupid, but I never knew there were so many ways to steal. Heart in mouth I'd watched; accidental stealing, left handing, receipt passing, swapping barcodes, fitting room scams. I'd soaked it all up. Now I just had to do it.

They'd chosen something 'easy' for my first job. A general 'shop' at a mini supermarket. I was glad it was Skye coming in with me and Chip outside on watch. If things went wrong, Skye was the master of distraction. I stepped inside, crossing the line of no return.

The shop was only three aisles wide. I wandered up and down them, forcing my mind to focus on what I was supposed to be doing. Sweat gathered in the small of my back. With every step, blood pounded in my ears. I grabbed a shelf to steady myself. Head swimming, I was seven-years old again.

Hungry, the last of the chicken nuggets gone. Mum must have been hungry too, but she'd never say. I'd been afraid then too, and like now, I'd told myself I wasn't really stealing. Ginger biscuits and Super Noodles pushed deep in my pockets. I thought Mum would've been pleased, but she cried. I hadn't seen her cry like that before. The next day when I came home from school the cupboards were full of food. Crisps, biscuits, pot noodles, even ice cream. It was only now, remembering, I wondered, where had the money for all that food come from. That all happened before things got really bad. I'm not sure she'd cry now. I'm not sure she'd even notice.

A light nudge in the side from Skye walking past brought me back to the present. A flick of her eyes, checking I was okay. I pulled myself together and pulled a smile across my face. Arms swinging, I carried on. Skye had said don't rush, keep it chilled. I picked up a few items, turning them over in my hands, making out I was reading the labels, then put them back on the shelves. Every so often I'd drop something in my bag. A bag with a false bottom. The bag got heavier. Nobody seemed to notice me. My nerves steadied. This wasn't so bad. I was doing okay. It was when it was time to leave, the pounding in my ears returned in full force. Taking the stuff off the shelves was one thing, it was another getting it out of the shop.

I repeated in my head what Mike had said, *walk straight*

and tall, look like you belong. I snatched a bottle of washing up liquid off the shelf and strode over to the checkout. I plonked it on the counter and forced myself to look the woman stood behind it straight in the eye. My bag felt like a millstone around my neck.

'That'll be one pound and three pence, please,' she said.

I'd already got the correct money out. I passed it over. If she noticed my shaking hands, she didn't say anything.

I breathed and headed for the door.

'Hey you!' It was the woman behind the counter. I stopped mid-step, my throat tightened. Shit! Was this it, first time and I'd been caught. Keep calm, just keep calm. I thought I was going to pass out but turned to see what she wanted.

'You've forgotten this!' she shouted, holding up the washing up liquid.

I held back the manic laugh trying to break out as I walked back and collected the bottle. Leaving the shop, I still expected to hear footsteps behind me, a grab to the shoulder, a wailing siren. There was nothing, only Skye's breath in my ear as she passed by.

'You did it.'

My head was light again, but this time giddy with happiness. She was right. I'd done it.

Chapter Eighteen

On the way back to The Warren, adrenalin kicked in. I could do this. I just had! Pound signs chinked in my head. Once I moved up to bigger stuff, the debt would be paid in no time. Mum and me, back home. It was going to be worth it.

Chip was flying as high as me.

'You did it man, you did it!' he screeched in a not half bad American accent. 'All for the greater good, man!'

'All for the greater good!' I shouted back, sliding him a high five.

'Hey, you two, cut the partying. We need to get back. If we're late Grits will wonder where we've got to,' Skye said, trying to bring us back down to earth.

It wasn't happening.

'No worries, Mike said we could CEL-E-BRATE!' Chip squealed back.

'What? He didn't say anything to me.' Skye looked mildly annoyed.

'Didn't realise he had to run everything past you?' Chip's face twisted with a grin. 'Danny deserves a treat after his first proper job.'

'Oh, okay.' Skye didn't sound totally convinced. I wasn't going to disagree with her, but it sounded like the generous kind of thing Mike would do.

'And I know the place to go, somewhere my Dad used to take me.' Chip turned the corner, 'Follow me!'

We ended up at a swanky coffee bar, neon lights flashing above its door. *Coconut Grove.* Inside was all black leather and shimmering marble. Not the sort of place I'd usually hang out, but like Chip said, we were celebrating. Large jars of coffee beans were stacked at each end of the counter, labelled with placed I'd never heard of.

'What you having?' Chip asked.

I looked at the chalkboard on the wall behind the counter, taking my time to choose, mainly because I didn't know what half the stuff was.

'Just a coke.' I played it safe.

'Are you sure this is okay?' Sky asked, still looking uncomfortable.

'Course, Mike doesn't only ask you to do stuff.'

'I'm not sure that ...'

I made my way towards the nearest table. Still buzzing, I didn't want their bickering to spoil it.

'Not there,' Chip called over. His eyes swept round the café. 'There, it's a better view.' He pointed to a table next to the door, looking out of the front window. 'Do you want cake? The Victoria sponge is to die for!' he drawled, hands clutching his neck.

Skye's lips were pulled tight. She was still in a mood as she walked over to the table to join me.

'He never lets up, he does my head in,' she said, sitting down to join me.

'Talking about me?' Chip walked over, balancing a tray piled high with slices of cake, a hot chocolate lathered with cream and marshmallows for him, cokes for me and Skye.

It didn't take long for us to demolish it. I picked at the crumbs left on my plate. Chip was spot on, it was good. Skye's straw rattled as she sucked up the last of her drink.

'I'll go pay,' she said, holding out her hand towards Chip for the money.

'Don't worry, I'll sort it.' His chocolate moustache creased, but it didn't hide his nervous smile.

'I'll see you outside. Don't forget this,' he said, dumping my "shopping" bag on my lap. Like I would!

'Give us a chance!' Skye pulled on her coat.

'Chop, chop, we haven't got all day,' Chip's voice moved up a notch, like he couldn't wait to get rid of us.

'What's going on, Chip?' Skye frowned; she'd sensed it too.

'Nothing, just wait outside,' he laughed nervously.

Skye glared at him. She was going nowhere. Chip shrugged and walked up to the counter. My foot pushed against my bag of 'shopping' which I'd put under the table. Suddenly if felt like everybody in the café knew what was in there.

I could hear Chip talking to the girl on the till, his words steaming along like a train that couldn't stop.

'Great coffee... fantastic cake... come again... blah, blah, blah.'

I was relieved when he put his hand towards his pocket to get the money, but as he did, he flicked his elbow, sending the big jar of coffee beans, labelled Guatemala, tumbling from the counter. There was an almighty crash. Glass shattered across the floor, followed by the bounce, bounce of coffee beans.

'Oh my God!' Chip shrieked. 'I'm so sorry!'

All eyes in the cafe were on him, the girl ran out from behind the counter, got down on her knees, hands scrabbling, trying, and failing badly to gather up the scattering brown pellets.

Open-mouthed, I watched not sure what was going on, other than Skye looked like she was about to explode.

'Bloody idiot!' she hissed through clenched teeth. 'Come on, we're out of here.'

She grabbed me by the arm, propelling me towards

the door. I didn't have time to process what was happening.

'I should have known. Mike never said anything about treating anybody,' she hissed again, marching at full pelt. 'Chip had no intention of paying. Accident my arse, he pushed those beans over on purpose to distract.' My legs went heavy. We were going to get caught. 'Come on!' Skye pulled me again.

Out on the street, Skye still holding on to me, we ran. I let myself get swept along, legs lightening the further we got away from the café. When we rounded the corner, she yanked me to a stop.

'We'll wait for him here.' She pulled me towards a green electricity box partially hidden by bushes. We crouched behind it in time to see Chip run out of the cafe. Relief mixed with the feeling I wanted to punch him – not that I ever would! As he ran by Skye put her fingers to her mouth and blew the familiar whistle. Chip's head whipped round. He was grinning, but he didn't stop. A second later, we could see why. He was being chased by a man in an apron.

'Why does he do it?' Skye asked herself more than me, just as well as I didn't have any answers. Her jacket squeaked against green metal as she slid down to the floor. Her face paler than usual, eyes clouded.

'He's going to get caught if he doesn't stop it. Mike's not always going to be there to save him.'

I risked another look from behind the box. In the distance Chip was still running. Behind him the man's chunky body swayed from side to side, the space between them growing.

'I think he'll be okay,' I said, but Skye wasn't listening, her mind was somewhere else.

'Hey, come on, it's Chip, he'll be fine. That boy's like

a cat, he's got at least nine lives.'

'He can't keep chancing it. Someday it's going to go wrong for him, and I can't face losing anyone else.'

And that's when she told me her story, the reason she was in The Warren.

Chapter Nineteen

Skye pulled a crumpled photo out of her pocket.

'My brother, Jake.'

A blonde-haired boy, about five or six, smiled out at me. Sat on a red plastic tractor, his eyes sparked exactly like Skye's. His cheeky grin reminded me of Chip. Voice faltering, she explained Jake had been sick since he was a baby, something wrong with his immune system.

'We had to disinfect everything, so we didn't pass on any germs. He was in and out of hospital, but he was a fighter, and he always came bouncing back.' Skye smiled. A smile full of sadness. 'I got a virus, nothing too bad, we did everything we always did to keep him safe. It wasn't enough. He caught it.'

When she next spoke, her voice was so low I could barely hear her.

'He died. It was all my fault.'

A sharp ache cut across my throat as I tried to find the words to say. I wanted to tell her it wasn't, it wasn't anybody's fault, but I could see it wouldn't make any difference. She carried on. Her Mum and Dad were heartbroken. Knowing it was her fault, she couldn't bear to see the pain she'd caused, so she ran away. That way she wasn't there as a constant reminder.

I still didn't have the right words, but I couldn't keep quiet any longer.

'Skye, they don't blame you, how could they?'

'Mike said the same thing. He went to see them, thought if he spoke to them, I could go home, happy ever after.'

What she told me next was hard to understand.

'Like you, he was wrong. They said they never wanted

to see me again. I suppose it's no more than I deserve.'

I couldn't believe it. Her own parents. Whatever was going on with Mum, I knew she was always on my side.

'That's why I'm here. This is my life now. If it wasn't for Mike, I don't know where I'd be. I owe him everything,' she said. 'That's why I want to be a nurse, make up for what I did.'

I wanted to put my arms around her, hug her, do anything to make it better. The sound of traffic hummed hypnotically in the background as awkwardly I moved closer. I wanted to make her feel better, not make her think I was coming on to her. I bent my arm, maneuvering it towards Skye's shoulders, when a loud bang on top of the electricity box made it shudder. Skye and I looked up. There was Chip, his beaming face looming down at us.

'Ooh, what you two up to?' he laughed, as I quickly pulled my arm back.

'Nothing... I... we...' I was flustered, looking from Skye to Chip, afraid she'd get the wrong idea, too. I needn't have worried. Her face was redder than mine, but with anger, not embarrassment. The sadness in her eyes replaced with a fiery blaze. If Chip hadn't slid off the box to join us, she would have dragged him off.

'What the hell are you playing at?'

Squashed between us, Chip's body quaked, not with fear at Skye's fury, with laughter.

'That was class!'

'Class!' Skye erupted. 'You could have been caught!'

'Stop stressing. You enjoyed your cake, didn't you?'

'Cake!' she screeched again. After what she'd just told me, her anger didn't surprise me. 'We don't need cake. We've got enough to eat back at The Warren. What we need is to stay safe, trust one another. Not for you to act like a complete imbecile because you want to impress people.' She glanced in my direction. 'And drop us all in the shit.'

'All's well that ends well.' The funny voice didn't get any laughs this time. Not from Skye and not from me.

'It will all end well when I have to explain to Grits why we're late back and why people better stay clear of the Coconut Grove,' she spat the words out at him.

'You don't have to tell Grits, it's not like we got caught. I wanted to make it special for Danny.' Guilt pricked. It wasn't like I'd asked him, and it had been a dumb-arse thing to do, but he'd done it for me.

Skye looked like she was about to cry. 'What choice do I have?'

Chip's voice faltered. 'But you can't, I'll...'

'I'll think of something,' Skye said, but she didn't sound hopeful.

By the time we were back in the tunnel, the buzz from my first successful 'collection' had well and truly fizzled and evaporated. We made our way back in silence. The heaviness of Chip's botch weighed me down, and if I was honest, there was a tiny part of me that was disappointed, even annoyed with him. I'd done good, but it had lost its shine. Talk about pissing on your parade.

At the end of the tunnel, Skye focused her torch beam on The Warren door, ready to knock out the password. The light caught Chip's face, eyes wide, he looked like a rabbit caught in headlights. He knew what was coming. It made me feel bad for being hacked off with him.

Skye tapped the bar of metal on the door. Grits' voice boomed through before it fully opened.

'Where the hell have you been? I was about to send someone out looking for you.'

We stayed silent.

'Well?' Grits demanded.

It was painful to watch Chip squirm. Skye looked at him, her mouth fumbled, finding something to say.

'We had a bit of trouble ... ah, it was ...'

Grits looked at Chip, 'What balls up have you made now?' The prick of guilt I'd felt earlier stabbed harder. *I wanted to make it special for Danny.*

Before Chip had time to answer I stepped forward. My voice didn't give way to the trembling inside.

'It was my fault,' I said. Grit's look of surprise turned to satisfaction.

'Picasso. I might have known.'

'I wanted to celebrate my first job. We stopped off at a cafe.' I searched in my head for the name of the place, 'Coconut Grove.'

Grits looked over at Skye, 'And you let him?'

'I made them come,' I cut in before she could answer. I was in the shit anyway so I might as well go the whole hog. 'I didn't pay either. They weren't too happy.'

Grits' mouth opened, about to launch into me. Then he stopped, looking at Skye and Chip like he was trying to work something out. He walked up to me, putting his face close to mine.

'Watch it Picasso, this isn't a free for all party, it's about keeping everybody here safe. We're here to help others, not ourselves. Don't ruin it. I warned you.' He walked away, anger steaming off him. I wasn't doing much to make a good impression.

I felt a squeeze to my arm as I watched him leave.

'Thanks, you didn't have to do that.' It was Skye.

'Yeah, thanks. I owe you one,' Chip said. There was no funny voice.

'That's what friends are for,' I answered. It took a

second to realise what I'd said. Embarrassment burned as I waited for the laughter, like they'd consider me a friend. I'd given up on friends long ago.

'You're right, we're here for each other,' Skye squeezed my arm again, then looked at Chip, 'Maybe one day you can return the favour.'

Chip nodded, 'Sure thing mate, anything you need, whenever, just ask.'

The warmth I felt now wasn't embarrassment. True, Grits might hate me, but I had Skye and Chip.

I had friends.

Chapter Twenty

Other than taking the piss out of me about Skye, over the next week Chip was on his best behaviour, making up for the coffee bean incident. I carried on learning, and I was learning fast. I moved from food to sportswear. I even bagged a camera. It was weird. I knew it was wrong, but I was proud. It was like Mike said, *all for the greater good*. I wasn't hurting anyone and most importantly Mum's debt was going down.

But today I was on bog duty - again - the third time this week. I know we all had to take our turn cleaning the loos but usually it was once a week if that. I knew it was Grits' way of getting back at me. He'd not forgiven me for what had happened in the café. I could see it in his eyes when he read out the list of jobs in the morning. He was the same with Chip – only he was on kitchen duty.

'Picasso – bogs.' It was the pause, followed by the death stare that said it. I just smiled. No way was I letting him see it bothered me.

The grey water dripped from the mop, twisting in the bucket. I should have got used to the stench by now, but the smell of stale piss and disinfectant caught in the back of my throat. Chip had got off lightly compared to me. Fair enough, he had to do the stoves, pans, grills, and everything, but at least the smell was better.

It felt like I'd mopped, wiped, and scrubbed everything for the hundredth time, though the smell didn't seem to get any better. I looked around to see if there was anything I'd missed, anything to pass the time. That's when I saw it.

It was the rat that caught my eye first. I'd got used

to them by now, but this one had more cheek than usual. It was long and skinny, sat under the sink, beady black eyes staring at me. I pushed the mop in its direction expecting it to scurry away, but it didn't. It carried on staring. I picked up the bucket and sloshed a whole load of water over it. Triumph - it scurried away. Bending down to clean the puddle of water spreading across the tiles, my eye caught a groove in the line of the tiles on the wall under the sink, deeper and thicker than those between the other tiles. I traced round it with my finger. It was a hatch, about the size of a kitchen cupboard door.

From the grime caked in the grooves I could tell it hadn't been opened in a long while. There was a hole in one of the tiles, like it was missing a handle. I shoved my finger in and pulled. It gave slightly but I couldn't keep hold and my finger slipped out. I looked around to see if there was anything else I could use. I might as well see what was in there. If nothing else, it would break up the day, make a change from cleaning. Leaning against the wall was a broken toilet door. A metal strip ran down its side. I dug my nails under it, peeling it back easily from the rotten wood. Perfect! I bent the end over, made a hook and pushed it into the hole.

The door moved as I gently waggled the hook from side to side, easing it open. A final tug and with a loud creak, it sprung out of its casing, the force pushed me back on to the floor. Rubbing my back, I pushed myself up and stared into the gaping black hole.

Through the circling cloud of dust, I stuck my head into the darkness. It was pitch black. I pulled out my phone and shone the torch through the dancing particles of dust. It was nothing exciting, a ventilation shaft. It would be plenty wide enough and tall enough for me to crawl through if I'd wanted. I didn't - I pulled my head back out. I was about to put the hatch back in when a voice sounded through the tunnel.

I flashed my torch back into the darkness. Surely there wasn't anyone in there? The beam shone into silence and for a second, I thought I must have imagined it, then it came again. I stuck my head in further. The voice was a muffled echo, but I recognised it. It was Mike. I was confused. What was Mike doing in a ventilation shaft? I swallowed hard, filling my lungs like I was about to take a deep dive underwater, then eased myself into the space in front of me. All was quiet. Then the sound came again, only this time it was different, quieter, I pushed forward, straining to hear it.

'Food glorious food.' It was someone singing, but it wasn't Mike, it was Chip.

I laughed to myself. I got it now. There wasn't anybody in the shaft, their voices were traveling through the air vents from wherever they were in The Warren. I laughed again. Chip wasn't the only one who could wind people up. I imagined a ghostly voice, my voice, floating through the vent into the cooking area, scaring the living crap out of him. Chip's face, the stories he'd tell afterwards, *The Warren's haunted!'* and all that. I moved forward, already laughing at Chips' reaction.

I winced at the rubble pressing into my knees. This was a much smaller space than the tunnels, but I was getting used to being underground. There was none of the panic I'd first felt, and anyway, it was going to be worth it. Dust settled on my chest. I kept moving, trying to work out where I was in The Warren. I couldn't hear Mike's voice anymore, but I moved forward towards Chip's tuneless wail.

Through the torchlight I squinted, trying to work out

how much further the shaft went on. It seemed like forever. A slight breeze blew hair across my face. I shook it out my eyes. Maybe the shaft led to a way out. On the right-hand side of the shaft wall there was a thin sliver of light which didn't come from my torch. It was the grill of an air vent, the light shining through it was coming from somewhere in The Warren.

I still couldn't work out where I was, and Chip had stopped singing. Maybe he was in there, where the light was coming from. With as little noise as possible, I switched off the torch and moved towards the grill. Thin slits of light spilling through it lit my way. Lying flat on my front, I edged further towards it. Finally, at eye level, I peered through.

Shit! It was Mike's office! Double shit! He was in there. God! I hope he didn't see me. Everything he'd done and I repay it by spying on him. I took a deep breath, calming myself. He couldn't see me, there was no way he knew I was here, but I still lay rigid, afraid to move in case he heard me.

Gradually my eyes became accustomed to the glare of the office light. Mike was totally focused on what he was doing. Piles of money were scattered across the desk. The memory of Mike in the hazard room resurfaced, but this time there was even more money. My lips parted as I took in exactly how much was there – it had to be thousands. I hadn't realised The Warren made so much money. I squinted to get a better look. Mike picked up a pen and began to write in a book. That was strange - it looked exactly like Meggsie's book.

A knock at the door and my heart jumped - so did Mike. Now wasn't the time to think about the book or the money. I pushed my back into the wall of the shaft. Mike pulled out a briefcase, the one I'd seen him with before, from under his desk. He swept the money and envelopes into the briefcase, snapping it shut just as the door opened.

'Ah Grits, glad you're here. I've been going through the finances.'

I imagined the glow of my cheeks burning through the grill. It was wrong. I shouldn't be listening, spying, but any movement and they might hear. I squeezed my eyes shut, like that might block out their voices, but the darkness only magnified them.

'It's not looking good I'm afraid, we've got major cash flow problems,' Mike said.

All that cash? Surely I must have heard him wrong, but when Grits answered, there was worry in his voice.

'What? We're working as hard as we can, and if we up it too much we risk somebody getting caught.'

'Maybe it's time to accept that we can't go on.'

Grits voice lowered, but I could feel the panic, 'We can't lose this, I can't let everybody down again.'

'This isn't your fault Grits - not this time.'

A memory pinged in my head. When I'd first come to The Warren, Chip had said something about things going wrong for Grits before he'd arrived here. It felt wrong, but I strained to hear more.

The seconds of silence that followed felt like hours.

'No!' Grits sounded strong and firm now, 'We'll all have to work harder, get more stuff, turn it round quicker. We'll have to be even more careful. We can do this - we've got to. I can't let everybody down.' There was a gentleness to his voice I'd never heard before. Despite everything, I couldn't help feeling sorry for him.

'You're right, we shouldn't give up. I don't like to push the kids so hard, but we can't lose this.'

'I'm on it,' Grits paused. 'All for the greater good.'

There were footsteps, then a door closing. Mike let out a sigh.

It felt like the air was being sucked out of the tunnel. Losing The Warren! Grits was right. We couldn't let that happen. And it wasn't just The Warren. If that went, so did any chance of paying back Meggsie. The thought of it suffocated me. I had to get out of here. The idea of scaring Chip was long gone. Slowly and soundlessly, I edged back towards the hatch. If The Warren was short of money, what would that mean for Mum's debts? Worry ate away at me, but that didn't stop the questions ringing in my ears. Losing The Warren – but all that money? How could there be a cash flow problem? And the black book- if it was Meggsie's, why would Mike be writing in it? But what did I know about it all? If Mike said The Warren was short of money, it must be. I didn't know how much it all cost and there was no reason for him to lie.

I'd only been back in the toilets a couple of minutes when the door swung open. It was Grits, arms folded.

'What've you been up to, Cinderella?' he said.

My heart pounded; guilt written over my face. Maybe he'd seen me through the grill.

'Better get that mopped up.' He motioned to the water I'd sloshed over the floor earlier. 'Looks like you're going to the ball after all. Time to do some proper work.'

'Right on it Grits,' I replied.

He rolled his eyes, mistaking my enthusiasm for getting off toilet duty. It wasn't. I'd do whatever I could to save The Warren.

Chapter Twenty-one

Proper work he'd said, but I knew what Grits meant - *more stuff, quicker* - that's what he'd said and that's what I was going to do. We'd been given a longer list than usual and sent into unfamiliar territory. That on its own was enough to set my nerves on edge. The fact Skye wasn't here made it worse. She'd already been sent out on a job before Grits got to Chip and me. She was Chip's calming influence and even that didn't always work, so there wasn't much chance with just me.

Chip needed to know how important this was, but I couldn't tell him. Not that I didn't trust him, but I knew what Chip was like. Even if he didn't mean to, he'd blab it out by accident, then everyone would know I'd been spying on Mike. The Warren needed us - Mike needed us. We had to get the job right. The money and the black book I'd seen in Mike's office still hung over my head like question marks, but I pushed them aside. The tube pulled into Bethnal Green. Time for proper work.

I needn't have worried about Chip. He was weirdly quiet. I didn't know whether to be relieved or worried. Maybe the kitchen stints had taught him a lesson. We worked hard and fast, got good stuff. No problems, no cock ups, just four bags stuffed with quality gear.

On the way back to the tube I was on a high, thinking about the money it would bring in. Chip was still quiet, but there was an edginess to him, constantly craning his neck like he was looking for someone. He didn't speak until we got to the station.

'I need a drink,' he said. His face looked pale, maybe he wasn't feeling too good.

'A drink and nothing else,' I shouted after him, as he

111

slipped into the mini supermarket outside the way into the tube station. I didn't want him mucking things up at the last minute for the sake of a free packet of crisps.

Chip had barely been in the shop when he came flying back out, face panic stricken. He looked straight through me as he ran past, his face pale with a greenish tint, like he was about to puke. He raced up the High Street, then disappeared down a side road. Anger pushed aside worry. He'd done it again, he couldn't help himself, cocked everything up and what for?

Fuming, I waited for someone to come running out after him. No-one came. I took a chance and looked through the shop door. Everything was fine, no harassed shop assistant, no nosey onlookers. Chip's face as he'd run past floated in front of me. Terrified. That wasn't Chip, everything was a laugh to him, even being caught. Unease cooled my anger, making way for worry to set in. I set off to find him.

When I got to the street he'd disappeared down, there was no sign of him. Fingers to my lips I gave the whistle. It was a dead end. He couldn't have gone far.

There was no response.

'Chip!' I shouted, 'It's me, mate. Where are you?'

Still no answer. I walked up and down, looking for somewhere he might hide. A row of over-flowing green wheelie bins stood against the wall. Moving towards them I heard something. A sob? I heaved at the smell of rotting vegetables as I squeezed behind them.

There was Chip huddled in the corner. His body curled up and shaking, gasping like he couldn't breathe. I was no doctor, but I think he was in shock, and so was I. This wasn't the Chip I knew.

I knelt beside him. 'Hey mate,' I whispered, touching his arm. He flinched, drawing further back into the corner, like he didn't know me.

'It's me, Danny.' I touched him again. His body shrank back further. Other than the arsenal cap this wasn't the Chip I knew. I was more than worried now. 'Chip.' I said, trying to get through to him. He looked up at me, recognition seeping in.

'What happened?' I asked. Chip shook his head, unable to speak. Slowly I breathed, in and out, in and out, encouraging him to breathe along with me. I'd done the same with Mum. It calmed her. I was hoping it would do the same for him. His body relaxed. When he spoke, I could barely hear him.

'My Dad, I saw him. He was in the shop buying a paper.'

'That's great?' I didn't understand, it's what he'd been waiting for - his dad to come home.

Indecision flickered across his face, then he pulled up the sleeves of his hoody - he'd made up his mind. Dotted on his arms were clusters of round scars, some redder than others. I could tell straight away what they were. Cigarette burns.

'Your Dad did that?' I asked, sure I'd misunderstood.

A glimmer of the real Chip reappeared, 'Well, I didn't do it to myself. I don't smoke, do I?' It disappeared again when he said, 'These are the ones you can see. I've got a few fractures, broken ribs, all part of the collection.'

I didn't know what to say. I felt sick. I knew some kids whose parents gave them a wallop, and I'd been pushed around by Meggsie, but nothing like this.

'What about the army, everything you said?' I asked, still not convinced I was getting this right.

Chip's head dropped along with his voice, 'Made it up. He's never left London, never mind been to

Afghanistan. We lived round here, but I ran away. That's where I was staying.' He pointed towards an old derelict building, 'That's where Mike found me. The old umbrella factory, me and some other kids hung out there.'

'What about your mum and stepdad?' I was still confused.

'Would be great if I had one. She left Dad years ago, haven't seen her since.' He trembled again. 'If my dad saw me, he'll come and find me, he'll make me go back.'

'You need to tell Mike. He'll know what to do.'

'No!' The word came out with force. 'As far as everybody thinks my dad's a hero in Afghanistan, not some bullying saddo who doesn't give two shits about beating the crap out of his son. And that's how its staying.'

I got where he was coming from. Nobody wanted to be the saddo kid everyone felt sorry for, the one people whispered about behind their hands and gave each other the 'look'. The number of times I'd lied, not turned up for things, made excuses because I didn't want people to know about Mum. Yeah, I got it, but this was different.

'We've all got shit we don't want people to know, but sometimes you need to tell someone.' I thought about everything I'd told Mike, and what he'd done since. 'Tell him,' I said again with more force 'He'll help you.'

'It's a bit different from helping you with your drawing.'

The sourness in Chip's voice hurt. He wasn't the only one who had it bad, and I had to make him see sense, so I told him it straight; the drink, the drugs, Meggsie. I stumbled over the words. It was more difficult telling him than Mike. Every word was a knife in Mum's back, but if it made him see Mike could help him, it was worth it.

'Mike's helping me pay the money back, he's even talked about us moving house.'

Chip still didn't seem convinced.

'And you know he's sorting college for Skye to do nursing.' I added, desperate to make him see sense. 'Mike can make sure your dad doesn't find you, and even if he does, Mike will make sure he doesn't hurt you. He'll keep you safe.'

It did the opposite.

'You can't tell Skye! You can't tell anyone!' His nails dug into my arm, his grip tightened, 'Promise me!'

'I won't say anything, I promise.' I wriggled my arm free. 'But you should speak to Mike.'

'No!' His word was final.

There was nothing more to say.

Hoods pulled tight around our heads, we sprinted back to the tube station.

By the time we got there, Chip was back to his normal self - and more. He was Chip magnified, doubled, tripled even. Everything he did was bigger and louder. I think he was making up for before, like it would make me forget what I'd seen, what he'd told me. Stupid comments blasted from his mouth, not bothering if people heard, riding down the escalator on the handrail, singing at the top of his voice. He was making a point.

'Calm down,' I said it in a way I thought Skye would say it. Chip pulled a face. His voice got even louder. I wished Skye was here. A groan escaped from my lips. This was only going to end one way.

The platform was packed with late afternoon commuters. As the tube pulled in, Chip grabbed hold of me, pushing me forward.

'What's the rush?' I asked, pulling away from him. 'There's another coming soon.' I nodded towards the board. It's illuminated letters flashed *2 minutes*.

'No, I'm going to show you something really special!' he shouted. The manic look in his eye made me nervous as he dragged me toward the end carriage. When we got to the door, I was expecting him to push his way in, but he kept on moving towards the back of the tube. I pulled him back realising what he was about to do, but he yanked himself free.

'Don't be stupid!' I shouted. The hairs on my arms and the back of my neck lifted and it wasn't the breeze of the approaching tube.

Chip turned around and grinned.

As the tube pulled out Chip threw his head back. Legs moving like pistons, arms bent, thrusting backwards and forwards, propelling him towards the tube. For someone so small he moved quickly. At the edge of the platform, his legs bent into a seamless crouch, with a push firing him through the air. My heart leapt into my mouth as he leapt onto the back of the tube train. His body pressed flat against the metal, clinging on tightly, whooping wildly as he disappeared into the tunnel.

My mind exploded. What the hell? It was all I could do to stop myself jumping on the track and running after him. I felt sick at the reality that all I could do was wait. The two minutes it took for the next tube to arrive stretched like two days. I waited for the voice over the tannoid. "We would like to apologise for the delay due to an incident on the tracks blah, blah…" The image of Chip, mangled and squashed, fixed itself in my head. I'd joked he had more than nine lives, but I reckon he'd pretty much used them up.

As soon as it stopped, I was off the tube. What was I going to say to Mike? 'Hi, we had a fantastic day, but sorry Chip's dead.' I felt sick. I bounded up the escalator steps, two at a time, not bothered whose feet I stamped on or who I had to push out of the way.

Rushing out of the station, I didn't know which way to turn. I looked for the ambulances, police cars, Chip laid out on a stretcher. My mind raced. I needed to find Chip, find out what had happened, even though half of me wanted to run, didn't want to know.

I needn't have worried. He was there, large as life with the biggest grin on his face.

'What kept you?' he said.

Chapter Twenty-Two

'I'll have that!' Chip leaned across the table, snatching up the crust of toast left on my plate.

Yesterday could have been a dream. After his stunt on the tube, I'd not known whether to punch him or hug him. I'd done neither. Instead, I'd tried to reason with him, tell him how stupid he'd been, how he could have died. How unfair it was he'd put me in that position. How I never wanted to have to go through that again.

'You might fancy the pants off Skye, but you don't have to act like her as well,' he'd laughed, not taking a word I'd said seriously. He was more serious when I switched the conversation to Mike. I'd done my best to persuade him to tell him about his dad, make him understand he could ask for help, but the shutters were down.

'You okay?' I gave Chip a meaningful look.

He shrugged his shoulders, the usual wide smile spread across his face, 'Why wouldn't I be?'

It was like it had never happened, but to be honest, if Chip wanted to forget about it, as much as I worried for him, it suited me fine. I had other things to worry about. Grits was still ramping things up. Today I was on *Station Duty*. All I could think about was the first day I'd seen Skye. The day she'd nearly been caught.

It had been a laugh when we were practicing in The Warren, picking pockets, slipping my hand into Skye's bag as she pretended to walk along, plucking out her mobile phone and purse. Now it was for real, and as much as putting my hand in someone's bag or pocket freaked me out, what really bothered me was it wasn't some faceless multimillion pound store owner anymore. It was real people.

'Look for the suits with briefcases, they're the ones with the money. They could do with a lesson in sharing,' Mike had said, and when I looked at what they had compared to what we had, he had a point. But somehow, it still didn't make me feel better.

On the tube with Skye and Chip, shaking inside, I was ready to put all I'd practiced into action. The carriage filled as the train got closer to Victoria. Skye and Chip's conversation dwindled. When the tube stopped, we pushed through the crowds, staying within eyesight; together, but apart. A slight tilt of the chin, dip of the head. Our first mark. Smart shoes, well cut suit. I watched closely. Skye and Chip moved in unison, an invisible rope holding them together. I followed, hanging back behind them, so I could watch and was ready to make a distraction if anything went wrong.

Towards the exit the crowds thinned. Skye right next to the target, sidled up to him when he stepped on the escalator. Chip hung back, but not too far. Skye took out her purse, making out she was looking for something. She timed it just right. The man stepped off the escalator, she walked across his path. Her purse 'fell' to the floor, coins bouncing on the tiles.

'So sorry,' I heard him say as I walked past without acknowledging Skye. Automatically he bent down to help her collect up the loose change scattered across the floor.

'Don't worry, it was my fault.' Skye smiled as they crouched, scrabbling on the floor.

'Need any help?' Chip bent down towards them as he walked past.

Skye looked up at him, showing no recognition.

'No worries, I've got it, thanks.' She turned back to

the man, 'and thanks for your help.' She clasped her purse shut. The man gave a satisfied smile. Good deed for the day done, then went on his way. It was pure professional.

As arranged, we met by the ticket machine, Chip beaming ear to ear.

'Beat this,' he said, flipping open an expensive black leather wallet. The American Express Gold card shone as bright as real gold in the artificial light of the station.

'How?' I was asking about the wallet, not the bank card.

Chip laughed, 'Magic, my friend.'

He'd got it when the man bent over. He was right; it was magic. I'd seen nothing, and neither had the man.

'Right Danny, your turn,' Skye said, as Chip stuffed the wallet inside his jacket. 'You know what you're doing?' She walked back to the escalator, not giving me time to think about my answer.

'You'll be okay, you learnt from the Master,' Chip said, then ran to catch up with Skye. It felt like I was about to jump off a cliff, but I remembered that first time in the shop. I'd felt the same then, and I'd done that. I pulled in my chest. I could do this. I followed Skye and Chip back to the platform. I didn't want to do this. Whatever Mike said, the voice in my head was louder, saying it was wrong. Again, I summoned up a picture of Mum. I had to do it. I was doing it for her.

When the train pulled in, we mingled with the crowds getting off. Another tilt of the head and we'd got our next mark. A woman, middle-aged with immaculate hair.

On our way out again, I kept close to Skye and Chip, but not too close, giving enough room for our target to slip in front of me as we stepped on to the escalator. I was glad I couldn't see her face; it made it less personal. I focused on her expensive clothes; her perfume didn't smell cheap, either. The ride up the escalator was long, sweat gathered in the small of my back. I flexed my fingers. I had to be quick.

Chip and Skye stood in front of the woman, chatting, an everyday conversation. Then, out of nowhere, Skye's voice rang out.

'Yes, you are going?' she pushed Chip firmly on the shoulder.

Chip stepped to the side blocking the escalator.

'No, I'm not, you can't make me.'

'It's your last chance. I'm telling Mum.'

'If you do, I'll tell her about that party...'

'You dare ... '

So, it went on. I could feel the woman's exasperation. She moved sideways trying to make her way past Chip, but he wasn't budging. People backed up on the escalator and I pushed myself closer. The woman's bag wedged between us; I took my opportunity. The bag was soft suede, but it might as well have been barbed wire. I slipped my hand into the front pocket, wrapped it round a cold, hard object and pulled it out. As soon as it was in my pocket, I gave a loud spluttering sneeze. On cue, Chip stepped back. Seeing the space, the woman, with a huff of impatience pushed her way through and sped off.

I got back to the ticket machine before them. I was buzzing, waiting to show off what I'd got.

'Beginner's luck, and it's last year's model,' Chip said when I showed him the shiny iPhone. I didn't care about beginners' luck or not; it was all going towards paying off Mum's debt. Even though I knew it was wrong, a bubble of pride swelled inside me. I'd done it.

Mike would be well pleased, and to be fair, the woman didn't look like she'd have much problem buying another phone. Mum needed it more. *All for the greater good.*

'Whoopee! What a morning!' Chip shouted, jumping through the tube doors. We'd been working non-stop for nearly an hour. Up and down the escalators, changing platforms, moving around. We'd got what we came for, a nice collection of phones, wallets, and purses. Now we were heading back to The Warren, no hanging about, risking the chance of being caught. Get what you need, then get out.

On the tube Skye and me got seats opposite Chip. Skye gave Chip one of her 'calm down, stop drawing attention to yourself' looks. I knew what she meant even if he didn't.

'Yes Siree! We hit the jackpot!' He carried on anyway, giving his thigh a slap.

Skye looked over at me, 'Chip and his after-job craziness...'

Maybe it was because I knew what had happened yesterday, or maybe I was being extra sensitive, but it was more than Chip's usual craziness. He was manic. Surely he wouldn't do a repeat of yesterday, not with Skye here. The other people on the tube began to take a particular interest in the floor as his voice rattled on, louder and louder.

When the tube pulled into the next station more people dribbled into the carriage. The doors were about to slide shut when, at the last second, a hand pushed between them. The doors drew back, and the owner of the hand followed through. He was dressed in a suit which stretched tightly across his chest, his forehead shiny with sweat. In his other hand, he pressed a new model iPhone against his ear, while trying to clutch his briefcase under his arm.

'Don't be an idiot Michael, the board will not tolerate another downturn,' his voice filled the carriage. 'Sort it, pronto!' Phone call finished, his eyes darted around, looking for a place to sit. There were no spaces. His gaze fell on Chip.

'Move, I need a seat.'

It took Chip a couple of seconds to realise he was talking to him.

'Sorry, I hadn't noticed you were pregnant,' Chip joked, eyes on the paunch hanging over the man's belt. Inside, I willed him to move. I didn't want a scene. Chip sat firm. He wasn't moving for anyone.

'Look, I've got work to do and I need a seat. Now. Move!'

'And?' Chip's face flushed with anger.

The floor of the carriage got even more interesting to the other passengers. I glanced at Skye, hoping she'd know what to do. Her lips parted ready to speak, but the man's voice over-road anything she was about to say.

'I'm not telling you again. Move!'

The man's hand moved forward and flicked Chip's cap. No-one messes with the Arsenal cap. I held my breath as it fell to the floor. Chip bent down and snatched it up. When he looked up, his face was twisted and red.

Before he could say anything, Skye shifted in the seat next to me. Her voice shot across the carriage, firmer than I'd ever heard it before.

'Leave it, Chip!'

He looked at her, then back at the man. I could see the battle in his eyes. Skye won. I relaxed back into my seat. With a look that gave Grits a run for his money, Chip stood up from his seat. The man pushed past, sat down, and got his laptop out. The heat of Chips anger radiated across the carriage.

We stayed silent until two stops later, when the man stood up ready to get off.

'Thank God,' whispered Skye.

'No-one messes with my cap,' Chip said, moving towards the door.

'Leave it,' Skye replied, but her words disappeared after him.

'What the hell is he doing?' Skye looked across at me.

I didn't answer. After yesterday, I wasn't taking any risks. Heart pounding, I grabbed her hand and pulled her through the door before it swished shut. Round the corner we gained sight of him. He was making his way up the stairs directly behind the man.

'The idiot! He's going for his phone,' Skye said. 'There's not even a crowd,' she said, more to herself this time. I watched in horror. Chips movements were determined. I sussed what he was doing, bump and nudge. Skye was right, he was after the phone, and right again - to get away with it he needed people round him. 'Is he on a death wi...'

Chip banged into the man. In a flash, the man turned and grabbed him. He might be big, but he was quick too. I watched in horror as Chip twisted and turned, trying to pull away, but the man's grasp was tight on his hood. I almost cheered when Chip kicked him on the ankle. He winced, his hold slackening. Chip wrestled out of his grip. I glanced at Skye, her eyes set on Chip, willing him on. I held my breath as he ran for the barriers and leapt over them. Unbelievable! He'd done it again, the cat with nine hundred lives. Then, with the jolt of his feet on the floor, his hat flew off his head and fell to the ground. In the split second, he turned to pick it up, a black clad arm stretched out of nowhere. It belonged to a security guard. Trapped in a firm grasp again, this time he wasn't getting away.

Chapter Twenty-Three

A fog of unhappiness shrouded the clatter of plates and cutlery in the dining area. The smell of chicken korma, Chips' favourite, wafting across the hall should have had our mouths watering. This evening, it reminded us he wasn't here. He did our heads in, but right now we'd all have been happy to hear his shrill annoying laugh and never-ending chat. I pushed away the plate of food in front of me. Skye leaned over and put her hand on top of mine, even her skin against mine didn't bring me out of the mood I was in. My head was too full of Chip.

'He'll be okay. Mike will see to it.'

She squeezed my hand, her eyes bright with hope.

When we'd told Mike what had happened, the colour didn't drain out of his face; it was more like sucked out - flesh to ghost white in less than a second.

'When? Where? Did anybody see you two? Did you hear Chip say anything? Where did they take him?'

He fired question after question at us, barely giving time for an answer. Standing up, then sitting down, his agitation cracked the air. Then, with the flick of a switch, Mike was back to normal. He stood up, face focused.

'I'll go to the police station and get him.'

'Mike,' I called after him as he set off down the corridor. 'Can you give him this?'

I held out Chips' cap. He'd been shouting for it when the transport police had dragged him away. I knew how much it meant to him, so we'd waited around until the coast was clear. Covered in footprints by the time I picked it up, Chip wouldn't care, he'd just want it back.

'Of course, but don't worry, Chip will be back here,

126

cap and all. I'll make sure of that.'

Mike's determination gave me hope. If anybody could sort it, Mike could.

Five hours later and that hope had faded.

We waited, finely tuned, listening for the familiar clank of The Warren door. When it came a wave of anticipation swept across the dining area. It crashed when Mike walked in alone. I looked at Skye, the hopeful shine in her eyes had obviously gone off to join mine.

Mike began to speak, 'You all know Chip was arrested earlier today.'

The air remained still as he carried on. 'I've spent the last few hours at the police station supporting his release, and I have good news and bad news. The bad news is Chip won't be returning to The Warren.' My stomach dropped. The Warren without Chip? My friend Chip. It wasn't right. A collective intake of breath sucked the air out of the dining hall. Mike continued, 'It's bad news because we'll miss him. He was a big part of our family, but there is good news.'

I couldn't think of any part of Chip not coming back being good.

Mike carried on, 'While I was at the police station, Chip's dad arrived.' Murmurs rippled across the hall. 'And you all know that's what Chip was waiting for. I gave Chip the choice. Come back to The Warren or go home.' Mike paused. 'He's gone home!' I looked around, expecting to see my confusion mirrored on everyone else's faces. Then I remembered, nobody else knew the real story about his dad.

Mike held up his hands as the murmur grew to a loud rumble.

'It's exciting but let me finish.' Silence returned. 'I

can't describe the happiness on Chip's face when he left with his dad, but not everybody is as lucky. Not everybody has family waiting with open arms.' Beside me, Skye tensed. Mike was still speaking. 'But we have each other and we will continue with our lives here. Chip asked me to pass on his goodbyes and his thanks to you all for being good friends when he needed you. Leaving was a tough decision for him, but I know you'll agree it was the right one.'

When Mike finished, chatter filled the hall. Happiness mixed with sadness and maybe a bit of jealousy, but my brain was whirring, trying to understand what Mike had said. I'd seen Chip cowering like a frightened animal. Why would he go back to that? It didn't make sense. Had Mike got it wrong?

'Do you think he's really okay?' I whispered to Skye.

Tears glistened in her eyes, probably thinking about Chip and her own family, but she answered me with a forced lightness.

'Course he's okay. It's all he ever wanted, his dad to come back, and Mike would never let him go if he didn't think he'd be alright.'

'But what about…' My voice trailed off. Chip might have gone, but I still couldn't break my promise, not even to Skye.

Skye mistook my worry for something else.

'You'll get used to not working with him. I'll miss him loads, but we should be happy for him,' her voice wobbled. She took a deep breath, straightening it back out. 'Typical Chip, only he could make a happy ending out of being arrested.'

A happy ending? I wish I could believe it, but it didn't feel right. The trickle of worry running down my back grew colder.

After Chip's run in with the police, Mike decided we better lay low for a few days, but there's only so much card playing you can do to pass the time. On the third morning of us being grounded, there was a cheer when Grits announced we were back on full duties.

In the two days we'd been stuck below ground I'd not stopped thinking about Chip. I'd had plenty of time for painting and sketching, but even that couldn't get the picture of those scars out of my head. Why would he choose to go with his dad? My head throbbed. Skye was right, Mike wouldn't have let him go if he hadn't thought everything was okay, but Mike didn't know the whole story. Then again, Mike had said Chip was happy - more than happy. It didn't make sense. Chip was a bull shitter, but no way was what I'd seen behind those bins been bullshit. Maybe Chip's dad had changed, maybe Chip was okay. The argument carried on in my head. I couldn't talk to Mike about it, I couldn't break my promise to Chip, but I needed to know Chip was alright.

Circles filled the paper as I moved my pencil across it without thinking. My mind was too full of Chip, I had to do something. The pencil carried on moving in my hand, up and down now. My hand moved faster, lead pressing into the paper, frustration travelled down my arm through to my fingers.

'Nice,' said Skye, sitting down beside me. 'What is it?'

I looked down at the hole I'd scraped in the paper and shrugged my shoulders. I didn't know what it was, like I didn't know what to do about Chip.

'Come on, leave your masterpiece till later, it's time to go.' Skye sounded as unenthusiastic as I felt. Like mine, her spark had disappeared along with Chip. I wrapped my pencils up in my art case and shoved it in my rucksack, I didn't feel like drawing anyway.

129

Chapter Twenty-Four

Above ground again I breathed deeply, ridding my lungs of staleness. The smell of traffic fumes from the nearby road smelled refreshing after being stuck underground. Grits had told us to keep away from our usual haunts for a few days. We'd all been given lists for food shopping and essentials, stocks were low.

I left it up to Skye to decide where we were going. I didn't take much notice, my mind still on Chip, but as the tube rattled on, I realised we were on the central line heading for Bethnal Green. Visions of Chip running from the shop, cowering behind the bins flashed before me. Without thinking it though any further, I stood up. I didn't know exactly what I was going to do, but this could be an opportunity. It was Chip's old territory. If I was going to find him anywhere, it would be here.

'Let's get off, here's as good a place as any,' I said as the train pulled into the station.

Skye didn't have time to argue. The doors swiped open, and I darted through them.

'What's the hurry?' she called out behind me.

'Need some air, you know being cooped up and all that.' It was a feeble excuse, but Skye bought it.

'This way,' I said. I picked up my step. I wanted to know Chip was okay, I tried not to think that he might not be.

By the time we got to the mini supermarket where Chip had seen his dad, a plan had started to form.

'You wait out here and keep watch. I'll go in and get the stuff. Meet round the corner if anything goes wrong,' I said to Skye. Imaginary fingers crossed in my head, hoping she'd go with it. Usually, she'd have insisted on coming in, but Chip's departure had pulled everybody down.

'Fine with me,' she said.

I breathed a sigh of relief and got out the list Grits had given us, pretending to study it. I had no intention of getting any of it.

Inside the shop I wandered up and down the aisles. I wasn't looking for anything I was buying time. Skye would be suspicious if I left straight away. I let five minutes pass. I was ready. Heading towards the exit I picked up pace and ran into the street giving a sharp whistle. Skye didn't wait to see who was following me, which was just as well, as she wouldn't have seen anybody. She turned, heading off to our meeting place.

My rucksack, empty except for my art case, bounced off my back. A quick look over my shoulder, to check Skye wasn't following - no sign of her. I stopped running and got my bearings. I didn't have much time. Skye would only wait for so long then she'd have to go back to The Warren. Me, I was heading for the umbrella factory. Chip had said he was there with a bunch of other kids. Somebody might be able to tell me where him and his dad lived.

The KEEP OUT DANGER sign on the fence had done nothing to stop people going in. The gap where someone had pulled the wire away from the post gave way to a well stamped pathway. I followed it through. The door into the factory was thick, solid metal. Not that it mattered, it was part open and even if it had been locked there were plenty of broken windows to climb through.

Inside the smell was rank, like wet clothes left to dry and fester, but worse. My footsteps echoed as I picked my way through old rusty machinery and broken work benches scattered across the floor. I carried on until I came to a corridor, off it was an entrance to another workroom. I poked my head round the door. It was like the other one, except less tat on the floor. Someone had made an effort to clean it. Light shone through the window making it feel warmer.

Along one of the walls ran a row of makeshifts shelters. A mishmash of broken tents, cardboard, and wood. It must be where people slept, where Chip had slept. The Warren was the Ritz compared to this. It made me think of Mike and everything he'd done for us. It didn't feel good going behind his back. My step faltered when I saw a boy and a girl sat around a makeshift table of a broken door and broken benches. My foot hovered in mid-air - I had no idea what I was walking into, who these people were, what they might do to me. They might not even know where Chip was, who he was even, he'd not lived here for ages.

I glanced behind me, checking how far it would be to run back to the way out, thinking whether I should stay or go. I didn't have a chance to decide. Turning back my shoulder caught against a broken fuse box hanging from the wall. The boy and girl looked up at the sound of creaking plastic.

'What are you doing here?' It was the boy who spoke, and he didn't sound friendly.

I glanced behind me again. My instinct was to run, but I had to know that Chip was ok.

'I'm looking for someone, he used to hang out here. Chip.' I said it like Grits might speak, but inside I was shaking.

'Never heard of him,' His face gave nothing away, but I knew he was lying from the nervous side look the girl gave him.

'Are you sure? He's small, wears an Arsenal cap,' I pushed.

'I'm sure.' The threat in his words matched the look on his face, but it wasn't him I was concentrating on, it was the girl. When he spoke, her eyes flashed towards a tent leaning against the wall next to the door, not far from where I stood. Whoever was in there might know something?

'Okay, fine.' I made out I was turning to go, as I did, I reached over and grabbed the tent door.

'No way,' the boy shouted. Running at me, he grasped my hand which was pulling back the tarpaulin. Before I had chance to look a figure darted out under my arm and shot off down the corridor. I had no need to ask them if they knew where Chip was, although I couldn't see the boy's face, I knew it was Chip by his bright blond hair.

'Chip! It's me,' I shouted after him. The elation I felt at finding him plummeted as he carried on running. I didn't get why he'd run away from me? Pushing past the boy trying to block my way, I set off in the same direction.

Chip was nimble on his feet and had the advantage, he knew where he was going and the obstacles to look out for. At the end he rounded the corner, without looking back. I followed, swinging myself round the wall in time to see him disappear down a set of stairs. I followed, taking them two at a time. I didn't know where they were taking me, but I wasn't giving in - not yet.

When I arrived at the bottom, I turned my head left then right. There was no sign of him. I stood stock still, listening. Above the sound of my own breath, I caught a slight scuttle from a room to the left. Slowly and noiselessly, I edged towards the door. Peering round the corner I saw Chip, listening, waiting to see if he'd lost me. Well, he hadn't. I stepped into the space where the door had been. His eyes panicked, moving from side to side, looking for an escape, but I was blocking the way out, and I was bigger than him, he had nowhere to go.

'Chip, it's me,' I said, not that he didn't know.

He edged backwards, movements jerky, eyes wide, face full of fear. I was lost as to why he'd be frightened of me, but it wasn't that which made me gasp. His left eye was swollen, partially closed. A deep blue and purple bruise flowered around it.

'Did he send you?' His voice shook.

'Who?' I asked, confused. 'Your dad? I don't even know your dad.'

'Mike sent you, didn't he?'

'What? Mike? No.' I was even more confused.

'Don't tell him you've seen me. Please!' Desperation filled his voice.

'I won't, but Chip, come back to The Warren, if things aren't working out Mike will understand, he'd let you back, you know he would,'

'No!' Chip took a step further away from me, his voice almost a cry.

'I'm trying to help,' I reasoned, wanting him to see sense.

'If you want to help, forget you ever saw me and don't ever come looking for me again.' He was breathless when he spoke.

Before I knew what was happening Chip turned, pulled back a shutter blocking a window behind him, and jumped through it.

'And Danny, be careful,' he shouted back as I bolted across the room ready to follow him. But it was too late.

As I got to the space in the wall, Chip slammed the shutter door shut. I could hear him propping something against it.

'Chip, please!' I shouted, heaving my weight against the shutter to push it back open. It was no good, it was stuck firm and the silence from Chip told me he'd gone.

Chapter Twenty-Five

Back outside the factory I spun my head, twisting and turning, looking for Chip. There was no sign of him. I'd well and truly lost him. I stood still, but my head carried on spinning inside. I had to face it, Chip didn't want to see me, but why? Why wouldn't he speak to me? Why wouldn't he tell Mike? Why was he even at the umbrella factory? Questions bombarded me and behind them crept up the images of the money on Mike's desk and the black book.

I started to walk, trying to work it out. What was Chip so afraid of, and what did he mean 'be careful', careful of what? Mike had said Chip was happy. If he wasn't, that could only mean one thing - Mike was lying, but Mike wouldn't lie, why would he? I carried on walking. I didn't want to stop. I wanted to keep walking, out of London, out of England, out of this world. Somewhere I didn't have to think about Mike, about Chip, about Mum, about anything. I kept putting one foot in front of the other, trying to silence my mind. I hadn't planned to go there, but it's where I ended up. St Cuths.

Sat on a bench in the garden area opposite. I'd seen pictures of the building, studied every aspect, poured over it in detail. St Cuths. I knew every feature. It was still more impressive in real life. I reached into my rucksack and pulled out the folder Mike had given me and took out my sketch pad and pencil. The wood between my fingers was comforting. I began to calm, focusing on the brilliance of the white paper, shutting everything out.

We'd done some work with Miss McGowan about architecture. There'd been the usual moans from most of the class. I'd sat at the back, hiding my enthusiasm. Remembering what she said, I stroked the pencil against the paper, forming smooth lines, Corinthian columns holding up the decorated portico. Carefully, I wiped my thumb against the grey, smudging the shadow set by the sun edging its way from behind the clouds. Flicking lead across paper, I moved on to the jagged angular edges of the new building attached to its side. Built about four years ago, people either loved it or hated it. I looked down at what I'd drawn. Hard bold strikes of the modern contrasted with the sleekness of the old.

'Very good!'

A voice chimed over my shoulder. I turned to see a woman, grey hair pulled into a tight bun, peering down at my drawing. 'I'm Esther,' she smiled.

'Danny,' I muttered, not looking up, not wanting to encourage her. She didn't take the hint.

'Excellent.' She leaned in further.

'Thanks,' I said. What did she know, anyway.

'Can I make a suggestion?' she asked.

What I really wanted was to be left alone, but I nodded.

Her mouth pulled into a line of concentration.

'You've certainly captured the fluidity of the columns, your transition from the soft edging to the harder edging is seamless.'

I was wrong, she definitely knew what she was talking about. Without wanting to, I started to listen. I felt a sudden pang for Miss McGowan. I hadn't realised how much I'd missed chatting about art.

'If you want to create a more dramatic aspect you need to cast it in a harsher light.' Her finger swept across the paper. 'Here and here, increase the weight of your lines,' she pointed.

I hadn't seen it myself, but the way she explained made it seem simple.

'Give it a try,' he encouraged.

I pressed my pencil harder along the lines she'd shown. The difference leapt out at me.

She carried on watching and guiding me. I carried on drawing. It was like there was a direct line from her mouth to my hand. She said something, I did it. I soaked it all in. When I finished, I held it out in front of me. It was probably the best drawing I'd ever done. The lines and angles were almost perfect, the sketching bold, but with an underlying softness.

'You have what I call a raw talent,' she said.

A wave of satisfaction rippled through me. I don't know why but I was glad she liked it.

'If you've not thought about going to Art College, you should. St Cuthbert's is certainly the place to nurture an emerging star. It would be a shame to waste your talent.'

'Yeah, it's just not the right time.' I shrunk a little inside thinking of the letter in the pocket of my art case.

She looked at me, waiting for more. I surprised myself when I answered, 'It's my Mum, she's not well.' I gave her a massively edited version, I didn't tell her about running away, Mike, The Warren. I was just a boy looking after his Mum.

Her reply wasn't what I was expecting. Not the usual pity in her eyes, more determination.

'Sometimes we must make choices that aren't always easy. Things might be hard, but it gives us the courage to succeed.' Her voice was firm but not harsh. Not like she was telling me off, more she was telling me something important. I listened, ready to learn more.

'In many ways I was a lucky young woman. I came from a privileged background. I had everything, I didn't have to work, I didn't really have to do anything. My life was planned out for me, a good marriage, children and carry on living the high life. But what I wanted more than anything was to go to art college. Art was and is my passion. My family could easily have paid for tuition, lodgings, everything, but in their eyes, it was a frivolous dream and, more to the point, not considered a respectable thing for a woman of my standing. So, I gave it all up,'

'What?' I squeezed the pencil in my hand. 'You gave up art?' I felt her loss.

'On no, not that! I could never do that. I gave up that life, the lovely house, the parties, the smart clothes, left in disgrace and went to art college. I got a part-time job and lived hand to mouth, scraping together enough money for food and a bedsit and I completed my art degree.'

That's why she knew so much!

'Life is a journey. Sometimes, to get where we want to be, we have to take a different route, one that we didn't expect. I had a choice, I could have taken the easy option, had that easy life, but sometimes the easy option is not always the right choice. If I'd have done that, I would never have ended up here, a lecturer at St Cuthbert's.'

Party poppers exploded in my head. A lecturer, here at St Cuths and she thought my sketch was good – no, very good. I pulled her exact words out of my memory, *raw talent, emerging star.* I soaked them up. She knew what she was talking about. Maybe I was good enough to win one of the bursaries and Mike was wrong, maybe I did stand a chance. Maybe, like Esther, I had a choice. I didn't have to go back to The Warren, I could go somewhere finish my portfolio and submit it to St

Cuths.

'Do you have any other work you can show me?' Esther broke through my thoughts.

My work was back at The Warren, but I had a couple of sketches rolled up in my art case.

'They're not my best.' I said, passing them to her, nervous but excited to see her reaction.

She rolled it open and looked at them, her head nodding. The lightness I felt surprised me. If I got the bursary I wouldn't have to steal anymore, and the questions that kept coming back to me, Chip, the money, the black book, the briefcase, none of it would matter.

'You capture the light so well,' Esther said, inspecting each drawing. Handing the sketches back to me, a group of lads ran past, the paper caught in the gust of air and floated to the floor. I bent to pick it up, raising my head I caught a streak of red flashing by. The paper fell back to the floor, my heart missed a beat - Meggsie. I straightened up, ready to run. The lad turned round, it wasn't him, but my heart didn't slow.

'Sorry.' My pencils rattled in my fingers, gathering them to put them in my rucksack. 'I've got to go,' I said, standing up, already walking away.

'But what about your ...' I didn't hear what she had to say. I'd made my choice.

Chapter Twenty-Six

What was I thinking? It wasn't Meggsie, not this time, but it easily could have been. I needed Mike and I needed The Warren. For a minute I'd been sucked in by a dream. Mike was right, that's all it was - a dream. Art school doesn't happen to kids like me. And all that crap I'd been thinking about the money, there'd be an explanation. Just because I'd seen all that cash didn't mean The Warren wasn't in trouble, that money was probably for something else. And the black book - just because it was a black book didn't mean it was Meggsie's, there must be thousands of black notebooks. And if things hadn't worked out for Chip, if he didn't want to tell Mike about his dad, what could I do about it? My priority was Mum. Paying off her debt and getting things back to normal, and the only way to do that was with Mike.

Right now, I needed to think about getting back to Skye. I'd been way longer than planned. There was no point going back to the meeting place. She'd have given up and gone back to The Warren by now. I headed back, thinking of a good excuse to explain where I'd been.

At the entrance to The Warren, I pushed through the undergrowth, before I had chance to get out of the bushes a high-pitched screech pierced my ears.

'Where the hell have you been?'

It was Skye; she'd waited. The glow her being there made me feel was short lived. Tears hovered in her eyes, and they weren't tears of joy.

She didn't wait for an answer.

'Come on, we need to go. How could you be so

thoughtless. They'll be panicking something's happened to us after everything with Chip.'

The mention of his name pricked at the worry I'd pushed to the back of my head.

Back in the tunnel, the silence was suffocating. Skye's anger electrified the air. The questions I'd answered so easily before wormed their way back into my head and loomed in front of me like the darkness ahead.

'Do you ever think Mike might be lying?' My lips snapped shut. I hadn't meant the words to come out, but it was too late to take them back.

The air in the tunnel moved as Skye spun round to face me.

'What!'

'I didn't mean it like that,' I tried to backtrack.

'How exactly did you mean it?' she shot back at me.

'Maybe like things he's not telling us?' Shit, why did I even say that. I'd dug my hole deeper.

Even in the dark, I felt Skye's stare penetrating me. The sharp huff as she turned away was enough to tell me what she thought.

'Sorry,' I said. It floated down the tunnel behind her, the returning silence heavier than before.

When the door to The Warren clanged open, Mike was waiting for us.

'Everything okay?'

The concern on his face made mine flush at what I'd been thinking. I was ready to fess up that it was my fault when Skye butted in.

'Problem on the line. We got held up, that's all.'

I smiled at her, glad we were friends again - or not.

'Don't think I was doing that for you,' she hissed when Mike had gone. 'He doesn't need anything else to worry about. Unlike you, I think he does enough for us already.'

'Sorry …' I tried again. My apology bounced off her back as she walked away.

I spent the rest of the afternoon drawing, filling my mind with lines and angles, hoping they'd block out the questions that wouldn't go away. They were stuck in my head. My pencils didn't work their usual magic.

At dinner, I took the plunge and sat next to Skye, hoping it would force her to speak to me. It didn't. When Mike sat down to join us, he mistook the stony silence for something else.

'I expect it's all feeling a bit different being out there without Chip,'

I glanced at Skye who blinked away the tears gathering in her eyes. I blinked too, but I was trying to blink away the picture of Chip. He'd looked so different; smaller somehow. Then I realised, his hat, the Arsenal hat he never took off, he hadn't been wearing it.

'Was he glad to get his hat back?' I asked Mike.

If he thought it was a strange question, he didn't show it.

'Of course, you know Chip he'd never be without it.'

Mike was right. He'd never be without it, but he was.

'I miss him too,' Mike carried on, 'but we've got to console ourselves knowing that Chip is back with his family.'

Skye's head dropped. I knew she was thinking about her family. Mine dropped too, but because I didn't want Mike to see my face, afraid it might give something away. I thought about Chip and what he'd said about his family, about him at the umbrella factory and then about what Mike had said about his family. Nothing made sense. Had Mike got it all wrong? A knot formed in my chest. What if he'd got it wrong about Mum, too?

'Can I go and see my mum yet?' I asked. 'You said she'd be out of the main ward by now.'

Mike hesitated before answering.

'I didn't want to worry you on top of everything that's happened with Chip; your mum's fine, but she had a bit of a relapse.'

The knot in my chest twisted. My breath caught in my throat. A relapse? What did he mean? I felt Mike's hand on my shoulder.

'Don't worry she's fine now, she just needs a bit more time to recover. Give it another week and I'll take you to see her.'

The tightness in my chest eased as I released the breath I'd been holding. It was going to be fine. One more week and I'd see Mum.

That night I couldn't sleep. Money, black books, and Chip whirled around my head, but most of all, Mum. I know Mike had said she was okay, and it wasn't that I didn't believe him, but I needed to see her now. A week seemed a lifetime away. She'd already had a relapse. Anything could happen in a week. I needed to see her now, to know she was ok.

I lay in bed, eyes wide open, listening to the night sounds, thinking of a way I could get to see her. I couldn't pull the same stunt I'd done to see Chip. Skye wouldn't fall for it a second time. The distant flush of the toilet echoing down the tunnel sparked an idea. I turned it round in my head, eventually falling asleep thinking it might just work.

Chapter Twenty-Seven

It didn't seem much later when I was woken by the smell of bacon. Typical - choose a day when it was a fry up for breakfast, but I'd starve the whole year to make sure Mum was okay. When I got to the dining hall, Skye was already there. I slipped into the queue behind her.

'Hi,' I muttered a peace offering.

Still mad, she ignored me.

'Skye, I'm sorry,' I tried again.

Her answer was a hard stare. I wanted to tell her about Chip, make her understand that I hadn't acted like I had because I was a complete dork, but I couldn't. A promise was a promise. I tried to think of something else to say to make it better. Nothing came to mind, and it would have to wait. It was time to put my plan into action.

Even though I say so myself, I played a blinder. I shook my head at Mim, who was on breakfast duty, when she dangled an extra fat sausage over my plate.

'Not for me,' I said, looking as un-hungry as I could. Not easy with a full English slap bang in front of me.

Then, when she scooped up a fried egg, I shook my head again and started to gag.

'What's the matter?' Skye couldn't stop herself from asking, looking at my empty plate.

'Not feeling too good,' I mumbled.

'You don't look great, now you come to mention it.' It was difficult not to smile at her concern.

It would have been good to hang around and wallow in her sympathy, but I didn't have time. I started to wretch. For added effect, I puffed out my cheeks and spread one hand over my mouth, holding back a torrent of imaginary vomit about to explode over everyone. With the other hand, I pointed in the direction of the toilets, then ran.

Inside the cubicle I made out like I was chucking my guts up. I did it so well my eyes watered. No-one else was around but I kept up the act just in case. Good job I did. When I came out, through blurry eyes, I saw Grits leaning against the wall, arms folded.

'What's the matter, Picasso?'

Head down I went to pass him. Now wasn't the time to get into an argument.

'Not so fast, sick boy.' He barred my way with his arm. 'You need to go straight to bed and stay there. Don't want you spreading your lurgies and contaminating everyone. Twenty-four-hour lock down for you.' His finger jabbed towards my face. 'Stay out of everyone's way. Right.'

I wanted to fling my arms around him. He didn't know it, but he'd handed me the perfect excuse. Instead, I hung my head and looked as ill and hacked off as I could.

'Okay,' I muttered, slumping off to bed.

Back in the sleeping area I pulled some clothes out of my rucksack and started to roll them up. A noise behind the curtains made me dive straight under my sleeping bag. It was Skye holding a mug of tea and some biscuits.

'Here,' she whispered, carefully placing it on the floor beside me.

'Thanks,' I replied, inwardly cringing at my put-on croaky voice.

'Even if you don't feel like them now, you might want them later,'

'Thanks,' I said again, easing up on the croaking. I didn't want to overdo it.

A couple of seconds of awkward silence followed.

'I'm sorry ...'

We both spoke at exactly the same time.

'It's me who should be sorry,' I said. I was apologising for what I'd said yesterday, but more so for the fact I was lying to her again today.

'Forget it. All you need to think about is getting better.' Her hand felt warm as she touched my cheek. If I hadn't felt faint before, I did now. Our eyes locked. It was just me and Skye. Her breath smelled sweet as our heads moved closer. Her lips parted, so did mine. I leaned further towards her, hoping I wasn't getting this all wrong. A shudder passed through me, throwing me off balance. It wasn't anticipation, it was a tube passing above. With the movement of the ground the moment was lost, the spell broken.

'I better go.' Skye pulled her hand away from my face. 'Grits will go mad if he finds me here and you look like you could do with some sleep. I'll try to sneak back later, but it won't be till this evening.'

She turned quickly and I watched her disappear down the tunnel. Half of me wanted to call her back, the other half was desperate get on with my plan. I touched my cheek where her hand had been, to remind myself. Once I'd seen Mum, I could pick up with Skye when I got back. The more I thought about it, the more I began to convince myself it had never really happened, it was all in my head, I'd read the signs wrong.

I picked up my sleeping bag and started to stuff my clothes in it. I had to stop thinking like this, for now anyway. Now the focus was Mum, I could stress about Skye once I'd seen Mum. I shoved in one more hoody then stood back to admire my handiwork. Arranged on the mattress, it sort of looked like a body, and under

Grits orders it was doubtful anyone would dare come to see me. As a final touch, I arranged a woolly hat at the top. Anyone looking in would think I'd fallen asleep with it on.

The sounds coming from the dining area were dying down. My stomach was empty, but I didn't feel like food now I was ready to go. Snippets of conversation filtered through my curtain along with the noise of people getting ready to go out. When the familiar metal clank of the door sounded, it was time to put part two of my plan into action.

Clutching my stomach in case I bumped into anyone, I headed to the toilets. Once there I got straight on to it. With the metal strip I'd used before, I waggled the cover of the hatch from side to side. This time it fell out easily. I leaned it against the wall. My ears pricked up at every sound, paranoid someone would come in and find me.

I stuck my head into the darkness. I wasn't a hundred percent sure it would lead to a way out, and a small part of me hoped it didn't. I had to know Mum was okay, but I was going behind Mike's back and that didn't feel good. I pushed myself through before I changed my mind.

Scampering along like a giant rat, my torch beam lit the way ahead. There was no light shining from Mike's office this time. I'd overheard Grits saying he was out at some probation workers conference or something. Passing the air vent, the piles of money, the black book, and the doubts I'd had, rushed at me. I tried to brush them off, but they sat there, a devil on my shoulder, stubborn and unmoving. I ploughed on, thinking of Mum.

The same breeze I felt last time I was in here stirred

the air. When I got to the end, my hunch paid off – there was a way out. I was on my way to see Mum. The shaft opened out into a space big enough for me to stand up. Tubing and wires ran along the walls. I stretched my legs, shaking out the ache in my knees. I shone my torch up and down. It was the same as the entrance to The Warren, a ladder stretched up to the ceiling, a manhole cover at the top of it, next to it a grate. That was where the air was coming in.

Torch clamped between my teeth I pulled myself up on to the first rung. The ladder swayed as I moved up. It wasn't as secure as the one at the entrance. I stopped to let it steady itself, then carried on, stop-start as it wobbled.

At the top my grunts echoed down the chamber as I tried to jimmie the cover open. My arms ached and the torch which I held in my mouth made me gag. I had to get out. I hadn't come this far to go back again. A final surge of energy, fueled by desperation, I shoved with all my strength.

The torch dropped from my mouth; light snaked its way across the shaft as it plummeted to the floor. I didn't have time to go back down and get it. The cover was starting to move.

Chapter Twenty-Eight

The shaft brought me out on the opposite side of the road to the usual Warren entrance. Lines of cars told me I was in a car park. I eased myself out, pulled my hood tight and put my head down. I'd get the bus to the hospital, it was safer than using the tube, less chance of bumping into anyone from The Warren.

The nearer I got, the harder my heart pumped. Mike said she'd had a relapse, and she was over it, but what if she'd had another and I was too late. My grinding teeth echoed in my ears. I had to keep positive. Mike would have told me if anything had changed.

I stopped inside the hospital door. The gel from the dispenser washed away the sweat gathering in my palms. I loosened my hood but kept it up, just in case. One deep breath and I took a step forward. It felt like a bird was trapped in my chest, wings beating against my rib cage. When the reception desk came into sight the fluttering slowed. It wasn't Rosemary, it was a bloke I'd not seen before.

Another deep breath, I pulled myself up straight and tall. Looking confident didn't only apply to scamming and shoplifting. I pulled down my hood, lifted my head and strode towards the desk.

'Excuse me, could you tell me which ward Lisa Bennett is on please?'

The man at the desk carried on shuffling the papers in front of him. I coughed, sharp but polite. I wasn't going to lose my nerve now.

'Excuse me,' I repeated. 'Could you tell me which ward Lisa Bennett is on?'

The man, looking officious in his glasses and tie,

glanced up.

'I'm her nephew, I've come to visit,' I added, thinking there might be a marker on her name about me.

Without speaking the man tapped into the computer. The bird in my chest started flapping its wings again.

'No Lisa Bennett here,' he looked up, disinterest in his eyes.

I shook my head thinking I must have misheard.

'Lisa Bennett. She was on the intensive care ward, but she's been moved.'

The man tapped into his computer again.

'No. Like I said, no Lisa Bennett.'

Now there was a flock of birds in my chest.

'Maybe she's moved wards, can you check again?'

'I can check as many times as you want but there's no Lisa Bennett.' He put his head down and started shuffling his papers again.

'But she must be!' my voice heightened.

The man gave an exaggerated sigh and tapped into his computer again. The tapping echoed in my head. I was too late. Mike had said she was stable. He'd said everything was going in the right direction. If she wasn't here, that could only mean one thing. She was dead!

'There must be a mistake.'

My voice was a high-pitched wail.

'There's no mistake, she discharged herself last week.'

'Discharged?' I held on to the edge of the desk, confusion and relief weakening my legs. 'Where to?' I asked.

The man shrugged.

'She can't have just gone!' I shouted. Anger and frustration took over, I banged my fist down on the counter.

The man raised his head again, but his eyes weren't on me. He was looking over my shoulder. I turned to look. His eyes were locked with a security guard, silent communication passed between them. I had to go. The green exit sign swam in and out of focus. For a second time I was running out of the hospital, for the second time not sure where I was going or what I was doing.

Nobody followed, but I kept on running. Each thud of my feet fired a question in my head. What had happened to Mum? Where was she? Why hadn't Mike told me she'd been discharged? He mustn't know or maybe he was trying to protect me. I needed to ask Mike, I needed to find Mum. Something bad must have happened. Oh God, what if she was with Meggsie?

At exactly the same time that entered my head, I rounded the corner to the bus stop and stopped dead in my tracks. On the opposite side of the road was Meggsie. Shit! What was he doing here? Maybe it was something to do with Mum. Quickly I stepped back into one of the gardens. Positioned behind the hedge, I had a good view of him, but he couldn't see me. I checked my watch. I had to get back, but no way could I catch the bus while he was there. I had no choice; I'd have to sit it out and hope he didn't see me or that I didn't get caught by some randomer in their garden.

From the safety of my hiding place I watched; his head moved from side to side scanning the street. He was looking for someone. The two minutes which passed felt more like twenty. When a black Mercedes pulled up beside him, I crossed my fingers hoping he'd get in. My foot tapped impatiently as the driver wound down his window. The tap turned to a kick when the driver got out of the car. He wore a flash suit and looked as dodgy as Meggsie. They shook hands like they were bezzie mates. Then my jaw didn't just hit the ground, it slammed into it like a ten-ton truck. I blinked hard, refocusing, making sure what I was seeing was real. There was no mistake, the mousey hair, the tilt of his chin; he might be dressed differently but the driver of the car was Mike.

I couldn't move, it was like I'd been shot with a stun gun. Mike had told Grits he was at conference, but he was here right in front of me, laughing and joking with Meggsie. I could just make out Meggsie handing something to Mike. They shook hands again, then Mike got back in the car and Meggsie walked off. I watched the car disappear out of sight, not quite believing what I'd seen. When they'd gone it felt like I'd dreamed it.

I wish I had.

I had to find Mum.

The journey back was a blur. I didn't have time to think about Mike, about Meggsie, about what I'd just seen. My head was bursting with one question only, firing through every brain cell, pushing at the space between skull and flesh. One burning question, a touch light ready to ignite an inferno. Where was Mum?

As soon as I pushed the front door open, I knew she wasn't there. My stomach felt as empty as the house, skin as cold. With hesitant footsteps I crept along the hallway, like I was entering a stranger's house, not my home. The takeaway cartons were still in the kitchen. Green and furry they'd become a life form of their own. Nobody had been here since I left. Still, I ran upstairs with an empty hope that Mum would be sat up in bed, drinking a cup of tea. 'Danny, where've you been?' she'd say. When I threw open the bedroom door, the only thing on the bed was the half bottle of vodka I'd tossed there weeks earlier. I snatched it up. The glass was cold and hard in my hand. I squeezed it hard, waiting for the glass to crack between my fingers, its icy shards to slice my skin. For that pain to wipe out the pain in my head.

My knuckles whitened as I carried on squeezing. The bottle didn't give. My eyes burned – anger – not tears. It should be Mum here, worrying about me, it was all the wrong way round. I raised up my hand and launched the bottle against the wall. Glass shattered and the sharp smell of vodka filled the room. I watched the liquid slowly run down the wallpaper making up for the tears that still wouldn't come.

I sat down on the bed. My breath is hot as it snorts out of my nose. I rock to its rhythm, gradually calming as it slows. My eyes fall on the glass scattered on the floor. A wave of guilt passes over me. Mum could step on that. She's not here, but still. Another wave washed over me. There's no point being angry with her. That's not going to help me find her. It's not her fault, anyway.

Defeated, I flopped down on the bed. My mind as blank as the empty ceiling I stared up at. I had no idea where Mum might be or what to do. Automatically I think, Mike will know what to do. With that, the picture of Mike and Meggsie loomed before me. There had to be a logical explanation. Mike wouldn't do anything to put me in danger, he'd done everything he could to help me, keep me safe. The only reason he could have for being with Meggsie would be sorting out something to do with me and Mum. Maybe he was giving him money for the debt. But why the flash suit? Who's was the car? The money I'd seen in Mike's office. The black book?

I concentrated on the humming in my ears, trying to block out the questions darting round my head. I'd go back to The Warren. I'd see Mike, he'd know where Mum was. Everything would be okay. There'd be an answer.

There had to be.

Chapter Twenty-Nine

It wasn't until I'd stopped running, I realized the pounding in my ears wasn't the sound of my feet. It was my head throbbing. I stood above the manhole not sure what to do next. The questions I'd put to the back of my mind had pushed themselves forward again. The jury was still out when I dragged open the cover.

When I reached the bottom of the ladder, I picked up the torch I'd dropped earlier. It seemed a lifetime ago. Its beam was fading, I'd have to get a move on before the batteries well and truly died. Crawling in the semi darkness, visions of Meggsie and Mike loomed in front of me. Meggsie's laughter echoed in my ears, only to be drowned out by Chip's words *be careful Danny*. The light from the torch dimmed further. I turned it off as I got nearer the vent by Mike's office. The tunnel blacked out, there was no one in the office. Mike would still be out. I peered through the grill into an empty room. If I could get into the office, I might be able to find something which would explain what was happening, show this was all a big mistake, answer all those questions whizzing round my head. If I was going to do it, I'd have to do it now, I might not get another chance. If I got caught, I knew that would be it. I'd be out. But right now, all I wanted was to know the truth, I wanted to know what had happened to Mum, that she was safe.

Ignoring my shaking hands, I turned the torch back on and felt around the edges of the vent, working out its size. It would be tight, but I reckoned I could squeeze through. I pushed my fingers into the grill and shook it gently. I felt it give. I shook a little harder, moving it from side to side. The screws holding it in were rusty, and with no effort it pulled away from the wall. I'd worry about how to put it back later.

I pulled my hoody over my head. to make myself as thin as possible. I'd got it above my shoulders but struggled to get it past my neck. Heat rose in my body as I twisted and contorted in the confined space, wriggling my way out. With a sharp turn I broke free.

I shone my torch down into the office, looking to see if there was anything beneath the grill that I could lower myself on to. There wasn't. I'd just have to go for it. I dropped the torch on to the floor below, turned myself round in the shaft, then feet first eased myself into the gap. My t-shirt rode up my back as I forced myself through, metal scraping against my skin but I carried on pushing. The weight of my legs pulled me down. Hands gripping the top of the grill opening I gave a forceful shove then shot out like a cork from a bottle, crashing to the floor.

Dazed, I waited for somebody to come racing in to see what the noise was about. No one came. I picked up the torch, now even dimmer. I didn't have long. I cast its beam around the room. The desk was probably the best place to start.

Under the fading light, my hand passed over the papers scattered across the desk. They were mainly unpaid bills. I flicked through a pile stacked on the corner. Credit card applications, all in Mike's handwriting but all different names and addresses. Some sort of scam but they didn't tell me anything else until my eye caught a familiar name. Lisa Bennett.

I snatched the form up and shone the torch directly on to the paper. It must be a coincidence. Eyes traveling down, a sick feeling gathered in the pit of my stomach.

It wasn't only Mum's name, it was her date of birth, our address, and a really crappy attempt at her signature.

Thrashing filled my ears. I stared hard at the paper not wanting to believe what it was telling me. The desk drawers rattled as I pulled them open. On top lay some photographs. I picked them up and flicked through them; photos of Grits with some kids I didn't recognize. They weren't from The Warren. I looked closer. Someone had taken photos of Grits out on the nick. The memory of Chip telling me Grits had thought someone had snitched on him and his crew came back to me. Surely it wasn't Mike. I stared down into the drawer, afraid of what else I might find. It lay there, taunting me, Chips cap. Mike said he'd given it back to him. Chip hadn't been wearing it when I'd seen him at the umbrella factory. Not sure what this meant, I snatched it up and stuffed it in my pocket.

Underneath where Chip's cap had been, my eyes fell on two passports. I opened the first one, Mike's face stared out at me, only it wasn't Mike, it was someone called David Thornton. I threw it down and opened the second, Mikes face again, only this time he was called Clive Seddon. I wanted to scream. I rummaged through envelopes, more credit cards, more application forms. My hands dug deeper, then I saw it, nestled between a box of tissues and a stash of credit cards. The black book. This time there was no mistake; it was Meggsie's.

Frantically I flicked through the pages until I came to what I needed to know. Scrawled across the top in Meggsie's spidery handwriting "Lisa Bennett". I read the figures scratched in pen beneath her name, the thrashing in my ears got louder. With one swoop of my arm, I swept everything off the top of the desk and placed the book flat out in front of me so I could see it clearly.

My lips curled. Short, sharp breaths snorted from my nose. The money Mum owed wasn't going down, it was going up. There was no record of any of the money I'd 'earned' paying off any of the debt. The only change - the book was now full of Mike's handwriting. Did this mean Mike was working with Meggsie? A volcano of fury erupted, I ripped out the pages with Mum's debt written on them, stuffed them in my pocket, then launched the book across the room. I couldn't deny what I was seeing any longer.

Everything had been a lie. I kicked the wall, kicked it again and again, but the pain in my foot was nothing to what I felt in my head. Gradually my kicks softened, and my breathing slowed. An exhausted numbness settled over me. Mike was a total fake. I was no nearer to paying off Mum's debt. I grabbed the pages with Mum's debts written on, out of my pocket and stared in despair. I'd made a mistake, believing Mike. And Mum's debts were still there, staring back at me. I sank to the floor. What was I going to do?

I could have sat there forever. The torch flickered. The batteries didn't have much longer. I pulled myself together. I had to get out of here. I looked at the papers and credit cards I'd scattered across Mike's desk, Mike couldn't know I'd been in here. I'd put everything back, act like nothing had happened and then get as far away from The Warren as I could. I gathered them up in my hands. Then everything fell into darkness.

I pressed the button on the torch. Nothing. The batteries were dead, but I pressed again and again. The room exploded with light. Confused I looked at the torch in my hand. There was no light coming out of it. It was the strip light on the ceiling, and stood at the door, hand on the light switch was Mike.

Chapter Thirty

The torch hitting the floor broke the silence. Mike's mouth twisted with fury. If he was furious, Grits stood beside him, was raging. A mad dog on a chain straining to get at me. When he stepped forward my body cracked like ice, not because of what he might do but because stood behind him was Skye, staring at me her face a mix of shock, anger, pain.

'It's not what you think!' I blurted out, looking down at the papers and credit cards clutched in my hand.

Mike seized the opportunity, 'Danny,' his head moved slowly from side to side. 'So this is how you repay me? Stealing from me? If only you'd spoken to me, I would have helped you. I still can.'

Concern and sadness oozed out of him, but now I could see something sinister lying beneath it. I'd just chosen not to before.

'It's not like that, you've got to believe me!' I shouted, looking at Skye not Mike, my desperation to make her believe me overtaking my anger towards Mike. I remembered, a few hours ago, her face close to mine, the warmth in her eyes. Now all I saw was disappointment.

Skye's voice wavered, 'After all Mike's done for you, how could you?'

Mike's pure sugar voice had cast its spell over her. Her eyes brimmed with tears and anger as she turned and ran out of the door.

Anger reignited, I spun round to face Mike, as Grits bounced forward. Fists clenched, spit shot out of his mouth, 'Picasso! You arsewipe. I knew you were trouble.'

Mike shook his head, his voice still syrup, 'Don't worry Grits, I'll sort this out. You go see if Skye's okay.'

Grits looked at me then back at Mike. 'Say the word if you need me.' Then he turned to find Skye.

Now it was me and Mike. I looked at him, trying to understand who he was. In front of me was the man who'd helped me, given me hope, made me believe everything was going to be okay. All of it built on lies. The anger inside me rose, fueled by a gut-wrenching sadness. I wanted Mike to be the man I thought he was, I wanted it so much. The world was crashing down on me, until he put a hand on my shoulder. My body went rigid, my spine steel, inside pistons fired.

'Danny, I can explain.'

The pistons pumped faster, I waited for more of his lies. I wasn't disappointed.

'It's all a simple misunderstanding. Everything I've done has been in your interests. I'm only trying to make things right for you and your mum.'

The pistons exploded.

'Misunderstanding! I haven't misunderstood anything!' I shouted back. Fireworks went off in my head. 'Make it better for my mum!' I screamed, 'How are you making it better? I've seen it in all - in black and white.' I threw the papers at him along with the black book. 'Her debt's going up not down!'

'You see Danny …'

I didn't give him chance to finish. I couldn't believe he was still trying to get out of it. I played my trump card.

'I've been to the hospital. I know my Mum's not there, and I've seen you with Meggsie! Why can't you admit it – you're a liar!'

He faltered, but only for a second.

'I may not have been exactly honest with you, but I

was only trying to protect you.'

'Protect me from what? More of your lies?' I threw back at him.

'No, Danny,' he paused. 'It's your mum. She's gone back to Meggsie.'

Humming filled my ears, and it wasn't the sound of a train in the tunnel above. My legs buckled, body crumpling, any hope I had drained out of me.

Mike carried on. His words took shape as the ringing in my ears faded, 'And you know what that means, she's taking drugs again. That's why her debts have gone back up, it's not interest.'

I swallowed hard, it felt like a metal bar had lodged itself across my throat. *No! No!* I repeated the word over and over in my head. I hated Mike. He was a liar, but the one time I wanted him to be lying, he must be telling the truth. That explained why Mum wasn't in hospital. She'd promised, she'd said this time it would be different. With the rumble of a train above, my world caved in. I had no idea where to go next. A yawning emptiness swallowed up my anger. I sat on the floor, drained of everything.

'I can still help you,' Mike's voice crept into the void I was sitting in, hovering above me.

Was he for real?

'One last job. It will pay off your Mum's debt.'

I didn't trust him, but I couldn't help listening. Whether I liked it or not, I still had Meggsie to pay off.

'Just one thing, then you can go home. Our paths never need cross again.'

Just one thing. Just one thing.

It repeated over in my head. I wanted to tell him where to go, but the truth was I was right back where I'd started. No money, no plan. The sickness I was already feeling grew. It didn't matter what Mike had done, the debt still needed paying and until it was, Meggsie would have a hold over Mum. However much I hated Mike, however much I didn't trust him, it might be the only way of getting the money. Pay Meggsie back, get him out of our lives and I'd never have to see him or Mike again. If there was a chance, I had to take it. What else did I have?

'I'll do it.' My body felt empty when I said it.

Mike walked over to his desk, pulled a rolled-up piece of paper out of the drawer, and spread it across his desk.

'It's a straightforward job, there's nothing to worry about. You'll be in and out and nobody will be the wiser.'

I looked down at the sheet of paper covering the desk. It was a blueprint of a building. At the top I read Wellbeck Pharmacy, Rowangate Shopping Centre. It was the floor plans for the chemist in the arcade.

Mike took a pen out of his jacket pocket and tapped on the thick outlines of the blue boxes drawn across the pages.

'See here, it's out of view of the counter and the camera.' His pen stabbed at various points on the plan. 'What you need to do is get in here.' He circled a small square, labeled the cloakroom. 'Once you're in you need to wait until the shop is empty, de-activate the alarm system so the doors can be opened.'

I waited for what was to come next.

'And that's it. Once they're opened you can go,' Mike said.

He made it sound so simple and technically I wouldn't be breaking in because I'd already be in there, and if it meant paying off Mum's debt it had to be worth it.

'It has to be done tonight, so we don't have much time,' Mike said.

That was fine with me, the sooner the better, then I could forget I'd ever been here.

'Listen carefully,' Mike said. I was all ears as he set out exactly what I had to do.

Chapter Thirty-One

It happened like Mike said it would. I left The Warren, everything packed in my rucksack, sleeping bag strapped to the top. There was no going back. Mike wouldn't let me see anybody before I left, didn't want me talking. It tore at me that I couldn't see Skye, that I couldn't explain, tell her the truth, and make her see what was happening. Not that she'd want to see me anyway, God knows what she thought of me, what lies Mike would tell her about me. Her face, full of disappointment and anger, was imprinted on my mind. If I'd misread any signs before, it didn't matter, it was clear she hated me now.

In the chemist, nobody noticed me wandering up and down the aisles. I breathed paranoia out through my nose. I couldn't mess this up. It was my last chance to get the money. If I blew it, I blew everything. It wasn't just the money now, if I got caught it wouldn't be social workers and care homes, it would be young offenders. I'd never see Mum. There was no way I was getting this wrong. I breathed again, slowing down the adrenaline coursing through me.

I picked up a bottle of shampoo, turned it over in my hands, then put it back on the shelf. I walked a bit further and chose some cotton wool. All the time eyes sweeping the shop floor, matching it up with the blueprint I'd memorised in my head.

At the top of Aisle Two I saw the door to the room Mike had circled. I needed to check it was open. I glanced over my shoulder. Everybody was engrossed in their shopping. I reached out and pressed down on the door handle, sighing with relief when it gave in my hand.

'Sorry, can I help you?' The voice came out of nowhere.

I spun round to see a smiley girl, hair dyed pink, not much older than me. She was wearing a white overall with a name badge attached.

'I'm looking for the loo.' The excuse bumbled out of my mouth.

'Sorry, we don't have toilets for public use,' she replied still smiling.

'I don't suppose you know where the nearest ones are? I'm desperate.' I smiled back at her.

She looked towards the counter at the older woman behind it, busy serving a long queue of customers.

'I shouldn't really, but there's a staff toilet you can use if you're quick. We don't want you to have an accident,' she laughed at her own little joke.

She beckoned me to follow as she shot another look at the woman.

'Come on, best be quick before the Dragon sees us,' she whispered as if the woman might hear. She opened the door I'd just tried and unhooked a key from the wall. Through the door I could see a row of coats hung up and stacks of shelves. She shut the door, and I followed her to the back of the shop, trying to look like someone about to wet themselves. To the left of the back door was the toilet which she opened with the key.

'Thanks,' I said, hoping I wouldn't get her into trouble. She was helping me, and I was repaying her by setting the shop up to be robbed. Behind the closed door, I stood for a few seconds calculating how long it would take to pee, flushed the loo, washed my hands then went back out.

'Thanks again,' I said watching her lock the toilet door.

'No worries. I better get back to my stock orders or I'll be in trouble.' She nodded towards a tower of deodorants stacked against the back wall. 'It's not going to finish itself, is it?'

I made as if I was going back into the front of the shop, but I couldn't waste any more time. I needed to be in that cloakroom. I took my chance. The Dragon was still busy serving, pink hair girl was busy counting deodorant. I didn't bother looking around. I walked up to the cupboard door and went straight in.

Leaning against the closed door, a tremor ran through me. I could do this. I looked at the shelving I'd spied earlier. If I pulled it slightly forward, I could squeeze behind it and hide. It creaked as I moved it towards me. I held my breath, waiting for someone to come and see what the noise was. Nobody came. Carefully, trying not to knock anything over I pushed myself round to the back of the shelves. Snuggled against my rucksack all I had to do now was wait – and keep quiet. It wasn't long before voices floated through the air.

'Get a move on, Pam! We want to go home tonight.'

My heart leapt to my mouth when the door clicked open. The light flicked on. I held my breath for what seemed like an age.

'Just getting my coat!' Whoever it was shouted into the cupboard. Through a gap in the shelving, I watched a hand reach around the door, patting the wall searching for their coat and grabbing it. The light flicked off. I breathed again.

A few more "Byes!" and "See ya's!" followed, then the bleep, bleep of the alarm being set, then silence. They were gone.

I ran through Mike's instructions. All I had to do was sit and wait for a couple of hours, enough time for everywhere to shut. Mike had given me a phone and would text me the code to deactivate the alarm. All I had to do was push a few buttons, then I'd be out of here. Easy. Even so, my whole body was on high alert. I wanted to get this over and done with. I shuffled from side to side to make some room and pulled my drawing pad and pencils out of my rucksack, hoping it would calm me down as well as pass the time while I was waiting.

I was just finishing the smile on Mum's face when the phone buzzed in my pocket. I pulled it out. It flashed a message from Mike. The code for the alarm - CB**1275. I stuffed my drawing things in my bag. I had exactly six minutes to turn off the alarm. As soon as I stepped out of the cupboard my movement would trigger it. I pulled my hood up in case of cameras and eased myself out from behind the shelves.

My heartbeat beat raced against the monotonous beep of the alarm. Quickly I walked to the control panel on the wall. I could do this. I steadied my trembling hand and began to punch in the code. This was it. I was on my way home.

The panel's lights began to flash. I wasn't sure that was supposed to happen, but I carried on until I'd entered the last digit. Then I waited. The lights carried on flashing and the beeping got louder. On the panel in front of me a message flashed across the screen. 'Error 04'. What the hell did that mean? Panic rose. On the inside of the alarm door there was a table of numbers. Quickly I scanned down. *Error 4 = incorrect code*. Shit. How did I get it wrong? I was being so careful. I gathered myself together. It wasn't a problem, I still had time. Slowly I punched in every symbol and number, checking and rechecking before I moved on to the next.

I stood back waiting for the flashing and beeping to stop. It didn't. Error 04 beamed out, laughing at me. Even though I knew it was no use, I punched the code in again. My heart and the alarm were pulsing in sync. The timer on the panel said I had two minutes and thirty-eight seconds left before the alarm went off.

I pulled out the number Mike had given me to ring in case anything went wrong. It was answered with a flat drone. Invalid number. I didn't bother trying again. I knew Mike wasn't there. I wanted to punch myself. There wasn't anything wrong with the code, or the phone. I'd been set up. How could I have been so stupid? My body and mind froze, eyes fixed on the alarm panel. My heart pumped harder with each passing second.

One minute – thirty seconds – twenty – ten – five.

Clang!

My heart exploded and I snapped back to life. Desperately, I tried to block out the clanging in my ears. Escape was the priority.

I ran to the back of the shop and shook the door handle. I don't know why. It wasn't like they'd have left it open, but I had to do something. I ran at it, full force. Pain shot through my shoulder. The door stood firm. My whole arm throbbed but that was the least of my worries. Over the sound of the alarm, I heard police sirens.

Frantically, I ran to the front of the shop and tried the door. It was no use, there was no way out. The blare of sirens was getting nearer. Desperation flooded me. Head twisting, I looked around, hoping an opening I'd not noticed might suddenly appear. It didn't, but my eyes fell back to the cloakroom I'd been hiding in. I rushed over and flung open the door. The key to the toilet hung there. A shiny silver prize.

I snatched it off its hook. As I rushed past the counter my eye caught a charity collection tin. With a twinge of guilt, I pulled it off the counter and stuffed it into my rucksack. In the toilet, I slammed the door shut and locked it behind me. The window above the toilet was small but I could get through it. I jumped onto the toilet and reached for the window. The catch was stiff but not locked. I forced it open and squeezed my rucksack through. It hit the ground with a satisfying thud. Now my turn.

I hoisted myself up, the metal shutter door being rolled up sounded through the shop. They were coming in. I stuck the top half of my body out of the window. I couldn't fit. I threw off my coat. I started to wriggle through when there was rapping on the door.

'Come on, we know you're in there. You might as well come out. Save us breaking down the door.'

With a final push I forced myself out and crashed to the floor. My head pounded but I didn't care. I was out. I jumped up, looking around for my rucksack, ready to run. I didn't get far.

'Got you!' My arm was yanked up my back. Turning round I came face to face with a bearded policeman.

'You're not going anywhere!' He tightened his grip on my arm. I wriggled trying to pull myself free, but his grip was vice like. He held on to me with one hand and grabbed his radio with the other. Panic made me pull harder, but I was going nowhere.

'This is 2278. I've apprehended the suspect. My location is directly behind the building. If you can bring a car round, we'll get him down the station.'

A trapped animal, I froze. How could I have been so stupid? I'd failed big time. I'd never pay off the debt,

Mum would be on her own, I'd be locked up. That couldn't happen. Spurred back to life I pulled harder. My breath sharp and shallow, I felt like I was choking, wheezing like Gizmo, back on the estate when I first met Mike. That was it! I put my hands around my throat and gasped for air.

'In..ha…ler. I need …' I puffed out the words, my cheeks inflating. I followed it up with a rasping sound.

'I really -' *wheeze, wheeze,* 'need it.' This time I even managed a throaty whistle. I relaxed in his grip, my body feeling loose. I rolled my head towards my rucksack. Indecision flickered across 2278's face. 'Plea..se, plea..se, inhaler, in my rucksack' I rounded it off with a coughing fit.

The policeman looked concerned and pulled me towards a stack of pallets.

'Sit down there.' Gentle now, he guided me, but he still wasn't letting go. 'I'll get it and I'll call the medics for support.'

He only let go for a moment, but I took my chance. I didn't have time to think whether it was wrong or right. I had to get away. With full force I kicked him on the shins. He wasn't expecting it. In my head I apologised, then kicked him again, harder, and snatched up my rucksack and ran. Heart soaring, I was free.

Chapter Thirty-two

Elation at my escape was quickly overtaken by anger, firing through me with every footstep. Anger with Mike, but more anger with myself. Why had I believed him, why had I fallen for it again? Rage powered me on. I kept on running. It was late but there were still people about. I didn't care if they were looking at me. My chest was on fire, exertion, and fury. I had to keep running. I didn't know where to, only that I had to get away.

When I got to the bridge by the canal, I stopped. My fury was a solid mass, glowing in the pit of my stomach. It burned as I watched the ripples of water flash beneath me. I had no money and nowhere to go. Again, I was back where I started. The ball inside me exploded. It was worse than that. I didn't even have the chance of the bursary, today had been the closing date.

I ripped open the side pocket of my rucksack. The box of Blackwings caught on its side as I tugged it out. The pencils scattered on the floor, each one a reminder of Mike, a reminder of how stupid I'd been. I snatched one up, the crack of wood as I snapped it stabbed my heart. I picked up another, then another. Snap, snap, snap until they were splinters on the floor. I gathered them in my hands and launched them into the water. They scattered then floated away along with my dreams.

When the mass inside stopped burning, numbness weighed me down. Back on Main Street, under the light of the lamps, I checked out the shop doorways. None looked inviting, but for tonight I didn't have much choice, I needed to sleep. Up ahead I could see a shop with a canopy over it, good for extra shelter. I was about to set off towards it when I saw a cop walking towards me. Blood pulsed to the tips of my fingers. My step faltered, the memory of kicking PC2278 shot in front of me. I couldn't believe on top of everything else I'd assaulted a police officer. My head twisted, looking for an escape. There was an alley way running alongside a betting shop. Before the cop had a chance to see me, I slipped down it.

The smell of dog piss engulfed me. Drifts of rubbish had settled against the wall, I kicked at them, making my way to the bottom of the passage. The end was blocked by a metal fence, peering through I could see a delivery yard. There was no-one about. I threw my rucksack over and followed. The yard was full of weeds, a padlocked gate opened up on to the road behind. It had an abandoned look, but I suppose a bookie didn't have much need for deliveries.

A set of concrete steps ran along the back of the building. I spotted a gap between the wall and the stairway and squeezed my way in. It was like a little concrete room, dry, free of rubbish with a sloping roof. I peered back through the gap. I was safe, no-one had followed me. Sliding down the wall, I slumped to the floor. Despair had taken the place of anger.

The wetness rolling down my cheeks woke me. I wiped away the tears. I don't know how long I'd been sleeping, but a sliver of morning sun filtered through the gap between the stairs and the building, lighting up the stairwell. A shiver ran through me, reminding me I'd left my coat behind. I sunk my head deep into my hands as yesterday's events came back to me.

Now, on top of Meggsie, I had the police and Mike after me. I couldn't go back home, Mum was with Meggsie, she'd discharged herself from hospital, the social would be all over us. If they didn't get me first,

Meggsie would. How could everything have gone so wrong? I sat there trying to numb my mind and body, wishing the world would swallow me up. It didn't. Instead, the smell of fags drifted into my shelter followed by a woman's voice. I stiffened.

'She's a right one, she is. I'm always covering for her. Well, I'm fed up with it, this is the last time.'

Murmurs of agreement came from whoever was standing with her. Rigid against the wall I risked a peek through the gap. Two women and a bloke stood at the back door of the betting shop. The two women sucking on rollies, the bloke stuffing a bacon butty in his mouth. I sat back against the wall, not really listening to what they were saying. After a few minutes the voices faded. The slam of a door told me they'd gone back inside.

The lingering smell of bacon reminded me I hadn't eaten since yesterday. I wasn't hungry but maybe I'd feel better with food inside. I dug into my rucksack and pulled out the collection box. The plastic was cold, but my skin burned like fire when I touched it. Stealing from a charity, I couldn't get much lower. I stared at its bright greenness, summoning up the courage to break it open. *"Barnardo's"* was blazoned across the front. Something shifted in my mind, sparking a memory. History lesson Year Seven. Thomas Barnardo. The boy he'd turned away, Carrots. His real name was John Somers. Same as the boy Mike had told me about, the one he'd turned away. Another one of his lies. He'd made it all up. It would be funny if it wasn't.

I picked up a stone lying beside me and stabbed the plastic. I stabbed it again and again until it began to crack. A hole appeared, big enough to tip the money through, but I kept on stabbing. My anger returned, only this time spurred on by determination.

Determination that I'd find a way to help Mum. I didn't need Mike; I didn't need anybody.

Shards of green plastic lay strewn across the floor, loose change scattered between them. I pushed the plastic to one side and scooped up the money. If Dr Barnardo was looking down on me, I hope he wouldn't be too hacked off. I needed his help right now. I needed somewhere to stay, somewhere dry, sheltered, hidden away, where Meggsie, Mike or the police couldn't find me. I didn't have a clue where to start. I stared at the grey wall in front of me, trying to think. I very nearly smiled when I realised I'd already found it. I was sat there.

With that realisation I was filled with a sense of purpose. I pulled my sleeping bag out of my rucksack and spread it across the floor. Clothes followed, pulling them out my hand fell on Chip's cap. I turned it over in my in my hand, sadness rose within me, thinking about the last time I'd seen him. I knew what he'd meant when he said *be careful,* I wished I'd listened, but it was too late now. I missed him. I put his cap on my head and pressed it down firmly. I might never see him again, but he could be with me in spirit. I was no way an Arsenal fan, but hey, I'd wear it for Chip.

I carried on folding my clothes and placed them neatly on a small step that ran the length of wall. I left my art stuff in my rucksack, that was too precious to leave behind. I stood up and surveyed what was going to be my new home, for now anyway. Rucksack on my back I squeezed back out through the gap. Today was a new day.

Back on the High Street I weaved through the early morning shoppers and people on their way to work. I wasn't in Warren Crew's territory, but I pulled my cap down just in case. I carried on till I found a newsagent. It was strange handing over cash for my meal deal, it had been a long time since I'd paid for anything. A pang of regret passed through me; I couldn't help it. As much as I hated Mike there were parts of The Warren I missed. Skye's smiling face floated into my head, then it morphed into the last time I'd seen her. I picked up my crisps and left.

Next stop was the charity shop. Inside I rifled through a rack of coats. There wasn't much choice - a puffer jacket or some old geezer overcoat. The puffa jacket won hands down in the fashion stakes but rubbing it between my fingers it was thin and worn. You could feel the warmth of the overcoat looking at it. I could wear it when it was cold and use it as a blanket at night.

In the queue I avoided eye contact, fixing my gaze on the picture hanging on the wall behind the cash desk. A portrait done in pencil, signed J.M Hughes at the bottom. Light strokes of lead created fine lines around the eyes, shading gave the eyelids a drooping effect. It made me think of my sketches.

My sketches! The ones at the cafe. If I got them back maybe I could sell them myself. In my head I repeated the name of the cafe Mike had spoken about. How could I forget it, I'd been so chuffed. Cafe Lucia, London Fields. It couldn't be that difficult to find, I just needed to be careful. It was a risk, but at the moment, it was all I had.

Chapter Thirty-Three

Cafe de Lucia. The sign shone down like a ray of hope. I'd found it no problem. Butterflies danced in my stomach, anticipation of getting my sketches and fear Mike might be around. I pulled Chip's hat down further and pushed open the door. From beneath its peak, I scanned the walls. I couldn't see my sketches. For a minute I thought they'd all been sold until I realised there was nothing on the wall at all.

'Are you ordering anything?' The man behind the counter asked.

'Do you sell artwork?' I asked.

'We're a cafe not an art gallery,' he said, irritated.

'I know, but do you sell paintings, drawings, that sort of stuff?' I asked again.

Eyebrows raised; his irritation grew. He didn't bother answering.

'Is there another *Cafe de Lucia* near here?' Maybe I'd got it wrong, but I knew before he shook his head I hadn't.

Outside, I sat on the grass. I don't know why I'd bothered coming here. I should have known selling my sketches was just one more in Mike's long line of lies. He'd probably binned them. They'd be rotting away on some landfill. I remembered how excited I'd felt. How stupid more like. Who'd want to buy them anyway? The sounds of the park banged in my head as I tried to think how I was going to get the money. Nothing came.

I stood up, trying to stop myself spiraling down into a black hole. What did Mike know about art? Shit all, that's what. I thought about the woman I'd met outside St Cuths - Esther. I pulled myself back up, thinking about what she'd said, r*aw talent, emerging star.*

Even if it was too late to apply for the bursary there might be another way I could use my drawing to raise the money. I stared ahead waiting for inspiration to hit me. A mother pushed her child on a swing, higher and higher. I remembered when Mum had done that with me. We'd been happy. It seemed a long time ago now, but I had to hold on to it. We had to get that back. We'd been there before, we could do it again, I knew we could - well not the pushing on the swing bit.

At the gate outside of the park a bunch of kids were running around, jumping up and down. When I looked closer, I saw they were circling a gold figure, one of those people who painted themselves and stood still for hours on end. The kids were trying to make him move. As hard as they tried, it wasn't happening. His reward was a hat full of money, people throwing in their loose change, I even spied the brown of a tenner. Esther's words came back to me again. *Life is a journey. Sometimes, to get where we want to be we have to take a different route, one that we didn't expect.* If a man could make money by being painted gold and standing still, there must be something I could do.

And I knew exactly what!

Chapter Thirty-Four

The Embankment was already buzzing by the time I got there. Plenty of tourists milling around. Street artists already doing their stuff; jugglers, acrobats, some girl doing sand sculptures. The whole place brimmed with energy. My nerve faltered. They were all so good. I hung back watching, feeling an impostor.

Like a mantra I repeated Esther's words over in my head, then I summoned up a picture of Miss McGowan's smiling face. They believed in me, maybe I should start believing in myself. I might not be as good as these people, but I could try. What's the worst thing that could happen? I'd make a complete idiot of myself, never come back and no-one would know any different. And although I didn't want to admit it, it was Mike's words ringing out the loudest. *Walk straight and tall, look like you belong, and people think you do,* I bigged myself up and walked across, looking like I belonged.

I found a space to work, a gap a bit away from the main crowds but still plenty of people passing by. I wasn't sure how this all worked, whether you bagged a place because it was free or if there was some sort of rights thing going on - my patch and all that. I'd just have to go for it and find out.

The Warren crew never came south of the river, one of the reasons I'd come this side. Even so, I did a quick check, reassuring myself that the feeling someone was watching me was only paranoia.

I'd got in my head what I was going to do. Keep it simple to start with, something that would go down well with the tourists. A school project we'd done, "Art in Urban Spaces", gave me the idea. Most of the class had gone for Banksy, I'd thought that was a bit obvious. I'd researched this bloke, Julian Beever. He did amazing, freaky 3D pictures on pavements. There was one of a swimming pool. Looking at it from a certain angle was like you were dipping your feet in it for real. He made a mint out of doing it and traveled all over the world. No way could I do anything that good and I wasn't expecting to make millions, but it was a start. A start at getting some money together, a start to paying off Mum's debt and getting things back to normal. I pulled Chips' Arsenal cap out of my bag and laid it on the floor, then the chalks and pastels I'd bought on my way here with the last of the Barnardo's money. I was ready to start.

Nerves and the dryness of the chalk set my teeth on edge, scrapping it against the concrete, but once I got going, there was no stopping me. My hands flowed. Still embarrassed, I kept my head down, but my confidence grew at the chink-chink of change dropping in Chip's cap.

I'd gone for a straightforward optical illusion. A tunnel that looked like you could walk into it. Simple, purple, and white, but effective. Half finished; I glanced up. The look on people's faces made me feel less shy about my work. Interested, smiling, heads tilting trying to work it out. They liked it. I flexed my cramped fingers. I'd have a quick break, get something to eat, then get back on it, filling in the detail. I was starting to enjoy this.

The smile hurt my face when I finished counting how much money I'd made so far. Lots of change, mostly pound coins, but two fivers as well. I couldn't believe it. I stuffed it into my rucksack pocket and headed off to the burger van I'd seen parked up the road. The burger barely touched my mouth, I wanted to get back as quickly as I could. I was on a roll, and I didn't want it to stop.

I carried on into the late afternoon before I decided to call it a day. I'd added a set of steps that looked like you walked down and a never-ending oval. My hands were aching, and the chalks were running low. I'd get some more on the way back. Happiness brimmed over like the cash in my hat, altogether I'd made over eighty quid! In the bigger scheme of things, it wasn't mega bucks, but it was a start. I hadn't felt this good in a long while.

The plan was to make an early start tomorrow morning. If I got a better spot who knew how much I'd make? On the walk back, I stopped to look at the display in a library window. It was the colour that caught my eye. It had been done by some school kids. *Famous Artists*. At the centre of it were some pictures done by Class 4CN. Each kid had picked an artist and tried to copy their style - Van Gogh's sunflowers, Degas's ballerinas, Da Vinci's Monalisa. It gave me an idea.

The sign on the library door said it closed at 9pm, late night opening. I wandered in, headed straight for the Art Section, and found the book I wanted straight away. The Art of L.S Lowry. I flicked through it. Scenes from up North. Factories, city streets. People, painted like matchsticks, going about their everyday business. I could do something like it, but with a modern-day twist, set in the familiar landscapes of London. That could be my thing. I got my pencils and pad out of my bag and started to sketch a plan. For a second, I regretted throwing away the Blackwings, but only for a second. My old pencils were fine. I didn't need anything from Mike. I didn't need him.

When I looked at my watch, there was still an hour before the library shut. I wandered over to the vending machine. I might as well sit and have a drink, enjoy the warmth and luxury of the library until I had to go. I got hot chocolate. I could afford it. It was only a quid but buying it with money I'd earned felt good. I found a quiet corner and sat down. I wasn't doing anything wrong, but I slunk down in my chair under the gaze of the librarian. I didn't want to be noticed. I picked up a newspaper someone had left on the table in front of me, opening it up to hide behind, leafing through the pages to give the impression I was reading. I wasn't taking much notice as I turned the pages until I saw something that made me do a double take. Turning back to the page that had got my attention, I peered at it, not believing what I was looking at.

Same black hair, slightly longer. Same sparkling eyes, I could tell even through the dullness of the black and white print. My heart fluttered at the memory of her. I didn't care if the librarian was looking at me now. I sat bolt upright and spread the paper out in front of me. I squinted harder, checking it wasn't my imagination. The picture was a bit grainy, but it was the smile, the same. There was no doubt - it was Skye.

Well to be exact it was Skye, but it wasn't. The print beneath the picture said the girl's name was Ellie Murray. Further down the page was a picture of two adults. A man and a woman, her mum and dad. No mistaking, Skye was a younger version of her mum. There was another photo, a little boy. There was no red tractor but the boy, with blonde hair and cheeky grin, was Jake, Skye's brother. I read on. It was the same story Skye had told me, but there was a difference - a big difference. Whereas Skye said her family blamed her, the whole reason for the article was her family were looking for her, devastated about her brother's death, but as devastated that she'd gone missing, that she blamed herself for what had happened. There was a quote in the article from her mum.

'Please Ellie, if you're reading this, we just want you to come home. We love and miss you so very much. Our lives are broken without you.'

The rage I'd felt in Mike's office bubbled inside me. It was Mike who'd tried to get her back with her family. It was Mike who'd come back saying they didn't want anything to do with her. Another lie, another life he was playing with. That day behind the electricity box I'd felt her heartbreak. Mike was evil, there was no other word for it. I didn't care about the librarian now. I ripped the page out of the newspaper, stuffed it in my pocket and left.

I couldn't let her carry on believing her parents blamed her and didn't want her back. She had to know the truth. I'd find her and tell her. By the time I got back to my shelter under the stairs, I realised it wasn't going to be that easy. The look on her face in Mike's office, the pain and disappointment. She'd seen me breaking into his desk, his papers in my hand. Why would she believe me over Mike? The person who she believed had saved her. He'd reeled her in like he'd reeled me in. I'd have to find her first and what if I got caught? It was a risk and there was a tiny bit of me not sure if it was a risk I could take. Skye needed to know the truth, but I had to think of Mum, too.

I shuffled further down into my sleeping bag, overcoat on top for extra warmth. It wasn't cold but I shivered. Sleep wasn't happening anytime soon; my head was too full of Skye. Ghostly shadows danced across the wall of my concrete bedroom making my eyes droop. Sleep was almost there when a bright light blasted the shadows away. I froze solid, unable to move. It was the security light. Someone was in the yard.

I lay for a second longer, ears straining, then slowly eased myself out of my sleeping bag, careful not to make a noise. Head turning, I wasn't sure what I was looking for, if I should stay or run. I pressed myself against the wall, skintight against my bones. I peered into the light to see who was out there.

Fear flipped into laughter when I clocked what it was. Two fox cubs scratting about in the rubbish. They must have triggered the automatic light. Wide awake again, I watched them play. I reached for my sketch pad, ready to capture their movements, their faces.

I carried on watching, mesmerised. A third cub poked its head out from beneath a stack of wood. Its nose tested the air, a cautious paw reached out, summoning the courage to join his play mates. The smaller of the other cubs didn't seem to notice him but the bigger one's eyes locked on to him, encouraging him to join them. Ears twitching nervously, slowly but surely, out he came. The small cub sensed his presence and rushed over. Although a lot smaller, he knocked the shy cub down in his excitement. The larger of the three cubs bounded over, taking charge, playfully pulling the smaller cub to one side but the smaller one wouldn't give up, he wanted to play.

The littler one reminded me of Chip, the way he darted around, how he moved his head. The middle sized one was me, unsure, a bit on the edge, that was until the bigger of the foxes, Skye, got me to join in, showed me the way. That was Skye all over, looking out for us, sorting us out. Sadness crashed down. I missed them both.

The foxes lost interest before I did and went off to find something else to do, sleek bodies slipping through the gaps in the fence. The automatic light flashed off. I stared into the darkness thinking about Skye and Chip. Chip had made it clear he didn't want anything to do with me, but I had to help Skye, whatever the risk. She was my friend.

Chapter Thirty-Five

The rest of the night I tossed and turned, thinking about how I was going to find Skye. In the end the only thing I came up with was hanging round places I thought she might be and hope. I knew the routine, so it was easy enough to try and work out where I might find her. I needed to keep a low profile and a bit of luck to catch her on her own.

When I woke to the familiar alarm call of early morning smokers I was knackered. The thought of meeting Skye sent a shiver down my back. I wished it was for different reasons.

Back in the Underground, the shivers returned. I'd avoided being down here for obvious reasons. Eyes wide open and ears tuned in for that high pitched whistle, I was on edge. I merged into the crowds, this time I wasn't looking for marks, I was looking for a head of black hair and a pale face. I spent a good hour going up and down the northern line. My heart leapt the first time I thought I saw her. A false alarm, someone with similar hair and the same jacket. But a few more false alarms and my patience paid off.

Squashed on the tube towards the end of rush hour, boredom mixing with despair, I wasn't concentrating as much as I should have and when I looked up, she was there, right in front of me. It reminded me of the first time I'd seen her. That felt like a different life now.

My mouth couldn't help breaking into a smile. I swear she was about to smile back when something flashed in her eyes, then she looked straight through me like I wasn't there. I moved closer.

'Skye, I have to tell you something. It's important,' I

said, my voice hushed.

'Go away.'

It's what I expected, but the words still cut.

'You need to hear this,' I pleaded.

'I don't need to hear anything from you.' Her eyes were cold. 'You're not one of us anymore.' She stared straight at me, 'Judas!' she spat. The tube pulled to a stop and the doors swished open. Skye pushed past me onto the platform.

'Skye,' I called, following her out of the carriage. She carried on walking, I carried on talking, unsure if she was listening but I wasn't giving up. Whatever she thought of me wasn't important now.

'Please, Skye.' I pulled the cutting out of my pocket. 'Let me explain.'

She stopped short and turned round, her face in mine.

'What do you need to explain? I saw what you were doing with my own eyes, Mike filled me in on the rest. I can't believe you'd betray us, after all Mike's done.' Anger flashed in her eyes. 'But do you know the worst thing? I thought you were my friend.' Her words twisted like a knife.

'Please, Skye.'

I thrust the paper at her. Her hand reached out for it as a familiar whistle sounded.

'I've got to go. I can't be seen with you.' She turned to leave, then turned back, eyes burning. 'Meet me outside the newsagents at Kings Cross tomorrow afternoon, three o'clock.'

Then she was gone, the paper left flapping in my hand.

The journey back to the Southbank took forever. I missed my stop, re-playing the scene with Skye over and over in my head. Picturing her face, the anger in her voice filling my ears. I don't know why I was shocked. I should have known Mike would have fed everyone some bullshit story about me. It was the fact she believed it that wrenched my insides out. I thought she knew me better than that. At least she'd agreed to meet me. I clung to that, maybe deep down there was a chance.

By the time I got to the Southbank, the spot I had yesterday had already been bagged by a trumpet playing mime artist. I found another, not prime position but there was still a steady stream of people. I got my chalks out and set to work. My mind had been so full of Skye, I'd not given much thought to what I was going to do. Every time I pictured the Lowry paintings I'd looked at in the library, all I saw was the fuzzy black and white photo of Skye.

Drawing didn't bring its usual calmness. Chalk jagged against the concrete, awkward in my hand. Still, the coins clinked into my hat as the picture took shape, matchstick families watching a matchstick Queen leaving Buckingham Palace, but even that didn't have the same excitement as yesterday. I was on edge, thinking about the meeting with Skye tomorrow, but there was something else. I couldn't shake off the feeling I was being watched, constantly turning to see a flash of red, or somebody from the Warren crew. I kept telling myself to stop being paranoid, the Warren Crew didn't come south of the river, and the Southbank wasn't exactly Meggsie's scene. When I'd finished, my muscles ached. Not from kneeling on the pavement, but from the pure tension in my body, strained, ready to run at any moment.

Back at the shelter, the feeling stayed with me. It was probably seeing Skye that had done it. If anybody was after me, they'd have got me by now, but I still stuck my head out of the shelter to check. There was no-one there. The stiffness in my body began to ease, it was all in my head. More relaxed, I counted out the money. It hadn't felt like it, but it had been a good day, better than yesterday, I had over ninety-five pounds. I should have been pleased, but it wasn't happening. There was a time when that sort of money would have bought the world for me, but looking at it now the notes and coins were swallowed up by the grey of the concrete floor, like it would be swallowed up in a debt of three grand. What I had was a drop in the ocean.

I scooped up the money with my gloominess and folded it up in Chip's hat. I stuffed it in the bottom of my sleeping bag for safe keeping. It might take time, but I was going to do this. Like Grits had said - ramp it up. I was going to earn the money to pay Meggsie if I had to draw my fingers down to the bone. It felt good and it felt even better that tomorrow Skye would know the truth.

Chapter Thirty-Six

I thought it was the foxes out playing again that woke me, but as sleepiness fell off, I sensed a presence. Through bleary eyes and darkness, a figure, shrouded in black, crouched at the bottom of my sleeping bag, rummaging through my things. In the seconds it took me to realise it wasn't a dream, the scream had already blasted out of my mouth. It wasn't a scream of fear, it was a scream of anger. This wasn't some loon come to murder me in my bed, it was worse than that- he was after my money. Chip's cap was grasped firmly in his hand.

In answer to my scream, a face, masked by a balaclava, looked up at me. All I could see was a set of eyes, staring. All dressed in black I couldn't make the rest of him out. I didn't even take time to consider if he was bigger or smaller than me, the thought of losing my money fired me into action.

'What the hell?' I shouted, struggling to get out of my sleeping bag. My whole body shook. I leaned forward, arms flaying. Through the darkness I made a grab for his trousers, losing my grip as my sleeping bag tangled round my legs.

'You thieving git!' I yelled as he pulled away, turned, and bolted.

I yanked at the sleeping bag twisted around my ankles. Free, I scrambled to my feet. Fury took over. I'd had enough. No way was he getting away with my cash. Back on my feet, I ran.

I could see now that he was smaller than me, and even with no shoes or socks I was gaining on him. Adrenalin was driving me on. With every step my anger rose.

191

We shot across the yard. Blood pulsed through my head. I wasn't going to lose that money. I nearly had him. My chest burned. He was nearly at the gate, ready to launch himself over it. I gave a final push. He must have felt the full force of my anger as I dived at him, grabbing him round the legs and pulling him to the floor.

There was no pain when I hit the ground. The pain came with the punch to the side of my head. I wasn't expecting it, but it made me even madder. My hold on him tightened as he struggled to break free. Grappling on the floor, I felt his body weaken. Still holding on, I managed to position myself astride him. I relaxed slightly. I'd got him.

Taking advantage, he pulled his knee from under me and forced it hard into my groin. Vomit welled up in my throat. When my hands shot down to protect myself from further attack, he gave me a hard push. Already dizzy, I fell off balance. Taking the opportunity, he writhed out from under me and jumped up to his feet, giving me a sharp kick in the back as he did.

Clutching my crotch, I clambered up and hobbled after him. I blocked out the pain searing from my groin to my head and concentrated on moving one foot in front of the other. Focusing on the rhythm of my feet, I started to build up my speed again. As I quickened, he seemed to be losing power. The distance between us shortened. Suddenly he darted off to the left down a small alley. I carried on following. The pain in my chest took over the pain in my balls. I was so close now I could hear his breathing, but he kept on going. He wasn't giving in, but neither was I. Then I saw it, right ahead, a high wall. I had him, there was no way out. The laugh bubbling inside me dissolved before it made it to my mouth. He was scrambling up the wall.

I hurled myself at him and grabbed the back of his coat, jerking him backwards. Grip loosened, he let go of the wall, I felt the weight of his body against me. He twisted, falling to the ground. As soon as he touched the floor, I was on him.

I wasn't the fighting type, but all my anger, with Meggsie, with Mike, with the lies, with myself, flooded to my fist, and I pulled it back, ready to land it on his thieving head. No one was taking my money. Not now. The balaclava still masked his face. I wanted to see him. I wanted him to remember me. I yanked the balaclava back. My hand stopped in mid-air, steaming anger evaporated. My fist hovered, not knowing quite what to do.

The person lying beneath me was Chip.

I collapsed on the floor beside him, energy sapped. We lay there listening to the sound of our breathing, both of us too exhausted to speak or move. My brain stretched, not knowing whether to laugh or cry. It was Chip. Chip, who I thought I'd never see again. Chip, the thieving shit bag who tried to steal my money - never mind the throbbing through my trousers. My anger resurfaced with the thought of my money, how I could have lost it and what it would have meant for me and Mum.

Pulling myself to a sitting position, I looked down at Chip.

'Why do you want to rob me?' I asked, not realising how much it hurt until I said the words.

Chip sat up in a flash.

'What? I wasn't robbing you!'

Chip's eyes followed mine, looking at the cap still clenched in his hands. Even by his standards he'd have to come up with a pretty amazing story to get out of this one.

He turned the cap over in his hands. Even in the dark I could see the confusion on his face. He started to unroll the cap.

'Tosser,' he said, looking down at the notes which had been hidden inside. 'I wasn't after your money, I wanted my cap back.'

'Sorry, mate,' I said.

'Mate? Call yourself a mate? A mate wouldn't think his friend was nicking off him?' His voice was heavy, no trace of its usual lightness.

'I know. I'm sorry, but hey, we've found each other.' I tried to lighten the mood.

'Not sure that's a good thing.'

Heavy silence returned, but not as heavy as I felt inside.

'Ha! Got you!' Chip's manic laugh broke through it. 'Good to see you, mate.'

I winced as he slapped me on the shoulder, but I didn't care. I'd found my friend.

Walking back to the shelter, I realised it wasn't only Chip stealing my money that I'd got wrong.

'So, you're living at the umbrella factory again?' I asked.

Chip nodded.

'Didn't work out with your dad?' I gave a meaningful look at his eye. In the light of the streetlamp, I could see the bruise was turning yellow, but it was still there.

'What didn't work out with my dad?' Chip replied.

I gave him a look. I knew about his dad, remember, he didn't have to pretend with me.

'Don't know what you mean. I haven't seen that thug since that day in Bethnal Green - thank God,' he answered, in response to my raised eyebrows.

'But you were living with him?' Even as the words left my mouth, I knew they weren't true. More of Mike's bullshit.

'That's what Mike told you,' Chip confirmed.

'Yep,' I said, feeling stupid, one more thing I'd been taken in by.

'Like I'd ever go back there,'

'I should've known, you'd never …' My thoughts raced ahead of me.

'If you've not seen your dad, who…'

Chips thoughts were travelling in the same direction as mine.

'Mike,' he said, flatly.

'What!'

I'd been sure there wasn't anything else Mike could have done to shock me. I was wrong.

'Yeah, he came and picked me up from the police station. Told me I was a liability and if I ever came anywhere near The Warren, he'd break my legs.' Chip jabbed his finger towards his eye, 'This was a taster of what I'd get if I ever told anybody about The Warren.'

For a minute I was silent, taking in what Chip was saying. Mike was a scheming, lying, manipulative, two faced git, but violence - I hadn't thought of violence - and I hadn't thought of Skye.

'Skye!' Her name burst from my mouth. All this happening, she'd gone out of my head. She wasn't safe at The Warren, we had to do something.

'What about Skye?' Chip asked, picking up on my urgency.

I pulled the paper out of my pocket and handed it to him,

Chips head shook as his eyes moved across the paper.

When he finished, he looked at me, his paled face glowing in the dark.

'We've got to tell her!'

'I've already seen her,' I said.

'What? She knows? She's okay?'

'Not exactly,' I replied.

By the time we'd walked back to the shelter, I'd explained what had happened.

'I'm coming with you,' Chip said. He was decided.

He pulled his cap tightly on his head.

I could feel the smile stretching across my face.

We were back in business.

Chapter Thirty-Seven

Chip came back with me and slept at the shelter, tucked under the old geezer coat. In the morning we didn't need the smokers alarm call, we were wide awake, the anticipation filled the small space under the stairs. It was early, but the day was already dragging. We were ready to meet Skye. Three o'clock couldn't come quick enough.

Even though every part of me was taken up with thoughts of meeting Skye, I still needed to get earning, so I was going down the Southbank. Hopefully it would make the time go quicker, too. Chip was coming with me. As much as we were in this together, I wanted to keep an eye on him, make sure he didn't go off on some crazy plan of his own. Chip was well up for it, and after half an hour I was glad he'd joined me.

'Roll up! Roll up!' he bellowed. The circus ring master, turning a few back flips, doing a few dances, some impressions. The money rolled in. He might not be able to draw, but he had a way with people. I drew the pictures; he drew the crowds.

'Come feast your eyes on the most fabulous, fantastical, drawings of the great, great grandson of the one and only Vincent Van Gogh,' he shouted.

Van Gogh didn't have any children but that didn't seem to bother anybody. The people came and the money chinked into the hat. When we counted our earnings, it was over a hundred quid.

'Slap up meal for us!' Chip rubbed his hands together. 'If we can earn this much money every day we'll be living like Kings,' he said. 'An honest living - who'd have thought it? We might even be able to get somewhere

197

proper to live. Who needs tosspot Mike? Me and you, and Skye when she joins us. It'll be like the old days, but better.'

Chip's mind was in overdrive, planning our futures. It sounded great. Drawing every day, enough money for food and clothes. Nothing to worry about. Me, Chip and Skye against the world. But that wasn't real life. He was living in a dream world. For a start, if everything went to plan Skye would be going home and me - it was great to be back with Chip, but my plans hadn't changed.

'You do what you want with your share, mine's for my mum – remember. Once I've paid off her debts it's a new start for us.' Now it was my turn to go into overdrive. I pictured me and Mum in new house, her old laugh back again. No Meggsie, no drugs. I could still come down to the Southbank on weekends, make some money, every bit would help. Skye could come round and visit, Chip as well ... I looked at him. There was me going on about my family, Skye was going back to hers, but where did that leave Chip. He had no-one. I looked across at him, but it was like he'd not heard a word I'd said.

'Some of the others from The Warren might want to join us. If they knew the truth about Mike, or some of them down at the umbrella factory? We could be on to something good here, you know. There's probably loads of stuff we could do,' he grinned at me. 'No more thieving - who'd have thought?'

'Chip, did you hear anything I said?' Exasperated, I interrupted his flow.

Chip nodded his head, 'Yeah Danny, I heard - your Mum. I know you want to help her but look at me. How many times did my dad say sorry, things were going to change? They never did. If you're gonna change, you've really got to want to.'

The way he said it was so matter of fact, but what did he know? Mum had gone back to Meggsie, but it didn't mean she'd chosen him over me, he'd have forced her, made her think she couldn't be without him. I knew what he was like. He'd got his claws into her and twisted her mind. Once I was home and paid off the debt, things would change. It was Chip living in a dream world, not me.

'It's time to go see Skye,' I said. That conversation was over.

The sick feeling in my stomach threatened to make it to my throat all the way to the station. I told myself it was stress at meeting Skye, but I couldn't get rid of the thoughts Chip had put in my head. Mum wanted to change, she'd said and this time I knew she meant it, but if I dug deep down enough, I was beginning to wonder.

At Kings Cross station, everything we learned in The Warren, we put to good use. Chip stayed out of sight, acting as a look-out in case things went wrong, ready to warn me of any danger. He even made up a new whistle.

Five minutes to go. Chip stood by the ticket machine, making a show of studying the map of the tube. Really, he was doing a reccy, checking nothing was going off. A brief nod in my direction; all was okay.

I stood in the doorway of *Pret a Manger,* doing a less convincing job of looking like I was waiting for someone. My nerves jangling like a xylophone, I was surprised no one heard. My stomach swirled, half of me wanted to see Skye, the other half wanted to run, remembering the last time I'd seen her; she'd looked like she wanted to kill me. I hoped this time would be different, I'd soon find out - she was walking towards me.

'Follow me,' she said without making eye contact. 'I can't talk to you here; we might be seen.'

I stopped myself from looking back at Chip, it might give him away. I had to trust he had my back. I followed Skye through the turnstile, desperate to explain things, tell her about her parents, but she was walking too quickly. She strode to the end of the platform where there was less of a crowd. I chanced a quick glance to my side, relieved to see a thin wisp of blue hovering at the edge of the crowds waiting to get on the tube. It was Chip.

Skye stopped and leaned against the wall, her eyes hard. As angry as she was, it was good to be near her again. I took my opportunity, pulled out the paper and handed it to her. That explained it better than I could. She snatched it out of my hand without looking at it.

'How could you?' Her voice was as full of hate as the last time, more if that was possible.

'How could I what?'

'Mike was right, he said you'd play the innocent, like you didn't know jack all.'

'Whatever Mike's told you, it isn't true. He's a liar. Look at the paper,' I pleaded.

Her eyes flickered, not towards the paper, but to the side of her. It was only a second, but long enough for me to see a movement in the shadow of the alcove behind her. The hairs on my neck prickled. Something wasn't right.

'Read the paper,' I shouted over the noise of the oncoming train, taking a step backwards, ready to run. It was too late. Out of the shadow stepped Mike. My mouth dropped; my heart dropped further. Skye had set me up.

I turned and tried to push my way into the crowd moving towards the train. I didn't get anywhere; my arm was clenched between sharp fingers. It was Mike. My skin bruised under the tightness. The more I pulled the deeper he pushed into my skin. My legs were moving but I wasn't getting anywhere. With the full force of my body, I pushed forward. I had to get away, but Skye had to know the truth.

'Read it!' I shouted at her.

I could see by her stricken face, she already had. Her hand flew to her mouth, head shaking. Mike looked at Skye, then at me. He reached over, trying to grab the paper out of her hands. As he did his grip weakened, I took my chance and pulled away. At the same moment the train pulled in everyone surged forward. A sharp shove on my back pushed me through a small gap in the crowd. I looked behind. It was Chip.

'Keep moving,' he said, still shoving me.

I'd almost made it to the door when my head was forced back by a tug on my hood.

'Got you, Picasso,' a menacing voice breathed in my ear. It was Grits. I should've known he wouldn't be far away. Chip was on the train, calling me, willing me on but I couldn't move. My hoody tightened round my neck. Grits pulled again with more force.

Chip was shouting but I couldn't do anything. My heart sank as the doors started to close with Chip on the other side. The next thing I knew Chip jumped through the doors as they were about to close, back onto the platform. He rolled like a tiny cannonball, knocking Grits to the floor. Then he was pulling me up and along.

'Run! Run!' He was screaming now.

'Picasso, you arsewipe!' Grits roared. He was up on his

feet again. Chip was still dragging me, but there was no point. Mike, holding on to Skye, blocked our way.

Chip didn't seem to notice or care, he kept on running, taking me with him. My sinking heart shot into my mouth when I realised what he was going to do – what we were going to do. The sheer terror I'd felt when I'd watched him disappear into the black hole of the tunnel clinging to the back of the tube carriage, was nothing to what I was feeling now.

I wanted to pull back, stop this happening. Mum, the money, Skye, Mike, Meggsie – none of it mattered if I was dead. But momentum was against me. Chip pulling and the wind from the train carried me along. Air hit my face as the train swooshed past. One final tug from Chip and I was flying, the train tracks passed beneath me.

My hands smarted, slapping against the cold steel bar on the back of the train. I held on for dear life; my grip so tight I didn't know where the metal began and my hands started. Terror widened my eyes, fear and wind made my hair stand on end, but I was alive. On the platform I could see Skye, Mike holding her back. She was shouting. Above the noise of the train and the thud of my heart, I couldn't hear a thing. I didn't need to. I could tell from the shape of her mouth.

'Sorry.'

Then complete darkness.

I was either dead or we were in the tunnel.

Chapter Thirty-Eight

Too stunned to talk, I nipped myself, checking I was still alive. Chip more than made up for my silence. He didn't shut up all the way back to the shelter.

'Whoa, Danny!' His voice had that manic edge. 'What a blast, can't believe you did it. Did you see their faces?'

I didn't know if he meant Mike and Grits or the transport police who'd chased us when the train had pulled into the next station. I didn't care. I was shaking, Chip was buzzing. Excitement was a drug to him. 'Let's do it again, Danny! The best place is …'

'Chip, stop it!' My shaking grew stronger, no longer shock, but anger.

'Listen to yourself,' I couldn't hold back. 'We could both be dead! And this isn't about me and you having a laugh. It's about Skye, she's still with Mike. God knows what he'll do now. We've got to help her, and Mike needs to pay for what he's done to all of us. If you want to go off dicking about on the tube, that's fine, go ahead. All I know is I've got to do something.' I don't know if it was the near-death experience, but I'd never felt surer about anything.

Chip looked down at his feet. When he looked up, I expected his usual smile, ready with some stupid comeback. Instead, his face was serious.

'You're right. What do we need to do?'

There was the problem - I didn't know. Mike might be a twisted liar, a thief, a complete and utter tosser, the names I could call him filled my head. He might be all those things, but he was clever. If we were going to get anywhere, we'd have to be clever, too.

'Come on,' I said to Chip. 'I know where we can make

a start.'

Back in the library, where I'd first found out the truth about Skye, we stared at a blank computer screen. Sandwiched between an old man who looked like he was researching his family tree and a young kid playing some dim game, I fired up the computer and typed in Mike Fielding. The list that came back was endless. *Facebook* pictures, Mike Fielding, Doctor of Science, University of Leeds; Mike Fielding, bass guitarist of some unheard-of thrash metal band, "Future Outlook"; Mike Fielding, Dentist. None of them were our Mike Fielding. I typed again, Mike Fielding Youth Justice, still nothing. The names on the passports I'd seen in his office were still fresh in my head. I tried those too. No luck. I tried Mike, Michael, Micky, Mikey. Still nothing.

'We'd probably have more luck walking round with a picture of him asking random people, 'Do you know this man?' Chip tried to joke, but like me, he was losing the will, but we couldn't give in.

As I thought about what Chip had said, the idea came out of nowhere.

'Chip, you're brilliant. It might just work!'

Chip looked at me like I was off my head. 'We're not actually walking round London with a picture of him, are we?'

'No, you prat.' I tapped the keyboard, searching for the app I needed. '*Facial Recognition.*' 'That's it!' I tried to contain my shout.

Chip still didn't understand.

'Look, I'll show you.' I was already walking over to the librarian's desk.

'Can I buy a sheet of plain paper, please?' I asked.

Back at the computer desk, I laid the paper flat on the desk and got a pencil out of my back pocket. Drawing a picture of Mike, I couldn't help thinking about the last time I'd painted him. The hope I'd felt then, now twisted to hate. I tried to make it as much of a likeness as I could, but I didn't have all day. Chip looked on as I carried on with the sketch. Finished, I held it up for him to see.

'What do you think? Does it look like him?' Mike's face stared out from the paper.

Chip gave a low whistle.

'Creepy! It's like he's looking right at me.'

I could feel myself getting hot staring into Mike's eyes. I had to admit, it was the spit of him. I'd done a good job.

Two quid later I switched on the scanner. The machine hummed in my ears as the picture uploaded on to the computer. I pressed search.

We pulled ourselves closer to the screen. I scrolled up and down, peering at the images as they moved across it. It didn't take long.

'It's him, it's him!' Chip jumped out of his chair.

'Shh!' I said, pulling him back down into his seat. The last thing we want is to draw attention to ourselves.

There was more than one picture of him, some had different names, but it was definitely Mike - or David, Thomas, Gary, whatever he was calling himself at the time. I clicked on the one at the top. A newspaper report, more than four years old, filled the screen.

David Garfield, under the alias Richard Cooper, ran a team of young shoplifters targeting chains of retail outlets in the Leeds area. He then sold the stolen items through an on-line account. He is estimated to have amassed more than £143,000 over a period of 18 months. Garfield, aged 29, from Fernley Crescent, Leeds was jailed for two years at Leeds Crown Court this week. He pleaded guilty. Investigating Officer, PC Ian Tompkinson, said; "It was a simple but effective scam, organising and directing vulnerable young people in an operation that netted him thousands of pounds. Garfield had supervised the fabrication of foil-lined bags to ensure goods made their way through security scanners. It was also revealed that recruited shoplifters would be punished if they failed to secure goods or tried to sell them on to other parties.'

I clicked my way through the rest of the links. It was more of the same in different places. A road map of Britain; Sunderland, Nottingham, Tavistock, Birmingham, it went on. The only difference was, he'd not been caught again, always managing to clear out before the police got to him. My anger rose as I read on. Everybody he'd taken in, everybody he'd made a mug of, but on the other hand it made me feel less stupid. I wasn't the only dim wit fooled by him. One article described him as a "criminal mastermind," building up a nationwide network of outlets for knock off goods. He'd made a living out of this, a living out of kids like Chip and me. I skimmed over the word *vulnerable,* that wasn't me. I was okay, I had Mum.

My stomach twisted and bile rose in my throat as I read on. It wasn't just stolen goods. It got far worse. He was suspected of money laundering, drugs, GBH. And Skye, what was he planning for her? We had to get her out of there.

I looked across at Chip. His grey-green face looked like I felt. We sat in silence, staring at the computer screen, as if the answer to what we should do might suddenly flash across it. We'd got all this information but all it told us was we were dealing with a complete psycho. The bile in my throat burned. I couldn't hold it in any longer. Stumbling on legs which didn't feel like my own, I ran out of the library.

Chip found me round the back of the library bent

double, wiping the vomit from my mouth. I felt like I was drowning. He'd got Skye, but there was something else, too. I grasped on to Chip's arm trying to pull myself out of it.

'My mum. He knows where my mum is. What if he does something to her?' My whole body was ice cold.

I waited for Chip to say something, to come up with one of his off the scale ideas, but one which might just work. He said nothing. Realisation suffocated me. There was nothing we could do. Chip voiced what we were both thinking.

'We're stuffed, Danny.'

Chapter Thirty-Nine

We sat for ages. The smell of sick stinging my nose was the least of my worries. We had to get Skye out of The Warren, and I had to get the money for Mum. But even if I could think of a way to do it, what then? Mike would still be out there; we'd be looking over our shoulders forever. We'd never be free. The police couldn't even catch him.

That was it!

'The police!' The words tumbled out of my mouth as the idea began to form. 'He's a wanted man. We need to let the police know where he is.'

Chip looked at me like I'd said we needed to zap him to another planet using my intergalactic ray gun.

'Are you serious? We walk into the local cop shop and say, "By the way, we know where Britain's most wanted is. If you'd like to follow us." They're after you for robbery, I've already got form, they'll lock us up before we can even say Mike's name.'

I shook my head slowly.

'We don't go to the police - we get them to come to us.'

Warmth crept back into my body as I started to think things through. Mike had once said to me, "Make it happen", well, that's exactly what I was going to do. It felt good using his words against him. An hour later we had the making of a plan. Now all we had to do was put it into action.

We spent until late afternoon in the library making lists. Things we had to do, things we needed. Everything had to be above board, we were not breaking the law. The only time we wanted to see the police was when they were dragging Mike away - and we'd be watching that from a distance. I'd had to argue with Chip about the air wave radios. Chip wanted to lift them, I had to admit it would hit hard handing the money over, but if it worked it was worth it.

By the end of the day, we'd got everything we needed and gone over the plan until it was fixed in our heads. Now we just had to do it.

Next morning. D-Day. I hadn't slept, but I was wide awake. Every muscle in my body twitched. My stomach was empty to its pit, but the thought of food made me queasy. Chip was up, sat on the shelter floor, hands running through his hair. We gathered everything we needed. We were ready.

We knew the routine of The Warren, what time people left, when they came back. We timed our arrival so we wouldn't be seen. The scrub land looked exactly the same but felt different. We were trespassers. Sadness crept up on me again. Whatever Mike had done, being back here made me realise how much I missed the place, missed what I thought I'd had. I tried to shrug it off, but it clung like an extra layer of skin.

The old mattress I'd first seen with Skye was lying exactly where it always was. We moved quickly, pulling out some of the crap from underneath it, making a gap. We squeezed ourselves inside, lying alongside rubbish and debris. The smell was disgusting. It cloyed the back of my throat, but I sucked it up. It was the perfect look-out point to see who was coming and going.

We were waiting for Mike. For the plan to work, he had to be in The Warren. After two hours, the smell was as rank as ever and there was still no sign of him. I told myself not to worry. The place ran like clockwork. He'd be here at some point during the day. I repeated it in my head, if I said it enough times it would happen, and even if it didn't, we'd come back tomorrow, and the day after and the day after. We had to.

'I think we should go get some burgers or something,' said Chip.

My empty stomach was churning, but not for food.

'How can you think about eating?'

'Nah, I'm not hungry. Thought we could be like cops when they're on a stake out. They're always stuffing their faces.'

We lay flat on our stomachs looking out on the empty scrubland. Nothing happened. Restlessness kicked in. Pins and needles buzzed in my leg. I could feel Chip next to me.

'Stop wriggling,' I said to him. 'You'll make the mattress move.'

'They'll think it's rats,' Chip said.

'Big rats.' I gave his leg a shove, trying to get him to stop.

'I need the loo,' he hissed.

Busy debating whether he could risk going to the loo or whether he'd have to do it under the mattress, in a bottle or something, we almost missed the slight movement of the bush.

As Mike's head pushed through, Chip stopped jiggling. Rigid, his fear and anger mirrored my own. When Mike stepped out and brushed down his jacket, my anger flared even more. It wasn't the usual tatty, brown thing he wore; it was the top-quality leather one he'd been wearing when I saw him with Meggsie. We watched him give a quick glance around, then pull something out of the plastic bag he was carrying. It was the shitty cord jacket he usually wore. He swapped them over, put the leather one in the carrier bag then headed towards our mattress. He was going to hide it.

Beside me I could hear Chip's intake of breath. He'd already had one beating, he didn't want another. He started moving forward towards to the opening we'd created, ready to run.

I pulled him back trying to signal to him with my hands which was difficult in the tight space beneath the mattress. But my jabbing fingers and rolling my eyes managed to get across what I wanted him to do.

Behind us, lodged at the back of the mattress were some black bin liners. If we pulled them forward, we could cover ourselves with them. We stretched our arms, grasping at the bags, careful not to move the mattress and give ourselves away. The black plastic ripped in my hands. Chip gave a quick look out of the gap in the front. The look on his face told me Mike was nearly on us.

I turned my body, pushing my foot under one of the bags, levering it up and catching it in my hands, then dragging it over both me and Chip. As I did, the rip I'd made earlier stretched open, covering us with the rubbish inside, wet, slimy and scaley. Fish. Now I knew what that smell was! Rancid, rotting fish, but I didn't care. It had done the job, just in time as Mike's hand appeared in the gap and pushed in the plastic bag he'd been holding.

The stench of fish wrapped round my throat. I wanted to throw back the mattress and breath in the fresh air, but there was nowhere to move so, retching, we waited until we were sure Mike had gone, then eased ourselves out.

After a quick stretch of arms and legs and a massive gulp of fresh air, we pushed ourselves back under the mattress. We had to go back under. Now we knew Mike was in The Warren, all we had to do was wait for midnight. By then everybody would be asleep. Getting a good night's kip, ready for 'collecting' in the morning.

Midnight couldn't come soon enough. Given the choice between being holed up under the mattress with Chip for much longer and meeting Mike head on, it was a close call. Though maybe not that close when the alarm on my phone sounded.

'Midnight – this is it.' I looked at Chip.

We pulled ourselves out of the mattress once more. I looked at Chip again. He looked at me. Silence hung between us. I leaned to give him a hug at exactly the same time he moved towards me. Our heads clunked as they collided.

'Idiot,' Chip laughed. The moment had passed.

The fresh air felt good, I tried to hold on to that feeling as we checked through our rucksacks. We'd got everything.

'Just one thing before we go,' Chip said, crouching back down to the mattress opening. He pulled out the plastic bag with Mike's leather jacket in it. He reached in further and pulled out one of the bin bags. He pulled open the bag with the jacket in it and poured in the rubbish from the black bag. He threw the bag, now full of jacket and fish, on the floor and started jumping up and down on it. I joined in. It was like some sort of weird war dance. When we finished, I looked down at the bag full of mushed up fish, Mike's jacket, and my hatred. This was going to work, I didn't want to imagine what would happen if it didn't, but if nothing else, Mike would be one leather jacket down.

Chapter Forty

I breathed easy. The manhole cover to the secret air vent lay undisturbed, still hidden by moss, entwined with weeds. I'd worried someone had found it, or worse, it had been sealed up. I pushed the green aside.

'Whoa!' Chip gasped when I heaved back the dull metal slab. 'Can't believe you never told me about this.' I felt bad for a second, until he added, 'We could've had such a laugh.' My point exactly. I bit back the words, but it must have shown on my face.

'No worries, I get it. No messing. It's in, get Skye, then straight out.' The determination igniting his eyes was as strong as my own.

'We're on,' I said, handing him one of the airwave walkie talkies.

'I'll be ready and waiting.' He grasped it tightly. 'One more thing, we need a word.'

I looked at him, puzzled.

'You know a code, a safe word, so we can let each other know if we're in danger.'

I wanted to tell him this wasn't some movie, but we didn't have time to argue so I said the first thing that came into my head, 'Fish.'

Chip smiled in agreement.

'Time check,' I said, heart thumping against my chest. This was it. We were ready to go. I gave the thumbs up then lowered myself into the shaft.

Rung by rung, I moved slowly. My stomach rolled with the sway of the ladder, the metal groaning each time I moved. It was looser than I remembered. My fists tightened, steadying myself as well as the ladder. Teeth gritted, I carried on. Four rungs from the bottom I jumped.

Crouched on the floor, the ladder swung from side to side above my head. I reached out, bringing it to a stop, gently giving it a shake. Yep, it was definitely looser, but it would hold. It had to. It was our only way out.

Head torch on, I moved through the shaft quicker than before, even with the added load of the rucksack on my back. Scrambling along, I wondered how Chip was getting on. To be fair all he had to do was sit and wait for me to give the go ahead. I'd drilled it into him; do nothing, absolutely nothing until you hear from me. But when had Chip ever listened?

Our first idea had been to phone the police with some bullshit story. We'd overheard a conversation, someone planning a robbery, something to do with the Underground, then give them directions to The Warren. Like that was going to work. Apart from anything, it sounded totally unbelievable.

It was Chip who came up with the idea in the end. We wouldn't phone the police. We'd get Skye's parents to do it. Their phone number was in the newspaper article about Skye – or should I say Ellie. The plan was simple.

Step One - I'd go down to The Warren through the shaft.

Step Two - When I found Skye, I'd radio Chip.

Step Three - He'd call her Mum and Dad, tell them everything- well most of it. He was a friend of Skye's, knew where she was, who she was with, all about Mike, what a shit he was, so on and so on. They'd call the police who'd come to The Warren and find Mike. By which time - Step Four, me and Chip would be long gone, Skye would be back with her parents. Mike would be banged up getting all he deserved. What could go wrong? I cut that thought dead before I had time to answer it.

Before I knew it, the hatch leading into the toilets was in front of me. The rough wood scratched against my ears when I pressed my head against it. Everyone should be asleep but there was always the chance someone needed the loo. All I heard was the trickle of water running through the pipes. I breathed deeply and pushed the panel.

Head poking out, my torch shone into empty darkness. Pulling my body through, I felt exposed. I suddenly panicked. If anybody saw me, I'd had it. I darted into one of the cubicles, shutting the door behind me. The sound of my breathing filled the entire space. I sucked in the air then pushed it out, in out, in out, slowing the rising fear. I could do this. I had to, for Skye, for Chip, for Mum, for me. I pushed open the door, stepped out and made my way to the tunnels.

Smooth tiles cooled my skin as I slid along the wall, moving forward, pressing myself as close as I could. I was heading for the main door. Back in the tunnel I'd expected to feel anger, fear, terror even, and I felt all that. What I hadn't expected was the crushing emptiness pressing down on me. This had been my home and despite everything I'd been happy. I gave my body a shake, throwing off the feeling. I didn't have time for this now.

When I got to the entrance door, I pulled the rag of material out of my rucksack. We'd thought of everything. I held it firm against the bolts, listening to their dull thud against the cloth as I pulled each one back. I wrapped it tight around the metal bar, my heart rose in my mouth when I lifted it up. I swallowed it down when the usual deafening clang came out as a muffled clink. When the police got here, they'd get in no problem.

I looked at the time on the airwave radio. We were on track. When I pressed the button to speak it felt like it echoed through the tunnels. I waited a second.

'Chip, it's me. I'm in. Step one complete,' I whispered, tensing as the radio crackled. There was no reply. I held my breath.

'This is Daddy Bear. Message received Painter Boy. I repeat message received.'

Even under the mass of pressure, I cringed. More of his movie stuff, he'd insisted on code names too. Painter Boy was his idea, not mine. The radio crackled again, 'Code names remember.'

'Sure thing.' Inwardly, my eyes rolled.

'Daddy Bear signing off,' Chip's voice whispered through the radio.

'Painter Boy, over and out.' I cringed again, grateful no-one else could hear.

Now step two - find Skye. I headed in the direction of the sleeping area, the most obvious place to look. I should have been bricking it, but it was like everything had been smothered by a heaviness as memories of my time in The Warren came back to me with every turn. The laughter, me, Skye, and Chip, filled my ears. It turned to a dead weight when I passed my bed, or what had been my bed.

Curled up in a sleeping bag was a boy. His rucksack stood where mine had been. Disappointment sliced me. I was gutted. Thrown out and replaced, no better than the shitty old coat I'd got from the charity shop. However much I hated Mike now, however much I knew it was all bullshit, at the time I'd believed him. He'd made me think I was doing something important, that I was important. The worst thing was it had been good, and even though I knew I was better off now, it didn't feel as good.

I looked at the sleeping figure, wondering what his story was, what crap Mike had fed him. The rip inside tore further. I was about to destroy this kid's hopes, his dreams, like mine had been destroyed. The thought grew, making me feel sick, it wasn't only this boy; I was about to demolish the lives of every single person down here.

I stopped myself, even now Mike was twisting my head. I'd almost talked myself in to thinking it was me who was the bad guy. I wasn't going to let that happen. This was all Mike's doing. I gave the boy a final look and carried on.

When I reached Skye's bed, I slowly pulled back the curtain. I didn't want to freak her out. The last thing I needed was her screaming the place down thinking there was some weirdo hovering over her. I needn't have worried. Not about that anyway. Her bed was empty.

Chapter Forty-One

Never mind freaking Skye out. I clutched my neck to stop the screech of frustration exploding out of me. My body shook with the effort. Where was she? We couldn't be too late. She must be here, she had to be. Then I saw it, pinned by the side of her bed. The photograph of her brother. She wouldn't go anywhere without that. She was still here. I had to find her. I had to focus. Now was not the time to lose my cool. I tried to think where she might be. Mike's office seemed the obvious place, but it was definitely empty when I'd passed.

Gentle snores buzzed in my ears, making it hard to concentrate. Think! I told myself, trying to block the sound out. She had to be somewhere. It made sense Mike would want to keep her away from everyone else, he couldn't risk her telling them what she knew. I racked my brain. Mapping out The Warren in my head. It had to be somewhere people wouldn't go, Other than Mike's office, which was well out of bounds, I couldn't think of anywhere.

That was it! Out of bounds! The hazard room, the one I'd seen Mike go in with the briefcase.

As soon as I got there, I tried the handle, moving it gently from side to side. No surprise it was locked. I leant against the door, listening for any sound that would tell me Skye was in there. All I heard was my own blood pumping. I gave the door a quiet tap. Still nothing. I gave another, this time a little louder. A muffled voice sounded through the door. I couldn't tell what they said.

'Skye!' 'Is that you?' I hissed. She was still Skye to me, I couldn't call her Ellie, 'It's me.'

'Danny?' Her voice came back, quiet, and hoarse.

I didn't have time to enjoy the relief that swamped me.

'Yeah, it's me.'

'Oh Danny, I'm so sorry. I got it all so wrong.'

She sounded weak.

'It doesn't matter, I've come to get you out. Chip's going to let your parents know you're here.'

Despite the news her voice was flat, 'You can't get me out. You need a key.'

And the only place that might be was Mike's office.

'No problem, hold in there, I'll be back in a minute.' My voice was more optimistic than I felt.

I headed back to the toilets. Chip would be wondering what was going on, but I didn't want to waste time radioing him. I needed to get to Mike's office and find that key. By now my eyes were accustomed to the semi-darkness. I moved quickly and soundlessly through the tunnel. Before I knew it, I was back in the shaft.

The screws on the grill over Mike's office were loose from the last time I'd been in. It came off, no problem. Like before, I squeezed my body around then lowered myself through the small space. I winced as my fall was broken by something hard. Rubbing my ankle, I could see from the glow of the computer on Mike's desk that I'd landed on a black briefcase, the one I'd seen Mike with. Stuffed in a back pocket were some papers. Although I didn't have time to look, I pulled them out anyway. Now they were in my hand I could see it was a passport and some plane tickets.

I flicked the passport open. Not that I needed to, it belonged to Mike, who today was Gerard Taylor and who tomorrow would be on his way to Spain. The ticket was one way. I stuffed the passport and tickets into my rucksack. He wasn't going anywhere.

I did a quick check of the other pockets to make sure there were no keys in there. Nothing. I clicked on the catches. When the briefcase sprung open a whistle escaped from my lips. It was cram packed full of cash. There must have been a few thousand in there. Enough to pay back Meggsie and more. I stuffed the money into my rucksack. Mike wouldn't be needing this where he was going. I smiled to myself. Paying Meggsie back with Mike's money - maybe karma was a real thing, after all. My problems were solved. Mum's problems were solved.

I'd got what I wanted. I should be flying, so why wasn't I? All I felt was hollowness, a gaping whole inside, getting wider and wider. I tried to shrug it off, all I needed to do now was find those keys, get Skye, and get out of here. I walked over to Mike's desk and pulled open the drawer. It had pretty much been cleared out, all the forms and papers I'd seen before were gone. There was a small pot with paper clips and drawing pins in it, among them I could see a filing cabinet key, too small for a door, but maybe if I looked in the cabinet.

The key turned easy in the lock. I yanked open the first drawer, empty. The second, empty. It was looking like Mike had cleared everything out. In desperation I dragged the last drawer open. There was no key, but the drawer wasn't empty, it was full of phones. Phones Mike had taken off everyone when they joined The Warren. Laid there on top was mine. I recognised it straight away. The scratch on the case, the dent in the left-hand corner. It wasn't much use down here, but I took it anyway. It made me feel closer to home. The emptiness inside me swelled.

I had my phone, but I still didn't have the key. Desperately I scanned the office, looking for anywhere the keys might be. I had to get into that room, I'd smash the door down if I had to. Then I spotted it, hung in the corner. Mike's other corduroy jacket. I rushed over, my hands straight in his pockets. Yes! My fingers clamped around cold metal. A bunch of keys. I snatched them up. I was out of here.

'Did you get them?' Skye whispered when I tapped on the door, signaling my return.

'Yes.' I whispered back. It wasn't until I pushed the key in the lock that it crossed my mind that it might not be the right key. My hands trembled as I tried each one. Get a grip, I told myself as the last key shook in the lock. Then click, it opened.

Skye ran straight to me, her arms were around me, 'I'm so sorry. I should have believed you.'

I held her close, not quite believing she was here, afraid if I let go, she'd be gone.

'It doesn't matter,' I whispered into her ear. Still holding on, I pushed her slightly away from me so I could see her face, and this time there was no mistaking the look in her eyes. I hadn't got it wrong. Gently my lips brushed against hers. The pressure of her mouth against mine increased. We were kissing and it was as electrifying as I thought it would be. I wanted to savour that moment for ever, but the crackle of the radio brought me back to reality. We had to get out of here.

'Daddy Bear calling Painter Boy. Are you receiving?'

Skye's face broke into a smile when she heard Chip's voice.

'This is Painter Boy receiving, loud and clear.' I answered, looking over at Skye apologetically before I continued. 'Rapunzel is out of the tower. I repeat Rapunzel is out of the tower.' I hoped Skye realised the name choice wasn't my idea.

'Step Three is go. The boys in blue will be on their way. This is Daddy Bear over and out.' Chip's voice disappeared and the radio went dead. Everything was set in motion.

'Let's go.' I said, checking I had everything. Radio clipped on the back of my belt, torch, rucksack, I'd almost forgotten about the money stuffed in there. Skye grabbed my hand and squeezed it. I squeezed her hand back. We were going home.

When I opened the door, the smile was ripped off my face. Stood there, right in front of us, were Mike and Grits.

Chapter Forty-Two

'Danny.'

Mike shook his head. Automatically I stepped in front of Skye. Mike's calm voice made him all the more threatening.

'Thought you'd pay us a visit? Came back to finish what you started?' He glanced over at Grits as he spoke. Grits' face was white. I couldn't tell if it was shock or anger. 'He's even managed to turn Skye against us. I didn't want to tell you, but you need to know the truth.'

Grits looked over at Skye. I didn't think his face could have got any whiter, but it did.

'It's not what you think, we ...' Anger and desperation fueled Skye's words.

Mike cut across her as she spoke, 'They're going to destroy The Warren, everything we've built.' You've lost everything before Grits, we can't let them take it away from us, from the kids again.' He threw Grits a meaningful look.

Grits' jaw tightened, turning away from Skye. He couldn't bear to look at her.

'It's not true!' I shouted. 'I found the photos!' It was my turn to look meaningfully at Mike. His cheek twitched slightly. He knew exactly what I meant. 'The ones of you, before you ...'

'Enough!' he shouted, before Grits had time to make sense of what I was saying. I edged backwards as Mike moved towards me. 'So, what are we going to do with you?'

Back pushed against the wall, the radio dug into my waist. Eyes locked with Mike, I sneaked my hand round, felt for the button, and pressed it.

'You're nothing but a fish face,' I shouted at him. 'Fish face,' I shouted again, then again, even louder, emphasizing the word fish. Our safe word. I couldn't spell it out any clearer. If Chip hadn't got the message now, he never would.

Mike and Grits looked at me like I'd lost it. So did Skye.

'Is that the best you can do, Picasso?' Grits said, a vein pulsing in his neck, he moved towards me. He pushed my shoulders hard, pressing me further into the wall. The radio crackled as it fell from my belt to the floor.

'Well, well.' Mike bent down and picked the radio up from where it lay at my feet, 'What have we got here?'

I stayed silent. Skye tensed beside me.

He thrust the radio in my face.

'I think you better tell me exactly what's going on.'

It dug into my cheek, still I didn't say a word.

'Nothing to say?' He pressed the button and in a muffled voice said, 'Come in, come in, it's Danny here.'

There was no answer, only a faint hum. Chip's idea of code names hadn't been over the top after all. With that and the fish thing he'd realise something was wrong.

Mike paced across the room, anger rising. 'Not playing, hey?' Mike looked at the radio, then at me, his face a mask of calm. Then out of nowhere, the radio flew across the room. As Skye ducked, my hands flew up to my face as it narrowly missed my head. It shattered against the wall, falling in pieces to floor. I wouldn't be hearing from Chip again. I didn't have a clue what he could do, I just hoped he'd think of something.

Before I had time to think what that might be, Mike followed the radio, launching himself across the room, grabbing me by the shoulders, shoving me hard against the wall. Pain split my back as the air shot out of me. Mike's face twisted with rage. I sank to the floor. The ache in my back was overtaken by a sharp dig in my side as Mike's foot connected with me. Then he bent down, his warm breath in my ear, 'I'm not messing about here. Tell me what's going on. Who's on the other end of that radio?'

Pain coursed through my body, still I didn't say anything. I wasn't going to drop Chip in it. I'd take the pain. Mike hauled me up from the floor. His body trembled with rage. Skye rushed forward, grabbing at him, trying to pull him off me. With a twist of his arm, Mike pushed her aside.

'Maybe this will make you change your mind.' Mike pulled his fist back. It was aimed at Skye. Grits leapt forward. I didn't know if it was to help Mike or Skye. I wasn't going to wait to see. I'd come here to save Skye, not get her hurt.

'It's the police! They're on their way, they know all about you! It's too late.' I shouted, hoping they'd cut their losses and run.

Mike swung round, the rage in his eyes now pure hate, but there was something else: panic, only for a moment, then he was back in charge.

'Grits, you stay here,' he snapped. 'I'm going to check the front entrance. I'll be back in a minute.' His glare penetrated me as he slammed the door.

As soon as he'd gone, Skye started shouting.

'Grits! You've got to believe us. Mike's a liar, you've got to see that.'

Grits, voice wobbled when he replied, 'I can't believe you've been taken in by him.'

He looked at Skye then at me, like he wanted to kill me, 'Everything Mike's done for us, for you.'

Skye was shaking now. 'Grits! It's me, Skye! Do you really think I'd turn on Mike for nothing? I trusted him, but it's all been a lie.'

Grits' lips started to move but no words came out, he wasn't sure. I knew the questions going through his head, the same ones I'd asked myself. I dug into my pocket and pulled out the passport and tickets. Maybe these would help him answer them.

'Look,' I pushed them towards him.

He snatched them out of my hands, eyes widening as he looked down at them. He shook his head.

'This doesn't mean anything,'

'I saw photos, too, in Mike's office, of you and your friends before you came here. It was him, he set you up.'

'That's not true, arsewipe.' He looked like he wanted to hit me. I didn't blame him. I knew he was trying to convince himself that Mike was the good guy he thought he was. I'd done exactly the same.

I took a breath. It was a risk, but it might be our only chance of getting out of here.

'Grits, the police are on their way. Mike can't escape. But you can if you come with us.'

Not for the first time, he looked at me like I was stupid.

'I know a secret passageway out of here,' I explained.

Grits looked across at Skye, searching for confirmation.

'You've got to trust us,' she pleaded. He looked back at me. I thought I could see a dilemma in his face.

'Take us to Mike's office, now, before he gets back. There's a vent in the wall behind his desk, we ...' before I had chance to finish the door flung open. It was too late. It was Mike and he wasn't alone.

'Look what I found while I was out,' Mike sneered.

Chip landed at our feet as Mike pushed him with full force. 'Thought he was the hero coming to rescue you, but as usual cocked it up.'

My emotions collided, never so pleased to see Chip, but at the same time so much wishing he wasn't here.

'Sorry., Chip mouthed silently, lifting his head to look at me and Skye.

'The police will be here anytime, so it doesn't matter,' I snapped at Mike.

'Ah yes, the police. I've put the bolts back on the door, so that will slow them down a bit. Enough time for me and Grits to get away, anyway.'

'Yeah, but you can't get out.' I looked nervously at Grits as I said it.

'Is that right?' Mike replied.

I hadn't noticed the axe he was holding in his other hand, which he now held up towards me.

Shit, he was going to kill us!

'That's the thing Danny. I'm getting out of here. It's you and your pals the police will find when they arrive – you and your pals and lots of incriminating evidence.' He waved the axe again, then looked over at Grits. 'This is our way out of here. The wall at the back of the dining room, we can knock our way through, but we need to be quick.'

He wasn't going to kill us, but he was going to get away, which was almost as bad.

'I'll get everyone else,' Grits said, already heading for the door.

'There's not time for that, it's just you and me.' Mike lifted the axe. 'Let's get going.'

Grits stared at the axe in Mike's hand.

'But we can't leave them?'

'There are times, Grits, when we have to put ourselves

first and this is one of them.'

Now Grits could see what Mike was truly like, and if he truly cared about the kids in The Warren this was the bit where he'd turn on him, overpower him. We'd get out and Mike would be left for the cops.

'No need for that, Mike,' said Grits. I waited. 'Picasso told me about a secret passage.'

Chapter Forty-Three

Skye's face looked like I felt. Broken.

'Grits, how could you?' Her voice was a whisper.

Grits stared straight ahead, face hard as stone. I hoped it was shame stopping him from looking at her, but I doubted it. He was as bad as Mike. All that crap about looking out for everybody. When it came to it, like Mike, he was in it for himself. Sourness filled my mouth. I wanted to punch him, but not as much as I wanted to punch myself. Why had I convinced myself he'd do the right thing? I held back the tears burning my eyes. I hated him. I hated Mike. I hated myself more. How stupid could I be? I was an idiot. I had to stop seeing the good in everybody, because however much I wanted it to be there, it didn't mean it was. Now Mike was going to get away and we were left taking the rap.

Grits had blabbed about the shaft, and Mike was all smiles again.

'That is a stroke of luck. You've got your uses, after all,' Mike sneered at me, then turned to Grits. 'Where to?'

'Your office.' Grits motioned at the axe Mike still had in his hand, 'Leave that here, we don't need it weighing us down.' Grits eyes swept over me, Skye, and Chip. 'We should take these three with us. Make sure they don't make any trouble till we're well on our way out of here.'

'Good idea' Mike nodded in agreement, then grabbed hold of Skye. 'No noise or funny business.'

He left the words dangling as he pushed Skye's arm up behind her back and moved towards the door. Grits grabbed hold of me and Chip. His heavy hands reminding me of the first time I'd met him down the tunnel.

We looked helplessly at each other as Grits dragged us along. My mind blank of any ideas as to how to get out of this. We fell to the floor when Grits pushed us through the office door.

'Tie them up,' Mike barked at Grits, shoving Skye down to join us.

There was no escape.

Roughly, Grits pulled the rucksack off my back and threw it across the floor. I thought of the money stuffed inside. Despite everything a sharp burst of happiness caught me. At least Mike wasn't going to get that. It fell flat when I realised it would be more evidence against us when the police got here.

'Put your hands together, all of you,' Grits ordered.

Like the three musketeers, our hands met. Grits pulled off his belt, the leather dug in as he wrapped it tightly round our wrists.

'Ready?' asked Mike when Grits had finished.

'Ready,' he answered.

Mike stood above us, mouth twitching, 'Enjoy your time in whichever juvenile institution you're locked up in. I doubt whether we'll be seeing each other again.'

My wrists pushed against the leather of the belt, burning my skin. It was nothing to the burning I felt inside. I wanted to get at him, but it was no use, there was no way I was breaking free.

Mike turned to Grits, 'Which way?'

'A vent in there.' Grits pointed to the door which led into the storeroom off Mike's office.

For a second confusion jolted my anger. I was sure I'd told him where the escape passage was. I stopped myself looking at the vent above Mike's desk, every second they wasted would count.

'Grab my stuff,' Mike called over to Grits, pointing to the black briefcase I'd found earlier. The thought of Mike opening it to find it empty rather than a shed load of money made me smile inside, even if it was only for a second.

Mike opened the door to the storeroom and Grits handed him the briefcase.

'It's all yours!' I was surprised by the anger in Grits' voice when, with full force, he pushed the briefcase into Mike's chest. Mike staggered backwards, eyes widening with realisation as he stumbled and fell into the room. Grits slammed the door shut and turned the key sitting in the lock.

'Arsewipe!' he shouted, only this time it wasn't at me.

The three of us looked up at him, mouths wide open.

'I was hardly going to have a go when he had an axe in his hand?' Grits said, bending down to loosen the belt he'd only just tied us up with.

As soon as her hands were free, Skye threw her arms around him. I wanted to hug him too, but even in this situation, that would be a step too far.

"We're free!' Chip sang, jumping up and down.

'Not for long if you don't stop dicking about,' Grits snapped. He'd come through in the end, but in a strange way it was good to know he was still the same snarky Grits.

'What's the plan? he asked. It took a second to realise he was talking to me, and another to realise Skye and Chip had the same expectant look on their faces. They were waiting for me to come up with the answers.

Above Mike's angry shouts sounding through the wall, I started to talk.

'The police will be on their way by now. We've not got

long, but it should be long enough to get everybody out.' I searched their faces for signs of disagreement. The original plan had been for us to get in, get Skye out and leave the police to get Mike. I hated Mike, I hated all that he stood for, but I didn't hate The Warren or the kids down here. I couldn't let everyone else take the flak along with Mike. They'd been taken in like me. Grits had been right; we couldn't leave them behind.

Skye and Chip nodded. I looked at Grits. I could have sworn his eyes were starting to fill up, before he said, 'Right Picasso, over to you.'

The thuds on the wall between us and Mike were getting louder. I raised my voice.

'Skye and Chip, you two go out through the vent here. Wait at the end of the shaft, then you can guide everybody out.'

If it all went wrong at least Chip and Skye would get out.

'Me and Grits will go wake everybody else and send them through the hatch in the toilets. When everybody's through we'll join you.'

'Where do we go when we're out of here?' Grits asked.

I hadn't thought that far ahead, but Chip had the answer.

'The umbrella factory?' he said without hesitation.

'Sounds good to me.' Grits almost smiled.

'Right, let's get everyone out of here,' I said.

The plan was back on.

Chapter Forty-Four

With Skye and Chip in the shaft, it was me and Grits. There was no time for awkwardness. We were a team, and we needed to get a move on. We left behind the bangs and shouts from Mike as we made our way to the sleeping quarters.

'Tell them it's a health and safety thing,' Grits said. 'That way, there's no questions. We can explain everything later.'

It made sense. Nobody would believe Mike could do anything wrong. We'd end up with a riot.

At the end of the corridor, we split. Grits went to go wake everyone, I went to the toilets to open the entrance to the shaft, ready to guide everyone through.

Excitement buzzed as they started to arrive, all up for the adventure, only they didn't realise the full extent of the adventure they were about to start. One by one I motioned them through. One boy with his bed head, rubbing his sleepy eyes. Another girl, who usually served dinner, clutching her sleeping bag like she was off on a camping trip. They went like sheep, one following the other, no questions asked.

'Everything go okay?' Grits asked as the last two disappeared through the hatch.

'No difficult questions, if that's what you mean,' I replied.

Grits snorted, 'That figures. Everybody believes what they want to believe. I suppose it makes life easier sometimes.' His voice trailed off. He wasn't just talking about everyone else he was talking about himself, too. Sympathy for Grits was something I never imagined I'd feel.

'Right time for us to go,' he said, snapping out of it.

I couldn't believe it. I was nearly there, Mike was going to get what he deserved, I was going to pay Meggsie back … Shit! Mum, the money. My rucksack was still in Mike's office.

'I've got to go get something; I'll catch you up.' I said, already turning to go.

'We've not got …' Whatever he was going to say was drowned out by an almighty bang. We looked at each other in the silence that followed. My first thought was Mike, but then with the second crashing boom, I realised it was the front entrance. It must be the police.

'Come on, Danny, we've got to go!'

I looked from Grits to the toilet door. If I ran back to the office, I could get into the shaft through the air grill. I'd have enough time. The police were going to get Mike, but there was still Meggsie. I had to get that money. It was the only way I was going to get rid of him.

'You go! I'll see you at the other end!' I shouted back and disappeared through the door.

I skidded into Mike's office, head throbbing. The crash of the police at the entrance merged with the banging and shouting coming from Mike. The door was shaking in its frame, loosening with every thud. The rage in Mike's voice sounded enough to blow it off its hinges. An earsplitting crack and the wood splintered. I could see Mike's fist now, punching its way through. I ignored the trembling that overtook my legs. I had to keep going.

My rucksack lay on the floor where Grits had thrown it. I snatched it up. I could hear Mike's voice more clearly now, but I didn't look round. With full force I pushed Mike's desk under the grill and jumped up. I was out of here. When my hands went up to the grill, I heard a familiar voice.

'Picasso!' It was Grits. He'd waited.

I pushed my rucksack through the vent, then hoisted myself up to follow. Grits twisted in the small space of the shaft, grabbed my arms, and started pulling me through. I was almost there when there was a sharp tug on my ankles. I felt myself slipping back out.

'Oh no, you don't!' It was Mike, he'd got out.

Grits held on to my wrists, pulling as hard as he could. My body yanked like a Christmas cracker ready to rip in half. I was slipping further. Blindly I kicked out my feet. Mike's nails dug into my skin. I kept on kicking and kicking. Bullseye! I heard Mike cry out and the pressure on my legs disappeared. With a final jerk, Grits pulled me through.

'Go! Go!' I shouted. Grits scrambled forward. I hooked the strap of the rucksack over my shoulder and followed.

Behind me I could hear Mike trying to squeeze through the hole. I didn't look back, I focused on moving forward.

'Think you've got something of mine!' Mike's voice echoed down the shaft. He was in, and he'd discovered the empty briefcase.

Grits and I didn't speak. We had a head start, so if we kept moving, we might stand a chance. Mike carried on shouting; we carried on crawling. As soon as we reached the shaft opening, we were on our feet.

'Up there!' I shouted at Grits, pointing to the ladder. The manhole was still open. No-one else was about, I hoped that meant everyone had got out. The thought of seeing them all back at the umbrella factory spurred me on.

The ladder swung sharply as Grits leapt on it. I jumped back, avoiding it hitting me. I put out my hand to steady it, then tried to jump on to join Grits. The metal groaned as it pulled away from the wall. Everybody going up it had loosened it even more. It might take the weight of both of us, but I didn't want to risk it.

You go first!' I bellowed at Grits. 'I'll hold it for you then when you're up, I'll come.'

Grits looked unsure 'Go!' I shouted.

With my hold steadying the ladder, Grits shot up. He heaved himself out of the manhole. For a minute he vanished, then the top of his body reappeared as he leaned back in and took hold of the ladder.

'Get a move on!' he shouted. I looked behind. Mike was in the opening now, getting to his feet. In seconds he'd be at the ladder. I jumped and pulled myself up on to the first rung.

'Hurry!' Grits shouted. At the same time the ladder lurched to one side. It was Mike. He was on it. I heaved myself up further. The ladder creaked under Mike's extra weight. Determination pushed me on. This time I wasn't going to let Mike get the better of me.

Looking up I could see Grits' face, screwed up with pain as he tried to stop the ladder swinging.

'I know you've got the money!' Mike shouted, clambering behind me, 'You might as well give it back to me. What's the point in paying off your mum's debts, she's never going to get off the drugs. Once an addict always and addict.'

His laugh echoed round the chamber, taunting me, but that wasn't all I could hear.

Shouting came from further down the shaft. Beams of light danced across the ceiling and walls. It was the police, their torch lights bouncing as they moved along. One last heave, I was nearly there. I could do this. I could get out - but so would Mike.

The police were getting louder as they closed in. The light of their torches as they moved into the opening was blinding. It lit something in my brain - that and Mike's words. Without thinking any further I pulled the rucksack off my back.

'Take this!' I shouted, holding it up towards Grits.

'What?' He looked confused.

'It's yours anyway. Yours and Chip's.'

My head, as well as my arms, lightened as I threw the bag up to him. Automatically his hand shot out to catch it. He let go of the ladder, I pressed my foot against the wall and pushed. The ladder moved slowly away from the wall.

'What the ...' Mike's voice echoed as the ladder teetered backwards and forwards. In what felt like slow motion, it moved towards the ground. My mind was as light and easy as my body soaring through the air. Any fear was drowned in the knowledge that I'd done the right thing. Mike was right. The money wasn't going to change Mum. I could pay off Meggsie but next week, next month, next year, I'd be paying him off again. It was like Chip had said, Mum had to want to change and deep down, as much as it hurt, I wasn't sure she did. At least Grits and Chip could use the money to help The Warren Crew; a new beginning at the umbrella factory. And if Mike got away, I'd be forever looking over my shoulder and he'd be free to cock up other people's lives. The only way to solve my problems was to face up to them and to get Mum to face up to hers. Whatever happened now I could deal with it.

The ladder plummeted. I crashed to the ground. Air

shot out of my body. Pain seared through my shoulder. Through the swirling dust, I saw Mike, and before I could move he was on me. Lights flashed in my head. I didn't know if it was the light from the torches or my brain exploding. Then in a split second the heaviness lifted. The weight of Mike gone. It was the police, dragging him off me. A mesh of arms and legs filled the tunnel as he struggled to get away, but he was going nowhere. Silver handcuffs flashed as they snapped around his wrists. His mouth moved but his words were a meaningless drone. The police hauled him to his feet. Through a swollen eye, I looked him straight in the face. The buzzing in my ears was getting louder, but I forced the words out of my mouth.

'All for the greater good Mike, all for the greater good.'

Chapter Forty-Five

From my seat in the police car, I watched Mike being bundled into the back of a van, then driven away in a celebration of blue lights. That's when it hit me. Our plan had worked. We'd done it. We'd gone and done it. The only thing hacking me off was I couldn't laugh, it hurt too much. My head throbbed, every inch of my body ached, but I can honestly say I'd never felt so good. I wished more than anything Skye and Chip, and even Grits, were here to share the feeling.

As soon as their names entered my head a wave of panic crashed over me. Had they made it out? The engine of the police car hummed as it pulled away. My neck jarred, twisting my head round to the back window, straining to catch a glimpse of the car park over the road where they'd come out of the shaft.

'Everything okay?' The policewoman sat next to me asked, in response to the sigh escaping my mouth.

I nodded silently while inside the cheering was deafening. The car park lay in darkness, no flashing lights, no movement. They'd made it. Chip, Grits, and the rest of them would be on their way to the umbrella factory and Skye would be on her way home.

The chill night air followed me through the door into the police station. On the ladder, when I'd made my decision, I hadn't really thought about what would happen next. All I knew was there was no escape for me, no moving forward unless I faced things head on. Now, standing in front of the custody desk, a social documentary of my future blasted through my head. Social workers, court, care homes, young offender's institutes. I blocked out the images, numbness taking over. I'd made the right decision, now I'd deal with the consequences - whatever they were. I went through the motions like it was happening to somebody else. Name, address, next of kin. I handed over my belongings. All my worldly possessions – everything I had in my pockets, sketch pad, pencil, phone.

I was taken to a room to wait. The only decoration was a no smoking sign, the only sound the tick of the clock, echoing off the dirty white walls. I'd been put in here while they tried to contact Mum.

Mum. Good luck there! The click of the door opening broke through my thoughts. It was the policewoman who'd sat with me in the car.

'We've not been able to get hold of your mum,' she apologised. Sadness, tinged with bitterness, churned my stomach. That was no surprise, but this time I didn't try looking for an excuse. I was done with that. There was no excuse. She was probably off her face somewhere with Meggsie. The policewoman carried on, 'We've informed Social Care, and the duty social worker is on his way over, he shouldn't be long. Can I get you a drink while you're waiting?'

I shook my head, a hollow laugh rumbling in the back of my throat. In the space of a couple of hours I'd made happen what I'd spent the last month or so desperately trying to avoid. The door clicked again as she left. Deja vu swept over me. Sat in the hospital waiting room, waiting for the inevitable, only this time there was no running away. I'd stopped running.

I settled back in my chair, trying to kill time, staring at the wall until my eyes hurt. When the door clicked again, it was a man I didn't recognise. He wasn't wearing a uniform, but I could tell he was a cop.

'Hi Daniel, I'm Detective Inspector Garner.'

To be fair, he looked quite friendly for a cop. He continued, 'And this is Paul Duffy.'

I hadn't seen the man stood behind him. He definitely wasn't a police officer. He looked like he'd just got out of bed, he probably had. He sat down in the seat opposite me.

'Hi Danny. I'm Paul, I'm the duty social worker and I'm also here to act as your appropriate adult. The police are going to ask you some questions and my job is to support you and make sure all the proper processes are followed.'

He flashed a challenging smile at Detective Garner.

'I'll leave you two alone so you can talk,' Detective Garner said.

He didn't need to leave us for long. I didn't have any questions. I didn't want to see a doctor; I didn't want a solicitor. All I wanted was to get this over and done with. Paul's disappointment filled the room. He wanted to help. No worries, I'd make it up to him. After this, I was going to need all the help I could get. There was a knock on the door, Detective Garner's head appeared round the door.

'Ready to start?'

His finger slowly pushed down the button on the recorder, its' click exploded across the room. My heart raced like I'd done a 100-metre sprint.

'For the tape, can you state your full name?' Garner said.

'Daniel Bennett.' I fired the words at him, looking him straight in the eye. Matter-of-factly, I answered every single question he asked, I gave him the papers I'd ripped out of the black book, I told him everything - about Mike, about Meggsie, about the underground. Well, almost everything - as far as Skye, Chip, Grits, and

241

the rest of the kids in The Warren, I barely knew them, had no idea where they'd gone or what had happened to them. The worry still lodged in my head that they'd not got away, eased its way out. Garner's face told me he knew nothing about them, either.

Garner's finger reached for the recorder button again, pressing it down. This time it sounded like a dull thud, echoing my stomach as it dropped to the floor. Interview over. This was it. The calmness I'd been feeling began to crumble. Garner's words were a meaningless buzz in my ears. I felt like was going to vomit, bracing myself for the feel of sharp metal clasping my wrists and the four walls of a police cell. Garner stood up, gathering his papers together.

'Okay, we'll contact you in due course,' he smiled as he left the room.

I looked at Paul, not understanding or believing what had happened, that I was still sitting here.

'You've been released while further investigations take place. It's not in your or anybody's interest to detain you. You know Danny, you're as much as victim in this as anything.'

The avalanche inside me stopped, setting like concrete. I was free, but there were no party poppers, no celebrations. We sat for a few minutes while Paul explained what would happen next. I listened from my void. Emergency placement while they sorted out what was happening.

'Right, time to go. If you want to wait here, I'll go get the car.'

I stayed in my seat trying not to think of anything. I looked up when the door opened again, expecting it to be Paul. It wasn't, it was the policeman who'd been at the custody desk. He put a plastic bag on the table in front of me.

'Here you go, if you want to sign here.' He pushed a form and a pen in front of me. I made an illegible scribble across the bottom. It could have been anyone. I felt like no-one.

When he'd gone, I opened the bag and took out the sum total of my life. I flicked through the drawing pad. It landed on a sketch I'd done of Mum. Anger mixed with sadness. I wanted to make it all okay for her, but she had to want it, too. She had to want it more than drugs, more than Meggsie. I couldn't do this on my own. We had to do it together, and at the moment, that didn't seem likely. I snapped the pad shut, closing with it any further thoughts of Mum. I'd always be there for her, but I needed her to be there for me, too.

I picked up my phone and switched it on. It flashed into life, there was still some battery left. The blank screen filled with an image of me and Mum, there was no escape. I was about to turn it off, but the ping, ping, ping of messages coming through stopped me. The numbers on the little envelope in the corner ramped up, three, four, five, ten. It kept on. I tapped on the icon. The same word rolled down the screen. MUM, MUM, MUM, MUM.

Heart racing, I tapped on a random one.

DANNY WHERE R U? REALLY WORRIED. TEXT BACK.

I tapped on the next. Same sort of thing.

PLEASE DANNY, WORRIED, PHONE OR TEXT.

I kept on reading, every single message saying the same sort of thing, until I came to a longer one.

DANNY, PLEASE GET IN TOUCH. I KNOW IVE LET YOU DOWN. PLEASE DONT HATE ME.

IM LEAVING HOSPITAL TODAY IM GOING TO THE RAGLAN REHAB CENTRE. PLEASE PLEASE COME BACK. I LOVE YOU. MUM XXX

The date on the message was when I'd gone to visit her in hospital. The day I'd found out she'd disappeared. The day Mike told me she'd gone back to Meggsie. Mike had been lying again, but this time I couldn't be happier. I was grinning so hard my face ached. I wished Mum was here, I wanted to give her the biggest hug ever. She'd done it. This time she really had meant it. I could feel my smile getting even wider, I was buzzing, ready to explode with happiness.

'Ready then?' I hadn't noticed Paul come back into the room. I jumped up from my seat, the smile still on my face. Paul looked at me, head cocked to one side, 'You okay?'

I was buzzing, I couldn't hide it. He probably thought I was on something. I was. Pure happiness.

'Yeah, I'm ready.' I replied.

I was going home, maybe not today, but I was going home.

Chapter Forty-Six

The rumble of voices faded to silence when the woman standing on the stage gave a polite cough. I shifted in my seat, navigating around the heads blocking my view. I didn't want to miss a thing. I breathed deeply, soaking it all in. The orchestra, sat below the stage, started up a slow tune. I took a quick glance down at the row of chairs. My eye caught Skye's, sat between her Mum and Dad, she looked as happy as I felt. We'd seen loads of each other since she'd got out of the Warren. I still had to regularly pinch myself to believe she was officially my girlfriend. I hadn't thought that life could get any better until I received a second letter from St Cuths.

'Good luck,' Skye mouthed.

Mum's hand slipped into mine, giving it a tight squeeze.

'Swap seats if you want, you might see better from here,' she said.

I smiled and shook my head I didn't want to draw any attention to myself. On the other side of me, Nadine, my foster carer gave a reassuring smile.

The music carried on as a line of other people joined the woman on the stage. Through the gap in front of me I saw Esther. As small as she was, somehow, she looked bigger up there. I wanted to wave, shout out, let her know I was here. Well, what I really wanted to do was throw my arms round her and say thanks a million times. That day I'd run off without my art portfolio, she'd found the letter from St Cuths and submitted all my work. If it wasn't for her, I wouldn't be sat here, in the Great Hall at St Cuthbert's School of Art.

The music ended abruptly, but its rhythm carried on

beating through my body. Mum must have felt it too, she squeezed my hand tighter. The woman on the stage gave another cough and started to speak, her voice echoed off the high ceilings.

'I'd like to extend a warm welcome and to thank you for joining us at our Annual Prize Giving ceremony. I am also extremely excited that today I will also be announcing the names of those young people who have shown outstanding promise and who will be awarded a scholarship …'

I moved forward to the edge of my seat, pressing the backs of my legs hard against its edge, making sure this was real, that I wasn't dreaming. It was weird being here, even weirder to think a month ago I was sat in a police station, my life plummeting into a black hole. Now life was good, not perfect, but it was good.

I was living with Nadine. It was only temporary. She was alright, though, and I could see Mum whenever I wanted. The plan was I'd go back home, Mum was back there now, but still going to the Raglan Centre every day. They wanted to make sure she was in a good place when I went back, strong enough to cope, and I got that. Mike was locked up and he wouldn't be getting out anytime soon. Even better, with the pages I'd ripped out of the black book as evidence, they'd linked him and Meggsie, so he was heading the same way.

A soft nudge on the side of my arm pulled me out of my thoughts. It was Nadine, her head nodded towards the stage.

'Daniel Bennett,' the woman's voice floated above the rows of seats. I froze. I couldn't move. That was me! For a minute I didn't believe it. I looked at Mum and at Skye, their faces told me it wasn't a mistake, it was my name she'd just read out. Nadine gave me another nudge.

'Go on, then,' she encouraged.

I heard the words in my head *Act like you belong.* I done it often enough in The Warren, I could do it now. I stood up, steadying the wobble in my legs. I fixed my gaze on Esther's face and set off towards the stage.

The sound of clapping filled my ears. My legs gave another slight wobble, I remembered Mum and Skye behind me, glad they were there, willing me on. I wished Chip and Grits could be here too. I hadn't seen them since that night. I doubted I would now, and if I thought about it too much it made me sad. It was nothing personal, I knew that. They lived in a different world to me now, they couldn't risk it. It was enough to know they were all safe at the umbrella factory.

The walk to the stage seemed to take an age. My stomach bounced, making me feel like I was walking on air. The clapping died down as I climbed the steps. The woman on the stage held one hand out to shake mine, in the other she held a certificate which she passed to me.

'Well done, Danny, and welcome to St Cuthbert's.'

With those few words, life's possibilities stretched out in front of me. Certificate clasped tightly in my hand, I left the stage and made my way back to my seat. Then through the sound of the clapping which had started up again, I heard it. An unmistakable whistle, short and sharp, followed by another. Chip and Grits! I looked around, trying to find them, but they were too good for that, and it didn't matter, anyway. They were here.

I sat down in my seat, looked down at the certificate, and it struck me, Mike was wrong. I didn't have to act like I belonged, I did belong. This was my life, Danny Bennett at St Cuths, Mum sat beside me, my friends around me. Life was good, and with help, it was going to get better. Inside I felt myself grow a little bit more.

Things like this did happen to boys like me.

ABOUT THE AUTHOR

Linda Nelson lives in North Yorkshire where she runs a Community Enterprise Company offering vocational training to young people with additional needs. Linda has spent her professional life working with children and young people, which has inspired much of her writing.

Linda's novels are aimed at older children and young adults. Her debut novel, Underground, is a modern-day Oliver Twist set in the disused tunnels of the London Underground. It is a gritty, contemporary, action-filled story, ultimately with a message of hope.

When not writing Linda enjoys reading, running, long walks in the countryside and being entertained by her cats.

All Linda's net royalties from the sale of Underground will be donated to the Harrogate Homeless Project.

THE HARROGATE HOMELESS PROJECT

The Harrogate Homeless Project has been a vital lifeline for vulnerable individuals in the Harrogate District since 1991, providing safe accommodation and essential support to those experiencing homelessness as they rebuild their lives towards independent living.

Central to its mission is offering a pathway of support, starting with emergency accommodation, and progressing through its hostel to move-on housing.

Alongside the accommodation offerings, HHP also provides a Day Centre, providing a safe and welcoming space where individuals can access essential support, including hot meals, healthcare, and pathways to accommodation. The demand for HHP services in Harrogate is stark and continues to rise. HHP works with a variety of people ranging from those in need of support through relationship breakdown or financial issues to individuals with multiple complex needs including substances misuse, mental health issues and offending behaviour.

The HHP vision is to make sure nobody in the Harrogate District has to sleep rough and that those experiencing homelessness have all the support they need to move towards independent living.